MADNESS

An Apocalyptic-Horror Thriller

M.L. Banner

Toes in the Water Publishing, LLC

To my wife, Lisa.
For your unending love and support,
even during my times of MADNESS.

Prologue

Santa Cruz de Tenerife, Spain – 1712

A scream sent him into motion. Aldolfo Suárez raced up the face of La Gomera, sure his son was seriously injured. He bounded deftly over the volcanic rocks, focused on not catching his sandals—there was no helping his son if he too were injured.

Halfway up the summit, his fatigued legs forced him to stop and find rest under the ancient umbrella of a dragon-tree. While trying to satisfy his oxygen-starved lungs with fitful gulps of the foul, sulfur-filled air, he took in the world's surreal textures.

Besides being colorless, like a charcoal drawing, it was soundless, not unlike a dense snowfall. Gray ash, instead of flecks of snow, quietly floated down from the murk, spotting the landscape.

He glared over his left shoulder to examine its origin. Only the thick plume of La Palma's volcano was visible now. An unending boiling geyser, belching ash from the depths. The townspeople blamed the eruption on God, saying that they were being punished for the sins of their past. Aldolfo knew it wasn't a vengeful God; evil was at the root of all of this and it was getting worse.

In the week since the eruption, the looming clouds thickened with each passing night. Daily, the sun's life-giving warmth was quelled by this cloak. And the skies grew more violent, with darker shades of crimson each afternoon.

He caught a glimpse of several sheep by his *granero*, the only building up on the hill. They had spread out from their normal confines, now testing the farthest reaches of his vast property. Sheep preferred to remain together for safety and not spread apart.

A tortured screech and several sheep dashed below him, not even slowing down, as if he wasn't there. They always stopped to gather around their shepherd.

Puzzled by this, he carefully studied them as they scurried along the well-trodden path, then around a corner into one of the two caves on his property. They disappeared inside.

However odd and troubling this was, he thanked his good fortune. At least those animals would be easier to gather.

Bleating pulled Aldolfo's attention once again back toward his *granero*. Above this, an undulating cloud of black dots fell from the sky, disappearing behind the building. Then the cloud rose again, where it clung to the air for barely a second and then tumbled downward. The chaotic dots then circled back to some unseen spot behind the building.

Movement to his right.

A winged shape emerged from the gray gloom. Black and angular. Bright red eyes. It flapped furiously, arched, and then dropped onto the back of a frantic sheep, which cried a labored bleat and burst past him. Its normal coat of alabaster—his flock's wool was well known throughout the region—was covered with tawny splashes. The winged shape rode on its back like death bridling a horse of the apocalypse. It lifted its head and shrieked back at him. Something fibrous hung from its orange beak.

Aldolfo gaped, dumbfounded.

Then he understood. The shapes, the clouds: these were *cuervo negro*, a black raven common around the island. Except their normally coordinated flights and wonderfully sinuous formations were erratic. Almost angry.

There were more shrill cries coming from behind the building. He ran again, to the sounds of his distressed animals. Making no connection to the birds, he became sure that one of the neighbor's mad dogs was attacking a few of the wandering herd. It had already happened twice this week. He clutched his staff, getting ready to wield it against the attacking *perro*. There'd be no warning this time; he'd beat the devil out of the animal, and demand payment for his injured or killed sheep.

Aldolfo arrived breathless, just off the side of his *granero*, and was once again frozen in his steps. What he witnessed stupefied him. For the first time, fear raced up his spine, faster than a cold December chill.

The *cuervos* were swarming three of his sheep; each lay in a dying heap on the rocky ground, wailing in pain. The birds pulled at the bloody flesh, frantically ripping at and plunging their heads into the moribund bodies.

Finally, the good shepherd in him reacted. Aldolfo jumped up, hollered a command at the offending fowl and swung his arms wildly.

The birds reacted instantly, the cloud breaking free from the mostly still carcasses—they were once his beloved animals. The haze of *cuervos* barely rose from the ground before quickly changing direction and flapping frantically, this time toward him.

They no longer seemed disorganized.

He yelped as each *cuervo* pelted him. One after another they hit, causing him to lose his balance. But he righted himself and swung at the thickening cloud, now swarming him en masse.

Their wild screeching was so loud he thought he might go deaf, if he even survived this.

Some of the birds fell from the swings of his staff, and a few others broke away, just avoiding being hit. But there were far too many. Each momentary hole in the black clog filled up again, as they continued their unyielding barrage.

Spikes of pain flared all over his body, and he caught momentary flashes of his own blood with each swing. A flood of panic rushed over him, causing him to thrash wildly. Losing his balance again, he dropped his staff and started to tumble toward the ground when he saw perhaps his only outlet of salvation.

The door to his *granero* was slightly ajar. If he could only make it inside there.

Using his headlong motion, he drove his legs forward, pushing through and into the comforting darkness, landing hard. Several cats bolted past him, yowling their own displeasure, and disappeared outside, just before he kicked the door closed.

The frame of the large building rattled and then, for a moment the world was a muffled quiet but for his own harried puffs for air.

A shaft of weak light nudged through the *granero's* single dirty window, illuminating a small lump in the middle of the floor, as if God Himself had reached in with His invisible hand and left a foggy thumb-print of light that split the darkness. The thumb-print crackled with movement.

His *granero* was not used much anymore, so the building should have been empty right now. He squinted at the abyss, fighting an inability to see anything in the dark.

One of his eyes wasn't working. He spat mental curses at the devilish birds for what they did to him. The back of his hand trailed over the nonfunctional eye, tentatively confirming nothing was blocking his vision. It felt sticky and moist. He purposely forced both eyes closed and attempted to reopen both again, hoping it might improve his vision. It didn't.

It was only then that he realized he wasn't alone.

With his one good eye, Aldolfo refocused on the illuminated lump in the center of the structure that he had first assumed was something his son had left there—he often didn't put things where they belonged. Maybe it was some more of those damned cats that were everywhere.

A spell of dizziness rocked him, and only then did he know how badly he was hurt. Yet he fought back the wooziness: he needed to know what this lump was. He felt drawn to it. An unshakable feeling, however irrational, that whatever the lump might be, it would offer him comfort.

He attempted to pull himself deeper into the building, using his elbows to propel his body forward.

A painful ringing crescendo in his brain, which already felt as if it might pop at any second. And yet above the internal din, he heard something else.

It was a dull murmur, coming from the illuminated mass.

The benign image of a litter of puppies jumped into his head; its edges fuzzy, like after a dream.

His son had watched over the neighbor's newborn pups, long before they had become vicious. Back then they were adorable, but when it came time to feed them, they showed their inner animalistic self, attacking their food, ripping at it and gnawing each morsel with untamed abandon. Their gnawing sounded like what he was now hearing, only raw.

As if something covering his ears were removed, he could hear better, the ringing barely noticeable. At the same time, the image became clearer. He halted his progression and focused. He could now see and hear this lump in motion.

He convulsed uncontrollably.

It was chewing sounds he was hearing, along with sounds of tearing and ripping at flesh. It was the evil *cuervos* eating from the mass...

They were eating his son.

His boy must have attempted to escape the birds inside, just like his father.

Aldolfo gave up all fight, fully accepting his fate. There would be no escape for him, just as there wasn't any for his son.

He watched the *cuervos* race toward him and wished at that moment, he could have once more told his boy he loved him.

Before everything went black, he marveled at the redness of the *cuervos'* eyes.

Part I

"If you gaze long into an abyss, the abyss will also gaze into you."
Friedrich W. Nietzsche

"It's a plague of madness that has infected most animals... a ticking time bomb, which could go off at any moment."
T.D. Bonaventure

DAY ONE

WE DIDN'T KNOW IT AT THE TIME, BUT IT ALL STARTED TODAY... THE BEGINNING OF OUR END.

01

Madrid, Spain

The red-eyed beast came out of nowhere, moving so fast they had no time to think, only react. And if it hadn't been for TJ seeing the creature and calling it to their attention before it struck, one or both of them might have suffered serious injury or a far worse fate.

Two days would pass before they'd come to realize that this was just one of many signs of an apocalypse that was about to befall the world. Until then, they would chalk up this event to just another part of the normal chaos that comes with travel these days. Technically, the chaos began over a week ago.

When they had boarded their transatlantic flight, they were mildly aware of some travel disruptions that had started earlier when Iceland's Bardarbunga volcano began spewing ash into the atmosphere. The volcanic ash plume slowly ballooned out toward Northern Europe causing flight delays and diverting air traffic across the continent—the thick particles of ash played hell with jet engine rotors.

This very thing had happened years before, and so neither Ted nor TJ Williams gave it much thought as they luxuriated in their first-class flat-bed seats and happily discussed their upcoming transatlantic cruise from Malaga, Spain back to the US. Their flight attendant added to their self-imposed detachment by topping off their glasses with seemingly endless sparkling wine.

An hour before landing, Sicily's Mount Etna blew its top as well, diverting more flights and adding to the already heavy air traffic coming into London's Heathrow Airport.

When they arrived, they received their first taste of the travel problems that lay ahead of them. Many flights had already been canceled, and further cancellations were mounting by the minute, as flights around Europe and Asia were being grounded. Their next flight was one of them.

Ted and TJ had only one more leg left on their journey to Malaga before Regal European's *Intrepid* would set sail at five tomorrow afternoon. Although Ted's agent set up the trip, TJ had done all the detailed planning, as she normally did for any of their vacations.

Now anchored at the American desk, outside their arrival gate, they were both scrambling for options. The gate agent busily searched for other air-travel possibilities on American, while they also searched on their phones for other available flights on competitor airlines.

"How about Madrid?" Ted spoke just below a shout, to be heard over the commotion. "There's a BA flight leaving in thirty. Ah... flight number 6-2-8-0." His eyes met TJ's for confirmation that this would work for them.

Instantly her face was awash with excited expectation. "Yes!" She turned to the gate agent. "Can you find us two seats?"

The agent furiously tapped at her keyboard, eyes drilled into her screen. "I have two bulkhead seats in coach, but at least they're next to each other," she announced with pride.

"We'll take them!" TJ threw back, without hesitation. In other circumstances, she might have been disappointed as a Platinum member of American's frequent flier program who just lost first-class seats on a canceled flight. But she was pretty sure they'd have no other choices if she waited even a few more seconds. This flight didn't get them to Malaga, but it brought them to within driving distance.

Once she heard the printer below the desk spit out their tickets, she asked the next obvious question. "Do you or anyone else have anything from Madrid to Malaga?"

"Sorry, there's nothing available. This may be the last flight in or out of Madrid," the gate agent responded fairly quickly, still not looking up.

Ted handed TJ his phone. "Here. I'll get our tickets. This is Cynthia with Hertz in Madrid." He flashed a Keanu Reeves sort of smile, which then broke into a grin. The curl of his handlebar mustache—the one part of his made-up British author persona she'd like to change—lifted high on his face.

At any other time, she might have smirked or said something about his appearance, made more out of place by his Cubs ball cap. Instead, TJ beamed at him, accepting his phone. After twenty years of marriage, he still loved making her smile.

They had to run to the gate to make the full flight to Madrid, with barely a few minutes to spare. Ted pulled their luggage, while TJ secured an economy car with Hertz in between harried puffs for air.

Relief turned into worry after they landed at Madrid's Baraja.

They made their way to baggage claims and customs, pacing silently, taking in news snippets from each TV they passed—most were tuned to BBC. The results of Mount Etna's eruption were devastating: it was the largest eruption in over a hundred years; several hundred perished in a giant swirling pyroclastic cloud that swept through Fornazzo; and air travel throughout Eurasia was now at a standstill.

They were the lucky ones, indeed.

At the Hertz counter, where lines of frantic travelers received the bad news, they were evermore thankful they had booked their car when they did, and that it hadn't been given to someone else. Yet a sinking nervousness gnawed away at their bellies. Something much greater than an immediate disaster was occurring and they were about to get their first taste of it.

Ted had volunteered to drive if TJ would navigate. She was far more adept at that than him, calling out approaching signs and anticipating their next turn. He didn't need a GPS when he had her. TJ was his GPS.

With both of their doors opened, they flashed each other smiles over the roof of the car. They had a five hour drive to Malaga, and maybe then they could relax a little.

That's when TJ called out, "What the hell is that?"

Ted's head snapped to where her finger pointed. "Get in the—" he yelled, cutting off his own command, as he threw himself into the driver's seat, and pulled the door closed behind him.

TJ, normally the one to react to a potential threat quicker than Ted, seemed frozen by bewilderment. It was fear. Her hesitation negated her ability to jump in on time. Reflexively she ducked behind the door's glass window, just as what looked like a dog made impact.

Both TJ and the dog yelped.

She remained fixed for a long moment, until Ted hollered, "TJ!"

Reacting as if being punched, she finally sprang inside, slamming her door behind her.

They watched in stunned silence as the German shepherd righted itself and shook its head violently, spewing blood and saliva across TJ's side window.

The animal momentarily scrutinized them, its eyes an unnatural and angry red. It seemed rabid with rage—without the foaming of the mouth—and yet befuddled at the same time.

Then the animal caught sight of something behind them, out of their periphery, and hurriedly limped away in that direction.

"What was that?" Ted squeezed his wife's hand to comfort himself, as well as her.

Time held its breath as they waited for their hearts to slow.

TJ, unable to find the right amount of air needed to reply, left his question unanswered. She didn't have an answer, even if she had had enough air.

Ted gazed at her and considered what must be going through her head right now. It was, after all, a dog attack that almost killed her and left her physically and emotionally scarred. Now just about any animal, big or small, caused his wife to freeze in fear. It had become such a liability to her now, she could no longer operate as a Bureau field agent, spending most of her time behind a desk. Even working out for her had to be done indoors, where there were no alleyways or streets where dogs could be potentially lurking.

She peered through her glasses at the side mirror, searching for the wild animal that just tried to eat them.

Finally, she turned to him. "Let's get out of this nightmare."

But their nightmare was only just beginning.

DAY TWO

WE WERE LOOKING FORWARD TO A PHYSICAL AND EMOTIONAL RESPITE: GOD KNOWS WE NEEDED IT. BUT MALAGA WOULD OFFER US NEITHER.

02

Malaga, Spain

This time, she didn't duck and the rabid-like dog got her. This time, he couldn't do anything to save her. He was forced to watch from a distance. The crowds of people swelled around him, holding him back, as she lay there alone and dying. When he finally broke free and made it to her, he knew he was too late. Her life-giving blood was everywhere, her eyes welled up in agony, pleading to him to answer why he wasn't there for her; why he couldn't have stopped this?

Then she was gone.

Ted sat up, swallowing back the bile that filled his mouth. He snapped his head to her side, desperately hoping she was there.

He couldn't see her.

But it was dark and he couldn't make out anything, really. A weak shaft of light from the coming dawn illuminated an unfamiliar desk on the other side of this foreign room.

He heard the distant sound of a car horn, which didn't make sense because they lived in the country.

Then he heard her.

She exhaled soft puffs of air, her breaths rhythmic and restful. She was asleep beside him.

And then it all made sense. She was fine. They were in their hotel room in Malaga, Spain. He didn't lose her. This time.

Ted continued to dry-swallow the bitter nastiness lingering in his mouth and the burn in his throat, while trying to keep from hyperventilating. He drew comfort in his wife's peaceful breathing and started to calm himself.

Many recent mornings he woke from a similar horror, with only the circumstances changing. Last week it was her drowning in their lake; the week before, she was being run over by a truck—that was the most common one. In each nightmare, a suffocating crowd flooded around him, holding him back with debilitating panic, so that there was no way to save her.

For over twenty years he'd been having this same damned nightmare, his author-mind only creatively interjecting different causes of death. But in the end, the result was always the same: some outside force caused her to die and he was held back by a swell of people.

He began to feel his breathing accelerate again, just by thinking about all the people.

"Same dream?" TJ asked, her voice heavy from sleep.

"Yeah," he huffed.

She slid over to him and wrapped her arms around his trunk, squeezing him tight. "Well, I'm very much alive, I love you, and we are now in the beautiful town of Malaga. Let's get up and go see the city."

"Sounds like a terrific idea."

And they did just that.

After checking out of their hotel, they stowed their bags in the trunk of their parked rental car and meandered through cobbled pedestrian thoroughfares bustling equally with tourists and locals.

Interspersed were city workers push-brooming away the fine layer of volcanic dust which had settled everywhere. Likewise, the Williamses pushed aside their worries about home, work and their travels, quickly wiring themselves into the vibrant culture and ancient history of Malaga, Spain.

Hand in hand, they walked quietly, each focused on their own thoughts. They were not unlike any couple who had shared twenty years of respect and love through marriage. Only as a couple, they rarely spent much time together, at least not lately. With TJ's and Ted's disparate schedules, they found themselves frequently apart. TJ worked late hours and often had to travel to other Bureau offices, sometimes for a week or more at a time. And Ted's agent often had him traveling around the US and the UK for book signings at small bookshops and radio and TV interviews. His schedule was especially busy around new book releases. His latest was apt to be his biggest. The cruise was to be their calm before their stormy schedule, already packed full of travel and appearances. And it would be a celebration of their anniversary.

Threading the needle of their already ballooning calendars, Ted's agent had recently booked this trip. He would have never chosen a cruise, because of all the people. But TJ insisted that they could spend most of the time in their cabin and it would give them some needed "us time." He relented, knowing their chances to be together would go away in less than a month.

At the *Teatro de Roman*—an ancient Roman theater excavated in the heart of *Ciudad de Malaga*—they turned right and ascended the centuries-worn ramparts leading up to the stone entrance of the Moorish palace known as Alcazaba de Malaga.

Originally built in the 11th century and continually expanded upon through the 14th, it was an impressive fortress pridefully peering over its Malagan subjects. The palace's occupants included Muslim rulers and Spain's infamous Queen Isabella and King Ferdinand.

And though the trek up from the city center was a calf-burning distance, the rewards were breathtaking vistas, flourishing gardens and ornate fountains which gushed sparkling streams, engineered into cascading outdoor water courses running through stairwells and walkways. An Andalusian Garden of Eden.

Just inside the towering defensive walls, they stopped to admire an impressive column of seagulls, which had corkscrewed up and into the complex, like one giant organism barking its excitement as it swooped overhead.

They passed tourists, young and old, including an elderly Spanish couple, their withered hands clasped together, their supportive canes on opposing sides, clunking against the polished stones in perfect synchronicity. Ted glanced at his wife, to see if she had the same thought as he, but she was preoccupied, as she had been the last several days.

Continuing along, just inside of the fortress's protective walls, they found themselves gazing up at a long walkway that crowned the top of the wall's buttresses, spanning the distances just five feet below the wall's lip. Bisecting the walkway periodically were lookout towers.

TJ couldn't help herself and took off like a jackrabbit, ascending a stairwell up to the closest tower's door. "What do you suppose is inside this tower?" She tugged on the obviously locked rustic door, which looked as ancient as the rest of the structure.

"Not sure you should even be up there," Ted stated tepidly, always amazed that someone in her profession so easily played fast and loose with other people's rules.

"Don't see a sign that says 'Don't enter.' Besides, it's locked."

Just as a large mouth might sense a new meal, the tower's knotty walnut door retracted inward. It was like a dried-up tongue pulled back to reveal a blackened opening surrounded by rotten stone teeth. The weathered appendage disappeared into the darkness, stopping with a clank.

A bearded man wearing official-looking work clothes of white and yellow stepped from the gaping orifice and jerked to a stop on seeing TJ there.

She quickly flashed her usual bright smile and added a warm, "Hola."

"Hola, Senora," the man replied, far more reserved than her.

"Can we, I mean, *podemos*..."

"You want to see inside?" the worker asked her, and then beckoned to both with his hand. "It's okay."

"Gracias, Senor," Ted replied from below, expending pretty much the totality of his limited Spanish vocabulary in one sentence.

TJ quickly stepped into the dark tower opening while Ted started up the brick steps, stopping just before the small doorway to glare at some point off the horizon, over Malaga.

"Come on in, Ted, you've got to see th—" TJ halted mid-sentence after gathering in her husband's demeanor.

She couldn't see what he saw because he was looking at something outside, past the tower. She bounced a little as she waited for him to tell her what it was, so she could resume her exploration.

Only a few hundred yards away, the same column of white seagulls continued its aerobatics, swooping around and around above them all, like a giant living corkscrew-shaped light fixture in the sky. But another larger swarm of gulls barrel-rolled from the west into the natural chandelier of birds above Alcazaba's grounds. The larger group of aggressor gulls broke through their brethren's columns, attacking each of the scattering birds.

Ted's chin started to sag. What he was seeing looked like a WWI dogfight between birds of the same feather, directly above. At first a surreal fascination, it quickly turned gruesome. After biting, ripping, and clawing at their panicked kin, sending their damaged bodies plunging to the ground, the aggressor gulls sought out new targets.

The people below.

Like a tsunami, panicked screams started to roll in, first one, then two, then four, as Alcazaba's visitors scattered to the four winds, each flailing at the terrorizing birds. The elderly couple they had passed hobbled toward an exit but then tumbled to the ground as one gull after another pounced on them,

That sight tore Ted from his moorings. He sprinted the rest of the way into the dark safety of the tower structure, nearly sending TJ—who was just making her way back out to see what was keeping him—to the polished brick floor.

"Close the door!" Ted yelled at the worker. "They're attacking."

The confused worker asked in Spanish what the crazy tourist was making such a fuss about.

"Per favore, close the damned door!" Ted hollered. He crawled along the floor and pushed with a shoulder to close the opening.

The worker, his foot blocking the door's closure, craned his head into the outside light, wanting to see with his own eyes why this tourist acted so loco. But then just as quickly, he pulled himself back inside and thrust his palms into the hard wood. Just before it loudly clasped shut, two thumps, like deep tremors, vibrated from the other side, causing both men to jump and exchange knowing glances.

"What the hell is going on out there?" TJ yelped.

"The birds; they're attacking!" Ted answered.

TJ was about to toss back a sarcastic comment about the Hitchcock classic, but held back after seeing Ted's face, and then hearing the screams outside. "What birds?" she stuttered.

"*Mira*," the worker said, now pointing to a long slit in an opposite wall, a few feet away from them. TJ studied the place where defenders used to shoot their arrows at attacking invaders centuries earlier. When the tower was open to tourists, this deep cleft afforded limited views out over the Puerto de Malaga and the inviting blue of the Med. Now, through the opening streamed terror-filled screams and shrieks from gulls, some of whom streaked by in flashes of white, gray, and blood-red.

The three of them tentatively ambled toward the opening to get a better look. TJ reached it first and stuck her face into the top of the six-inch-wide space.

Before the other two could reach her, she screamed and flopped backward onto the hard floor. A gull crashed into the opening with a thump, stopped short by its extended wings.

The men gasped at the red-eyed bird as it thrashed to gain traction with its claws and broken wings, but then fell away from the opening, out of sight.

"*Mierda*!" the worker panted.

They remained fixed in their places, for a moment, before TJ jumped back up. She quickly snatched up a pile of coveralls on the floor and shoved them into the opening. Ted and the worker followed her lead, snagging drop-cloths from a pile and completely sealing the opening.

They listened to the muffled shrieks from the birds and the occasional scream from a human, until there were no more of either. Waiting for what seemed like an hour, but was more likely just a few minutes, they carefully pulled the makeshift stopper from the opening.

They watched and listened for a longer period before they dared to brave the door.

Whatever had just happened was over now.

"*Se terminó?*" the worker asked them, still breathless.

"I think so," replied Ted, the first of them to tentatively descend the stairs, followed by TJ.

The cobbled walkways were carpeted in bloodied and mostly dead seagulls and a few other birds. Every fifth or sixth carcass flopped or fluttered with weakening brays. Splatters of blood were everywhere.

As they hurriedly navigated the ancient path out of the castle, Ted and TJ clasped their hands, clutching each other so hard their knuckles turned white. So fixated were they on the sky and getting out of Alcazaba, and then Malaga quickly, they didn't even notice the old couple they had passed on the way in. The two ancient lovers who had drawn Ted's admiration were slumped in a dark corner of the entrance, the first human casualties of the attack.

03

Puerto de Malaga

"Leave it," TJ demanded, her voice all wobbly. "We'll call the rental company from the ship. We can mail the key in when we get home. It'll cost, but I don't want to spend another moment in Spain."

Ted was already out of the car, double-parked outside the port entrance, and gathering their bags from the trunk. "How far to the ship?" He asked this partially out of a nervous need to say something, as he could plainly see three cruise ships in the distance. But the port also looked pretty big and he didn't want them to take a wrong turn. And although it was the first time either of them had been to the Malaga port, he knew she'd studied the map and knew by asking she'd be focused on where they needed to go next so they wouldn't dawdle out in the open.

"I know this is the way."

He slid a rollered bag into her hand, and they scurried across the street and into the vast Puerto de Malaga.

They walked in hurried silence down a long, straight pedestrian street filled with shops on their left, bustling with people. On their right, the boarded walkways of a dock ran parallel. Small but expensive boats were intermittently tethered, each gently swaying to the Med's incoming tide.

Their eyes continually darted toward the dark sky, tracking on any bird that fluttered above.

On their left, a small delivery van stopped in front of a store, making a delivery of supplies or perhaps picking up the few baubles that didn't sell well.

Glorious aromas of coffee from the street-side restaurants fought against pungent scents of decaying sea-life pushed in by the cold waterfront breezes.

It all felt normal.

Those not milling around the shops seemed to be ambling in the same direction as them, although at a much more leisurely pace: probably passengers on their cruise ship or one of the others.

As they passed each clog of tourists—all pulling giant bags on rollers—they'd attempt to catch a bit of their conversations. Only a few spoke English, and none of those spoke about anything of importance. All seemed jovial and unconcerned.

Ted and TJ maintained their constant pace in silence.

Their ride from Alcazaba had consisted of short bursts of navigational instructions, but no other words. The whole time to the port and even now, both their minds were mentally racing to keep up their anxious desire to get to safety, away from the outside, sure another attack was imminent.

But no one here was anxious. There was no panic.

It was human nature to discount an event that went against all measures of normalcy. And both were doing this in their own ways. Perhaps what they experienced only occurred at Alcazaba and nowhere else. It had to have been an anomaly, based on what they were seeing now. It might have been terror-filled, but only incidental. As their minds continued to discount the enormity of what they witnessed, the adrenaline stopped pumping and fatigue quickly caught up to their steady march. The endorphins had long since ebbed, and now they felt tired. Yet they didn't slow.

They found themselves coming up to their ship, the Intrepid. As if they needed any prompting to board, it let loose a long horn blast.

Between them and their destination was a giant terminus where a few other passengers calmly lolled inside. Most of the passengers, they suspected, were on board, as they had chosen to check in as late as possible, to as TJ said, "give them more time to enjoy Malaga." Of course, the bird attack scuttled that idea.

Only when they were forced to slow their pace, and feeling the safety of the giant building beckoning them inside, did TJ start to breathe just a little easier.

Ted's breathing increased the moment he saw the huge crowd inside. His eyes appeared to nearly pop out of their sockets; his posture stiffened, while almost shrinking.

She knew this look: he was about to go into a full-on freak-out.

Every time this had happened it broke TJ's heart. She couldn't imagine the pain her husband felt losing his first wife and child, all because of his enochlophobia. But she wouldn't let it run its course. She wouldn't let it conquer him. Not this time.

She snatched his hand and dragged him and their bags—leaving one bag with a porter—through the horde and the port security.

TJ did most of the talking for them at check-in, while he focused on his breathing.

They might just make it through without incident, or so they thought.

After receiving their Seacards they were told to head up to the gangway, which led to the entrance of the ship. They were definitely among the tail-end of the incoming passengers. Purposely avoiding most of the crowds was by TJ's design. And Ted was thankful for this.

Just inside the gangway entrance, they stopped at the rail to allow a small clump of passengers to move past them.

It was their first moment of inactivity since Alcazaba.

Each examined the other, faces still drawn tight. Ted brushed a lock of TJ's hair away from her cheek and flashed a warm smile. He breathed a deep and exaggerated breath. "Whew, we made it, huh?"

She returned his smile. Even though the gangway was mostly covered, she still felt anxious. Part of it must have been Ted, she reasoned.

They watched their fellow passengers, also in the gangway, slowly process onto the ship. The awaiting crew welcomed them on board with beaming faces.

Below them, a few of the ship's crew pushed carts of baggage into a much larger entrance. One cart even held kennels containing a variety of dogs: pets of the passengers who paid for the privilege of sailing the Atlantic with their animals.

It was all the normal hubbub of a cruise preparing to leave port. No one, not a single soul, appeared to reflect any of the angst or fear Ted and TJ had been feeling.

"It's almost like what we witnessed never happened, isn't it?" The ship's horns sounded again, with two long blasts, which were deafening this close, even inside their enclosed gangway. TJ watched the lazy movements of a couple more passengers ambling behind them, and still others being welcomed inside.

After a while, TJ noticed that Ted had not answered her. She turned to him, concerned that maybe he was still not dealing well with the crowds, even though they weren't that large at all.

That concern changed focus quickly when she saw him; he had that same look he'd had at the castle. "Ted?" She wasn't really after an answer.

He clutched her forearm, not diverting his gaze.

She followed his gaze, squinting to see what he must have been staring at. Her glasses were in her purse so she couldn't quite focus that far.

She felt the presence of a few other passengers on the gangway and noticed that they too were also seemingly mesmerized by something going on outside the port entrance where they had just abandoned their rental car.

She blinked harder and squinted tighter, wishing her eyes worked better.

In the distance, in front of a few plumes of smoke coming from the city center—which normally might have drawn a curious glance—there was a growing haze. The haze clung to the ground, like a smoke cloud rolling toward the port entrance.

It reminded TJ of the occasional haboob they'd see in Arizona, near where they lived: a growing billow of dust that would consume everything in its path, dumping tons of sand on homes, businesses, vehicles, people, and pets. This swelling wave was similar in that its dusty mass seemed to consume most everything in its path. Only this cloud didn't appear to be anywhere near as tall as a haboob. In fact it couldn't have been more than a few feet above the ground, whereas a haboob could reach a thousand feet, or more.

Also peculiar, this cloud was only moving down Paseo Reding, into the traffic circle of Fuente de la Tres Gracias. When they arrived, they'd noticed the streets of Malaga were covered in a fine gray dust, which had seemed foreign. Their hotel's concierge said this was from the Mount Etna eruption. A wind blowing the dust could create this rolling cloud. But that didn't explain why the dirty billows were tracking along only a couple of the streets.

At the traffic circle, connecting several streets, the cloud noticeably turned and blew into the port entrance.

It wasn't a weather event.

"Look, it's moving toward us, almost ..."

"... like it was sentient," Ted finished.

"What is it? It doesn't look like the birds up on the castle," she stammered.

As their hearts accelerated, they gawked in horror as this undulating mass of murk quickly churned down Paseo de la Farola, the main street through to the port—parallel to the one they'd just walked on.

A man crossing the street, seemingly unaware of the oncoming cloud, turned to look—it must be making a noise—and in his surprise, he tripped and fell onto the pavement. A small van veered off the road to avoid the man, crashing into a building.

The wave didn't hesitate. It blew closer, consuming all in its path.

Now, the pedestrians on the parallel street were running. Their frantic screams arrived in breeze-filled wisps.

Ted squeezed TJ's arm tighter and flashed a puzzled grimace at her.

TJ couldn't stand it. She had to see what this was. She snatched her glasses from her purse with her free hand and banged them onto her face.

She quickly averted her eyes and peered into his. Hers were filled with puddles. "Oh my God, Ted. What the hell is going on?" But neither of them could understand what was at the root of the cloud and why the people and cars were reacting this way. Dust blowing over you would not cause the fear these people obviously felt.

Finally, TJ could see what caused the clouds, and it sucked her breath away.

A younger woman beside Ted shrieked in horror.

But it was Ted who announced the cause of the pandemonium. "No! Those cannot be rats. What ... what are they doing?"

"Attacking," TJ answered, her voice cracking.

"What? What are they attacking.?"

It was a rhetorical question, because each of them watched the wave of rats attack everything with a heartbeat: men, women, children, dogs.

When the bile rose in his throat, Ted seemed to be the only one to understand what this meant to them. "Um... I think," he announced in a loud voice, "we should all get on the ship." He backed away from the railing, pulling his wife with him. They bolted toward the ship entrance at the end of their gangway, a very long hundred yards away.

But he and TJ were the only ones moving.

At least ten passengers lingered on the gangway, holding fast to the railing, gawking. Two even held up their cameras in an attempt to chronicle this oncoming spectacle. TJ shouted, "Let's get going, people, before the rats get here."

Apparently, the use of "rats" in a sentence had the same value as shouting "Fire!"

That moved them.

The final passengers trotted behind Ted and TJ, their heavy footfalls and squealing baggage wheels a deafening swell as they bounced toward the ship entrance: their mutual finish line.

"Slow down, folks," commanded a crew member who thrust out his palms to hold back the wave of worried tourists coming his way.

They slowed, with Ted and TJ still leading.

A muffled din grew in the background.

A few terror-filled screams ripped through their frenzied calm, breaking down their usual decorum, and they pushed forward faster.

They panicked when they could hear the cacophony of little squeals and the scampering of thousands of little feet, like heavy raindrops on a metal roof.

"They're coming," someone yelled and pushed past TJ and bounded into the crew member, sending both tumbling to the ground.

Other security crew members emerged from the door, thinking a fight had broken out.

Ted and TJ held at a bridge connecting the port's gangway with the ship's opening. Ted yelled to an approaching security guard, "We need to get on board and you need to close up the doors. See that? It's rats." He gestured behind them to where he could hear the roiling mass.

The guard could see a wave of movement stream up the gangway stairs and toward them. The remaining guests slipped past him, some abandoning their bags.

He blinked twice in sudden comprehension and pushed Ted and TJ toward the opening.

With everyone in, the guard halted at the entrance and glared at the open hatch.

"Can't you close this?" TJ asked, her voice growing more unsteady.

The panicked guard turned his glare to her and said, "Only the OOD, security director, or captain can announce the command to seal up early."

"Then call the fricking captain!" Ted howled.

04

Captain Christiansen

"Staff Captain, what am I looking at?" bellowed Captain Jörgen Christiansen.

All heads of the bridge crew rubbernecked in the same direction. They gawked through their starboard windows, down the gangway below, fixated on the fast approaching wave of just what they didn't know. None paid attention to the ringing phone, its light indicating it was from their starboard main guest entrance. It would ring when they wanted to close up, or if there was a problem.

"Sir..." Staff Captain Jean Pierre Haddock hesitated through his binoculars, "I think they're rats."

Captain Christiansen didn't need any other prompting. Jean Pierre confirmed what his own disbelieving eyes were telling him. He learned long ago not to worry about the reasons why something was happening. He dealt in facts, and not in what was unexplainable. He had no idea why waves of rats were streaming in their direction, but he did know he didn't want those damned things invading his ship, just as they appeared to be invading the port. "Sound the call to close up and to pull away from the dock."

The officer on deck or OOD, Urban Patel, didn't hesitate, slapping a big red button on a panel below him, which sounded the horns announcing their departure. The deep blare of their ship's horns was loud even in the protected confines of the bridge.

Usually Security Chief Spillman, who was MIA at this moment, would ring the second officer on duty at the gangway entrance. So Wasano Agarwal, the first officer of security and now senior on the bridge, followed protocol and picked up the ringing phone. "Close up, now! Pull in everyone waiting to board; everyone else who comes after will need to wait."

He hung up the receiver and picked it up again, punching another button on the comm's console. "Close up, leave whatever baggage isn't already on board... No arguments. Do it now!"

"I can confirm the doors are closing," said Jessica Eva Mínervudóttir, first officer of navigation, watching her panel. "The passenger door is closing. The freight doors are already closed."

"Release from the dock now," encouraged the captain.

"What about the pilot boat, sir?" Jean Pierre asked.

"We'll wait just off the dock. I don't want any of those rats on my ship." The captain's head and binoculars were one, aimed like a gun barrel pointed at the leading edge of the first wave of rats fast approaching along the gangway. They seemed to be surging toward them even faster.

He moved over to the exit onto the starboard-side swing deck, to get a better look and to hear what he was seeing. The bridge was soundproof as well as waterproof to protect it during the gales of the heavy storms they sometimes encountered at sea.

The moment the steel hatch cracked open, the frantic sounds of Puerto de Malaga poured into the bridge. The crew peered in the door's direction. For only a few seconds, they paid little attention to their monitors as the outside blared a violent torrent of screams, car crashes, frenzied horns, and something else.

It was a haunting sound: an escalating frenzy that built upon itself; a horrific drumbeat of hundreds of thousands of scampering feet and their corresponding squeaks. A crescendo that grew with each passing second.

The captain could only stand the nightmarish sounds for so long. But before he turned back into the bridge and sealed them once more into their orderly bubble, he caught a quick glance of a sight that would haunt his nights, perhaps for the rest of his life: a couple of dock workers and at least one crew member overwhelmed by blankets of rats.

He had once witnessed the decapitation of a crew member, back when he was a first officer. He always thought that was the most horrible sight he would ever see. This was worse.

Jörgen stepped back onto the bridge and slammed the door, sealing out the chaos. It was the one space over which he had some control. Outside, he had none. He felt the troubled eyes of his crew on him, all wide, and close to panic.

But the quiet was like a balm to their frayed nerves. And the strength of their captain was an elixir.

Captain Christiansen only momentarily flashed anything resembling worry before his usual stern presence stood before them. "Report, how many on board?" He didn't know what the hell was going on out there, but he knew his crew would be able to focus on their duties if he directed them. That would give them all a much-needed sense of control. Duties now; discover what's happening later.

"They're still counting the last few who squeezed aboard when we closed the doors." Jean Pierre fixated on his tablet. It flashed up-to-the-moment details about the ship, its passengers, and its crew. He kept his eyes glued to it for a prolonged period before giving the count, as if staring at it a little longer would somehow increase the dismal numbers. *"So far,"* he stressed, "728 guests and 501 crew. Only one cart of luggage didn't make it. And we're fully supplied."

The ship was supposed to have 1525 guests and 700 crew. Most of the missing could be easily attributed to the many flight cancellations. But he also knew others didn't make it because of the rat attacks—still, it seemed utterly ridiculous to even consider that supposition.

"Captain?" Jean Pierre asked. "What should we do now?" This kind of thing—rat attacks and departing early, leaving passengers and crew behind—was not part of their training or experience.

"First Officer Mínervudóttir, call the harbor master and tell them to get the pilot boat here in two minutes or we're plowing through the harbor without him."

"I'm on it, sir," Jessica fired back.

Jean Pierre held his gaze on the captain. "No, sir. I meant what do we do about the missing passengers?"

Captain Jörgen Christiansen looked at each of his crew, who returned his steady glare with apprehension. He'd served with these five men and one woman for almost four years now, and they'd been through a lot, including one hurricane, one rogue wave, even an attempted boarding by terrorists. But none of them had ever been through anything like this.

He learned a long time ago, as he was making the ranks on his way to becoming captain, to deal with what you know. These are the only actions over which you'll ever have control. Don't focus on those things you have no control over. They'll take care of themselves.

"We're going to do our one job now, which is to take care of our current passengers and crew. OOD Patel, please contact corporate and let them know, so they can get help on the ground and make arrangements for the stranded guests. We'll get through this together, okay?"

"Aye, Captain," they responded together.

"Mr. Haddock, can I see you in my ready room?"

T he two marched in and sat at the same conference table they'd met around hundreds of times to discuss everything from the highly significant, like which crew member to fire, to the insignificant, such as whether or not they should give a free spa package to a certain guest to keep them happy. The gravity of what they needed to discuss now weighed heavily on both.

Jörgen hovered for a moment over a side table, slowly pouring equal measures of coffee into two mugs from a carafe that was always kept full and hot by one of his crew. He mindlessly set the full cups down on the conference table. "I wanted to speak to you before the rest of the crew about some troubling issues ahead of us, which are going to come to light soon." He took the seat beside his number one, grabbed his Uffda coffee mug and sipped the hot liquid.

"You mean more troubling than a swarm of rabid rats attacking our guests and crew?" Jean Pierre didn't want any coffee. He was fully amped up at this moment, his body providing all the natural stimulant it needed, and so he certainly didn't need caffeine. Besides, Jean Pierre was barely hanging onto his wits, by the edges of his fingernails. He was mere seconds away from drowning in waves of his own fear. He took in quick shuddering breaths, trying to calm himself down.

Jean Pierre knew that it was important to look strong and decisive in front of the rest of the crew, especially on the bridge. His captain had taught him this. But in here, in the captain's ready room, Jean Pierre knew he could be himself, speak his mind, and let his hair down (assuming he had any). "Captain, what the hell is going on? If you have additional information, please tell me."

"That's what I wanted to talk to you about," Jörgen paused and gazed at his staff captain. "I don't mind telling you that I'm terrified of what we'll be dealing with in the next few days."

This caught Jean Pierre by complete surprise. He had never thought his captain was afraid of anything. Crazed terrorists proved that to him. Plus, he wasn't speaking about what just happened; he was speaking about what was going to happen.

Jörgen turned on his tablet, scrolled down the screen, and started to read off a laundry list of subjects which normally would be terrifying for any cruise ship, but seemed mellow by comparison to what they were witnessing right now in Malaga.

"We've already spoken about the Icelandic volcano, which is still erupting, and so is Mount Etna. We know these are causing all sorts of navigational difficulties to the north and east. And we must be prepared for the sea traffic, which will be abnormally heavy. But what has me most concerned is the report of tremors on two of the Canaries. There was one report that stated that La Palma might blow any day now. Here it is." Jörgen read the report dispassionately, like he was reading off the daily fuel numbers.

Although he had just said otherwise, Jörgen seemed completely calm. And it was having an effect on Jean Pierre. He could feel his blood pressure simmering and he pushed up straighter in his chair. He no longer felt the uncontrollable panic that was overwhelming him only moments ago, in spite of the terrifying news.

Just then, Jean Pierre realized this was by design.

Jörgen knew him that well, that he obviously saw he was about ready to break. This short time in the ready room was to enable them to take stock of what they knew, as well as what they didn't know. To focus on the ship-related issues and the corresponding actions they would need to take. It was all bad news. But it was factual. They could apply their years of experience to each of these data points and come up with the best solution available. And when new data arrived, they would render similar or different judgments. They would figure it out, together. Just like they always did. They would figure this out too.

"What do the reports for Gibraltar look like tomorrow?" Jean Pierre asked, preparing himself for the worst.

Jörgen tapped a corner of his screen and scanned through the summary provided by Jessica, who besides overseeing navigation looked at weather, currents, ship traffic, and anything else that might affect their successfully making it to the next port on time.

"Looks like smooth sailing. Since we're leaving a little early, we can take our time getting there and assess the situation in the Canaries as we get closer," Jörgen resolved.

"Okay, I'll ask about the horse in the room—"

"—you mean elephant?" Jörgen corrected, smiling at Jean Pierre's misstatement.

Jean Pierre was always trying to improve upon his American idioms, but he still had a ways to go. Since Jörgen was a lover of American culture, he taught Jean Pierre many he hadn't yet heard. This slip would be fast forgotten—Jörgen often kidded him about his slip-ups—because Jean Pierre was not on his A-game. *Another idiom.*

"Yes, the elephant, or rather, thousands of crazy rats..." Jean Pierre trailed off, unsure what to ask.

There was a knock on the door. It was Jessica.

"Sorry to interrupt." She nodded first to Jörgen and then Jean Pierre. "We've released from the port, but we had to abandon our stern line because the dock was overwhelmed by... by the..." She paused, her eyes welled and her lower lip quivered. She recalled the mental picture of the dock workers being attacked, and of the rats running up the line toward the ship. She shook her head. "Sorry. Also, there's no answer from the harbor master—or anyone at the port authority, for that matter. As far as we can tell, the port operators have left the harbor. But there is little to no large traffic right now. Just a few small craft. So I'd recommend we go, while we can." Jessica hesitated at the door, like she held a secret that she wasn't supposed to reveal. "And Staff Captain," she said to Jean Pierre, "Mrs. Williams and her husband did make it on board."

"Thank you, First Officer. Unless there's anything more, we'll be just a minute more," Jörgen replied and waited for his first officer to leave and close the door behind her. When the door clicked closed, he continued. "The rats at this point don't matter, Jean Pierre. I fear it's not the worst thing we'll witness during this cruise." He let his words sink in before continuing.

"But our job is still the same: to keep everyone safe, comfortable and happy. In other words, I want us to do everything we can to keep our guests and crew thinking about anything other than what's going on in the outside world."

"Aye, Captain."

"And find me Spillman!"

05

Robert Spillman

Security Chief Robert Spillman had a secret he was desperate to keep under wraps. His professional life depended on it.

Before his appointment, he waited for the monitor room shift change. When the incoming monitor stood in front of the MR door's small inset window, the outgoing monitor got up and left the room to "pass the baton" or hand over the MR key just outside the door. This process ensured that no more than one monitor was in the room at a time, which Robert argued helped to protect the ship's privacy policy. Actually, Spillman's procedure promoted the breaking of the ship's privacy policy, and that was on purpose.

Usually, the outgoing monitor took the opportunity at this point in the key exchange to also pass on stories about the passengers who did stupid things because they didn't realize they were being watched and recorded on one of the four hundred and sixty cameras spread throughout the ship. Discussing what passengers did on camera during work was against Regal European's policies. But that never stopped them.

Like Robert, the monitors attempted to keep their "non-work" activities outside the ever-present cameras' purview. Since there were no cameras just outside the

MR doorway, the exchange provided the monitors ample opportunity to trade stories and pass notes as to where to find the discussed videos. All video feeds were copied and retained in a multi-terabyte hard drive for the duration of the cruise. The drives were swapped out during the turnover, when a new itinerary started. And then new stupid passenger feeds would be copied and stored again.

While the two monitors were occupied with each other, Robert made sure he wasn't seen and flicked a switch that turned off all the deck 2 cameras. He was purposely quick and stealthy about this, as he only had a few minutes today before the captain noticed he was missing. He also knew the discussion outside wouldn't last as long, as there were no stories yet to tell about this cruise: the passengers were just getting on board.

Once the passengers' lips had become more pliable after the application of the ship's overpriced alcohol and they had tested out the boundaries of the ship, the stories between the incoming and outgoing monitors would be longer and more animated.

He closed the monitor room behind him. His two men's heads snapped to attention, their lips falling quiet at his presence.

He enjoyed this.

"Don't mind me, gents. It's pretty quiet right now, and I won't be back for a while." That was code for, *Screw off as much as you'd like, because I won't be watching over you.*

That would also give him at least ten minutes to do what he needed to do before being seen.

"Thanks Security Chief," they both acknowledged, having difficulty holding back their grins.

Robert took the public elevator down six floors to deck 2 and quickly moved forward through the port-side hallway to the first wall panel, using his master key to open a metal cabinet. Inside, multi-colored wires ran up and down the left side of the long foot-deep enclosure, some stopping midway at a circuit board. This was where various electronics for this hallway were connected to the ship's main lines. He reached in and without hesitation grabbed a blue wire and yanked it out of its board, leaving it just off its connector, as if it had somehow jostled itself loose on its own. This would disable only the port-side, deck 2 hall cameras aft of the elevators.

Soon, his on-duty monitor would notice that deck 2 cameras were black. After flicking them back on, if he was paying attention, he'd notice cameras 63 through 68 were still dark. Once it was confirmed that only these deck 2 cameras weren't working, and it wasn't a connection in the MR, maintenance would be called to investigate. Robert figured he had at least thirty minutes now.

He wouldn't need that long.

He shut the panel and casually walked aft, toward cabin 2071.

A couple lurked around their cabin entrance, in between him and his destination, causing Robert to stop in front of a restricted doorway. Using his card, he unlocked and pushed open the door that warned "Crew Only" and hung inside the small well which gave crew access to a separate elevator and stairwell. It was similar to the passengers' access, but far more utilitarian in design.

He pushed his back into the door, like he was holding it open for a crew member, and listened just out of view for the couple to leave or go back into their cabin. He craned his head forward and cupped a palm around an ear to block out the active chatter coming from above and below him.

The guests closed their door and he heard a female voice say something in German.

He waited for them to turn and exit to the public elevator, a few steps away. They shouldn't even pass by this doorway.

Robert examined his watch, feeling each minute ebb away deep in his groin.

"Hello, Security Chief," sang one of the seventy-five or so room attendants, who came from below and turned to ascend the stairwell like a light breeze on his way to a higher deck. Robert didn't recognize the young Croatian man and guessed he was one of the new crew members, reporting in late. His supervisor would cut him some slack this time, because several of the new crew were late or simply didn't make it because of the flight delays.

"Excuse me," a heavyset man said—everyone who took a cruise was heavyset in Robert's opinion. "Where pool?" The man had a distinctive German accent and obviously a poor command of the English language. There would be a lot of Germans on board this cruise, as the cruise line heavily advertised in Germany.

He almost grunted his reply, but corrected himself quickly. "Take the lift you just passed on your left, and go up seven floors to deck nine. Then walk aft maybe fifty steps and it's right there." Robert said this with a fake smile, pointing down the hall. He wanted to say to them, "Can't you read a fucking map, you stupid krauts?" He didn't like German cruisers much. They expected perfection from everyone, except themselves.

"Danke," said the woman, who had to be at least twice the man's size. They both waddled away, clutching their room towels. Cruisers always brought their room towels to the pool, even though the pool provided towels for them so that they wouldn't ruin the ones from their room. Not that they cared.

He closed the crew-access door and waited for the unbearably slow German couple to exit.

Finally, they left the hallway.

Robert moved abruptly, like a thoroughbred horse bursting from its starting gate.

Better yet, a stud seeking his mare.

There was no one else in the hallway, plus he had very little time now. He was anxious to get started and not suffer through any more delays that would lessen his time of pleasure. He almost jogged the hundred-yard space to the cabin door, tossing a quick glance at the mostly hidden camera above, which he knew wasn't working.

He pulled out a different card he'd retained from a fired employee and slipped it into the door, the lock blinking green, telling him he could enter. He let the door shut on its own. The cabin was mostly dark, with both the curtains and the sheers drawn. A small electronic candle pulsed a flicker from the desk area, casting just enough light to see the outline of the bed. This was funny since he didn't need any mood lighting. He just wanted sex.

"You late. You get in my bed now," said Chen Lee in her poor impression of a sultry voice.

He slipped off his clothes and slid into bed, instantly feeling her warmth as she wrapped her arms and legs around him.

He had barely fifteen minutes now, so their lovemaking would have to be quick.

06

Deep

"Dammit!" croaked Whaudeep Reddy, or Deep as the other crew called him, banging the flat-screen monitor, as if that would make it work again.

He grabbed the radio microphone, switched to the channel monitored by maintenance and said, "Hey, this is Deep in security. Buzz, are you there?"

"I'm here," crackled Buzz. He had a longer name that none of the Anglos could pronounce, and since he was the expert at making all things electrical work on the ship, everyone called him Buzz. Both were on their ninth contracts and they'd worked together on the Intrepid all nine years. "What's up, Deep?"

"The deck 2 hall cameras are down again. I thought your guys had fixed this." Deep wasn't accusing his friend, or his mates. But he did want him to know his level of frustration over one of the many things that didn't seem to work on their fifteen-year-old ship. And this was even after their ship had just come out of dry-dock, where so many things had been replaced and cleaned up.

"Sorry, Deep, I did too. I'll check it out myself this time."

"Thanks, Buzz. Hey, I have three for the game tonight."

Deep and Buzz had an ongoing card game almost every night in the crew living room, especially when they were on the same shift, as they were on this itinerary.

"Excellent. See you after the change. Buzz out."

Deep almost jumped out of his seat when he realized the staff captain had quietly entered the MR while he was on the radio. Or was it before? He immediately felt his mouth dry up like the desert: the second in command of the ship just heard him talk about their card game. They were not allowed to gamble on the ship, so they used a system of old ravioli noodles, colored to represent different denominations. Either Buzz or he kept a tally of winners and losers. All who played that week would settle up each Friday at the Slop House—the crew's mini-market—where the loser would buy the winner the equivalent number of desired products using their Regal European Seacards. They played the game in plain sight, so that everyone thought they were just playing for the fun of it. But he always wondered when one of their superiors would find out.

"Sir." He stood up to greet the ship's second in command, his right knee banging loudly against his work table. "I'm sorry, I didn't hear you come in." His voice cracked.

"Please sit down. I didn't want to interrupt you. What's going on with the deck 2 cameras?" Jean Pierre now stood over the young man and glared at the deck 2 monitor, which was black and then flashed images of the starboard cabins, then the forward cabins, aft, then it was dark again.

"Don't know exactly. When I came onto shift, the switches were off for Decks Two and Five. When I switched them back on, deck 2 never fully came on. We had this same problem yesterday and the day before. So I'm having maintenance look into it again. Well, you probably heard that part."

Jean Pierre seemed to think about this for a moment and then asked, "Is the security chief around?"

"Ahh, I saw him up here right when I came on shift, but I'm not sure where he went. Do you want me to call him for you?"

"No, that won't be necessary. Actually, I wanted to see the tape on deck 7, the aft suites, for the last hour or so. Can you pull that up for me?"

Deep tossed him a curious glance before working his magic. The staff captain almost never examined video recordings. That's what the security chief would do, and usually only after one of the passengers had done something to warrant the attention. Deep wanted to take advantage of this rare opportunity to show off his talents to his superior and he started to relax a little, thinking maybe he dodged a bullet on their illegal card game. He knew right where to look for this video, having brought up passenger recordings thousands of times at the insistence of Fish, who had the shift before him, especially tapes of the pretty ones.

Fish, or Fish-Eye as he was called by his mates, had already made a listing of the times and camera numbers for the feeds Deep needed to examine to see the beauties who had checked into their cabins. Today's listings were for the deck 7 aft and deck 8 forward cameras. Deep hadn't planned on taking a look at these until after he'd been on his shift for a few hours, when he knew no one else would be checking in on him.

"Here sir," he said, setting the video replay on 4X, so they could cover the span of an hour in fifteen minutes. Any faster and they'd miss something.

Less than five minutes later, the staff captain had him stop and view it in real time. Yes, Deep thought, just as his friend Fish told him. *She is beautiful, for an older woman. And she is blond!* He loved blondes.

07

TJ and Ted (4:27 PM)

Without missing a step, she flicked her blonde hair back over her shoulder.

They marched aft, down the long hallway, over the ridiculously-colored carpet. Ted trailed behind, their rollered bags squealing their displeasure behind him.

"I just want to get to our room and drink heavily," Ted said.

"I think 7652 is right down here," she mumbled, glancing at her Seacard once again for confirmation, even though she knew only the last two digits appeared on it.

"So the last thing I want to do is clink glasses with strangers tonight, or with the captain tomorrow, and all the while pretend everything is good with the world."

"Here it is right here, corner balcony," she emoted, all too chipper considering what they just went through.

"Have you heard a word I've said?"

"Yep, every one." She slid her card into the card reader. A little green light pulsed a confirmation that it was the right one, and she pushed the door open a crack.

"Fine, I'm dumping my bag and bellying up to the Irish pub I saw on the ship's map."

"Okay, if that's what you want to do," she said, not even allowing a wisp of emotion to salt her words. She took her bag from him, pulled it through the narrow doorway into the room and let the heavy door flop back, like a Venus flytrap. It thumped closed on her husband.

A few seconds later, the lock clicked open. Ted withdrew his card and pushed open the door. "Man, you piss me off sometimes." His voice imitated hot, but he wasn't really that fiery.

"I know, that's why you love me." She flashed a playful smile at him.

She was very familiar with this game. Ted often played the victim in circumstances such as these, when he didn't want to deal with other people, especially a lot of people. The victim thing—which he played rather poorly—was in hopes of garnering enough sympathy from her to release him from tonight's dinner with a table full of strangers or that he'd be let out of his obligation with the captain tomorrow night. But she needed him to keep up appearances and although she rarely participated, she couldn't completely shut him down now as she often would in these kinds of circumstances.

She snickered again, and then suppressed her smile, pretending serious. "Look, if you want to go on a binge or continue your anti-social behavior on my vacation, and on our anniversary, I'm not going to stop you. We can order room service tonight, but don't think you're going to abandon me to a dinner that was set up in your honor tomorrow. And don't forget the captain is a big fan of yours. You wouldn't want to let one of your biggest fans down, would you?" She batted her eyes at him for effect.

Then she did turn somewhat serious.

"And as far as the drinking goes, I'm the one who's going to be pissed if you don't take me with you drinking. After almost getting eaten by Cujo, then a flock of fucking seagulls and then a billion damned Bens, I need to do some heavy drinking myself."

Ted didn't say anything in rebuttal, pretending to examine the couch, while she quickly started the process of unpacking. She often would do busy things when she was anxious.

She paused and glared at him for a long moment before continuing.

"And before we both get slobbery drunk, you need to make sure I can call Mom. I can't figure out the damned ship's cell service. Even though we texted our families, I just want her to hear my voice before she reads about any of this, whatever *this is*."

Ted plopped into the couch and just nodded. They'd been married long enough for him to know when she was releasing her pent-up worries, it was best to just let her finish before he said anything.

She wasn't done, but flicked her hair once again, not for show but because it bothered her. It wasn't tied up into her normal ponytail, the way she liked it. She was trying to be a little more dolled up for their cruise.

"Finally, and speaking of almost getting eaten, are we going talk about what we've witnessed the last thirty-six hours and what's going on?"

Ted removed his ball cap and ran a hand through his thinning black hair. That was his tell that he was deliberately considering what she had said, and he was choosing his words carefully.

"Can we decompress about all of this later? I still need to consider a few things. Maybe tomorrow?"

It was the way Ted's mind processed things—like an engineer, very methodically. He never rushed to judgment. He was always stable like that. And although it was what she preferred, she sometimes wished he'd act irrational, just a little.

"Fine. I'm going for a run, then." She moved toward the bathroom, mumbling something unintelligible about needing a busy activity to occupy her mind and an errand she needed to take care of before dinner.

He watched her reach into her bag and precisely find and snatch out her running shorts and sport shirt, as if the bag had handed these items to her.

She disappeared into the bathroom, leaving Ted to himself.

Ted marveled at her organization. Even though their main checked bag, with all their formal clothes, hadn't arrived yet—he wondered if it ever would, based on their abrupt exit from the port—she packed exactly what she needed in her carry-on, and had it placed exactly where she needed it. She'd probably be fine if their main bag never arrived. His stuff was separated unequally between the checked bag and his carry-on; he couldn't even say what was in each. He'd unpack later.

Far more interesting to Ted was what awaited him on the small built-in desk/dressing table. It had mirrors and compartments too small to hold anything useful. More practical was the desk's center, where three bottles of red wine were displayed on a tray. And beside it, a leather-bound notebook.

"All right, now we're talking," he said, mostly to himself, since TJ was out of earshot.

A noise like a muted rocket ship engine blasted away from inside the bathroom. He couldn't help but break a smile at the sound of the turbo toilet, wondering how startling that must have been to some first-timers who used it. TJ had been on many cruises before they met, so that noise was probably old hat to her.

Enough of this. Time to drink.

He turned his attention back to the wine mirage and plucked an envelope sandwiched between two of the bottles. After noticing the RE logo on the top left corner, he pulled out a hand-written note card and paraphrased it loud enough so that she could hear him inside the bathroom. "The captain wants to welcome us on board with these three bottles of wine."

Using the corkscrew—also monogrammed with the solid white on dark blue Regal European logo—he yanked out the cork, and poured half a glass of the red cab. He'd prefer she'd join him in this, but knew she wouldn't have one until after she finished her run. He couldn't wait that long.

In the small open area of the desk, he unfolded his iPad, turned it on, and loaded a copy of his second-to-last book, along with all of his notes.

He sipped the wine and glanced down at the healthy streak left on the side of the glass. It was a bit harsh, but it would do just fine thank you. He took a larger sip.

With eyes focused on his iPad, he went directly to the Research area of his Scrivener program, and opened the document on toxoplasmosis.

Another sip of wine.

"Oh shit," he muttered.

He swallowed the rest of the glass of his wine, no longer tasting it or feeling its warmth in his belly. His ball cap came off again; he put his glass down and massaged his aching temples.

TJ popped out of the bathroom a new woman: her lipstick freshened, her hair pulled back into a tight ponytail, and her slim figure perfectly highlighted by her running outfit.

Ted watched her move with quick determination, briefly admiring his wife's athletic physique, before he turned his attention back to his iPad.

She thrust the clothes she'd been wearing—folded neatly, almost creased—into the already opened small closet, laying them neatly on a middle shelf, and walked over to Ted. "Save some for me, dear." She smiled and pecked him on the lips, turned and marched out the door.

He needed more wine.

TJ had intended to head up to the sun deck, two decks above them, and go for a run. Then she had a meet-up with a ship's officer. But she only made it three steps out of their cabin before she stopped dead. There were dogs barking.

Her head snapped in the direction of an open crew access door. A small man with a big smile was pushing a service cart her way. She wasn't paying him any attention, because her mind was busy attempting to confirm what she thought she had heard. Before the rats attacked the port, they had seen the dog crates being ushered on board. But only now did it connect: these dogs were on her ship, that was their barking, and they could be loose.

That's when the memory flooded back all at once. She had thought she had long since suppressed this, burying it deep down where it would no longer hurt her. She squeezed her eyes shut and desperately tried to think of anything else. Still the memories came: the images, the sounds, the smells... and the fear.

TJ had been in Chicago as part of a larger investigation of Cleavon Drummond, or *Cleavon the Cannibal*, as the media later called him. One of Cleavon's victims was from Tucson and so TJ had flown out to work with their team in Chicago. The next day, they had a warrant for one of Cleavon's suspected locations. Her Chicago equal,

Agent Little, and she were going to cover the back of the property. What their sources never told them was that Cleavon owned several vicious dogs tied off by the exit. Unfortunately for Agent Little, he surprised the dogs. More unfortunate was TJ's deathly fear of animals, and most especially dogs, since it was a dog which had viciously attacked her years earlier. She had hung back behind a dumpster when the animals struck. Even though she was supposed to cover him, she froze. She even retreated farther behind the dumpster to get away from the animals.

The dogs tore the agent apart, and she did nothing.

His screams were heard for blocks and other agents came running.

But it was too late.

Agent Little died on the scene and TJ remained in her spot, cowering behind the dumpster, shaking like a leaf in October.

A Chicago PD officer helped her up, though not before commenting, "I sure as hell wouldn't want you backing me up." Turned out that wouldn't be a problem anymore, because after that, TJ had been relieved of her fieldwork.

She froze, and Agent Little died.

"Ms. Williams," called a voice in the distance.

TJ blinked her eyes. She came out of her vivid daydream and found herself nearly hyperventilating.

"Ms. Williams, are you all right?" begged the little man standing in front of her. He'd swapped his willful smile for genuine concern.

"Yes. Thank you." she answered, in a voice that didn't sound like her own. "I'm sorry..." she tried to focus on the man's badge, but was having difficulty."

"I'm *Jagamashi*, but you can call me Jaga."

He was an Indo, she thought. She started to feel a little more... normal. *"Ah, terima kasih, Jaga,"* TJ replied.

53

"*Sama-sama*, Ms. Williams. *Senang sekali bisa ngobrol dengan orang yang bisa berba-hasa Indonesia.*" Jaga smiled genuinely. (Thank you, Ms. Williams. It's so nice to speak to someone who understands Indo.)

"*Bahasa Indonesia saya tidak terlalu bagus.*" TJ chuckled quietly and shrugged. (My Indo is not that good). She was surprised the language had come back from her time in Indonesia.

She took a deep breath. "Thanks Jaga. Speaking to you in Indonesian really helped. Ah, before you go, check in on my husband. He has some questions about room service and I know he'd like some ice."

"Of course. *Sama-sama*, Ms. Williams."

"*Makasih*, Jaga." She smiled and then jogged past Jaga in the direction he had come, tossing a side-glance at the now-closed crew access door. She was glad she had some work after her run. She needed to focus on anything but crazy dogs.

08

The Dogs

Allegro Palmigren Ramgoolam—guests were thankful he went by, Al—loved what he did, especially at times like this.

When he entered the giant thoroughfare known as I-95, the internal "road" which traversed the *Intrepid* from bow to stern, he only heard the muffled mechanical thrum of the ship's powerful engines. Maybe two hours earlier, these spacious halls had been a buzz of activity as many of the officers and crew found their way to all parts of the ship, out of sight of the ship's guests.

A noxious combination of grease and oil filled Al's nostrils. He shot a scornful glance at a chin-high box filled with mechanical parts and gave a tug on the master leash. His canine charges were unrulier than usual.

The box was one of many organized discards which awaited recycling when they ported in Miami fourteen days from now. Even though the cruise had just started, this stretch of hallway was already lined with pallets of various items slated for the same purpose: corrugated boxes, strapped tight into a human-sized square; a multi-colored rectangle of pressed aluminum cans, which reflected dull spikes of hallway light as he walked by; and maybe a dozen other various boxes, the contents of which he didn't know. By the end of the cruise, every square meter of wall surface throughout this vast network of hallways would be crowded with recyclables and other discards.

A crash and a series of thumps in the distance drew his and the dogs' attention.

An unruly toy poodle barked at the unseen clatter and it shot forward, pulling the collection of dogs and Al with it. Al gave a mighty tug on the master leash, which was connected to all the individual leashes, which were connected to each dog's choke-chain. "Heel," he boomed his command.

The pack halted instantly.

The little white poodle, the perpetrator of this undisciplined instigation, coughed twice and then sat its haunches on the gray laminate floor, panting its displeasure at being restrained roughly. The other dogs followed suit.

And so ended the first lesson in tonight's series of lessons, for Al to establish himself as the pack's alpha dog.

"Hello Al." A tall Croatian crew member in a black jumper strode by. The mechanic's head snapped forward after admiring the pack's obedience, and then he turned into a connecting hallway, the echoes of his black Dickies already trailing off into the expanse. Al didn't know the mechanic, other than he was probably from engineering based on his uniform. But the mechanic obviously knew Al.

A chasm-sized smile of bright white spread across Al's face.

Having one of the few pet kennels on any cruise ship, filled Al with a large measure of pride. He often enjoyed boasting on phone calls or on social media to his family and friends in Mauritius, as well as to other crew members, that he had the most unique job among all cruise lines. This wasn't an exaggeration, since other than

RE's *Intrepid*, the only other cruise ship that could claim a pet kennel was the QE2.

Al was also prideful of how well he did his job, the proof of which was evidenced by the generous tips he often received and the many positive comments sent into corporate about him and his pet spa. Regal European responded with elevations in title and pay, lots of praise, and recognition among his shipmates. Corporate even offered to give Al a number of staff befitting his position. He had heard that some in corporate felt a second officer shouldn't be walking dogs, or cleaning cages. But Al preferred to do this job himself. So he operated solo.

But the real secret to Al's success was in how he handled the guests. As he told his mother many times on the phone, it basically came down to giving guests what they wanted, at least in their minds.

Usually the guests stressed over their pet's wellbeing while on the ship, and this was where it would seem (to the guests) that Al focused most of his attention: what food the animal was eating—he ordered food in advance from many specialty outlets all over the world, for which RE charged a generous mark-up; how often they were being fed—he was very careful with this; whether they were getting enough sleep-time—"It's their vacation too," he'd tell the owners; if the other animals were being mean to their pet—"Absolutely not!" he'd insist to them; whether the animals were watching the right programs on TV—"Because they all had their own favorite programs," he'd mimic in a comedic voice to his family through their laughter; the number of times they saw a picture of their "mommy" or "daddy"—the pet's parents always had a specific number in mind; and so many more requirements imposed by the guests on him for the care of their pets. But this was where Al had a secret which helped him excel.

He learned to take copious notes of the guest's instructions and concerns and he made sure to repeat them back to the guests. That way the guests believed their wishes were going to be fulfilled to the fullest measure, even if Al was lax on some of their standards. As he had told his family, "What they don't know won't hurt them." And he could tell pretty quickly what he could get away with and what he couldn't, based on the pet and their owner.

And as a trained and certified vet, Al was also adept at caring for the animals' medical needs.

Most of these animals—typically dogs—were very pampered by their owners, and almost all just wanted attention: they suffered from separation anxiety, especially after being dumped at the kennel. But they also suffered from a sense of being the most important entity in the owner's household, sometimes to the detriment of the owner's own children. It was this pet-centric thinking and the lack of training that led to the pet's overall lack of discipline.

And so the first walk of the cruise was critical.

He always conducted the first walk late during the first night of the cruise. That would allow him to take control over his boarders without any interference from the pets' owners or any well-intentioned crew who might wander by and offer scorn for his seemingly rough methods. He never did anything to harm an animal. It wasn't in his nature. But since most of his boarded pets were undisciplined, just like their owners, he often needed to be aggressive by showing them who was in control.

And there was always that one pet that didn't do what it was told.

This time it was the white-colored toy poodle, owned by a wealthy Brit traveling to one of her homes in the states—he had yet to meet her. Her equally pampered dog, Monsieur, had its own ideas about where they should go. To prove this, the poodle rose and attempted to take off again. But Al wouldn't have it. Snapping back on just Monsieur's leash caused the little dog to once again gasp for air.

It would eventually learn.

Al looked up, and saw the signs pointing to various crew rest areas: The Living Room, the Slop House, and so many other areas all dedicated to the crew. From this point forward to the bow of the ship, he'd experience more crew than he wanted: he just didn't want to find himself under the scrutiny of others while he was training the dogs. And he still had a lot of work ahead of him. Al glared at the poodle, about ready to wander off again.

"Heel!" He tugged hard on the master leash. Two of the dogs yelped in surprise and instantly came to attention. Monsieur went the other way—again.

"Dammit!" he hollered as the little rascal once more tried to dart toward another hallway. *This dog has some of the worst shiny ball syndrome I've ever seen.*

Al did a quick 180, making sure what he did next wasn't seen. He reached over the other dogs' leashes to make sure he grabbed only the poodle's leash and gave an enormous tug. Like a giant rubber-band had broken, little Monsieur snapped back into the air and then tumbled to the feet of the others. A Shepherd in the group unceremoniously stepped on top of the dog—Al would have sworn it was vindictive. The little dog yelped and then attempted to dart away in the other direction, tangling all of their leashes into a web of leather spaghetti.

"No!"

He'd have to untangle this mess quickly, before he lost further control of the situation.

One by one, he unleashed a dog, untangled the leash and reattached the dog to the master leash. When he unhooked Monsieur's leash, the little dog unexpectedly bolted through Al's grip. A flash of white scurried away, then down the hall it had been angling toward the whole time.

Al knew why: this hall contained all the food storage on the ship.

Thinking quickly, he attached the master leash to an orange strap binding two boxes bursting with discarded wood furniture pieces. He trotted after the poodle. The dog, already out of sight, seemed to be hot on the trail of something: no doubt some of the ship's food.

That little dog is about to experience the wrath of Al, he thought as he stomped off after the mutt.

As Al came around several pallets of canned food, he found the poodle. It had stopped in front of the opening of the butcher's area, and was growling a face full of little teeth.

Al proceeded toward the beastie, figuring he could grab it while the dog's attention was on the doorway.

Cold from the refrigerated area met the warm hallway air, condensing it into billowing clouds of dense fog, making the inside invisible. The dog seemed fixated on what was inside.

Now was Al's best chance.

He slowed his pace, meticulously placing one foot in front of the other, to not startle the animal while it was preoccupied with the fog. When he was a couple of feet behind the unsuspecting pooch, he leapt. At the same time, Monsieur decided to dart inside the milky murk.

Al didn't even lay a finger on him.

He glared at the opening shrouded in white mist. He couldn't see a thing.

He had never been inside the butcher's area where they stored the ship's beef, in which one butcher cut up all the meat before sending the cuts to one of the ship's three galleys. Al was a vegetarian, so he'd never had an interest in venturing inside. Now he wished he had.

As he stepped into the vapor, he immediately ran into a table with lumps of beef randomly strewn around it. An icicle of pain dug into his hip.

It occurred to him then that the butcher couldn't have operated in this near invisibility. One of the freezers inside must be open and none of the lights were on. Al squinted his eyes tighter and could only make out that there were one or two large shapes further away. Their images were fuzzy, almost ethereal.

"Hello?" he begged, thrusting his hands out to block anything he might run into, and continued around the table. Now he could only make out the dark sticks of his arms and the two approaching shapes. Then he wondered how he would even see Monsieur. By every measure, he was blind.

"Monsieur," he called out as he moved deeper into the room. He remembered overhearing that it was three rooms in one: a preparation room that he was walking through, one refrigerated storage room full of meat, already prepared and ready to be cooked, and one freezer. He couldn't tell which or if both were opened.

The two shapes, he suspected, were by the cold storage. They were also bigger than he'd thought.

And they almost seemed to be... moving.

Al felt his way around until he reached one of the two shapes. His heart rose up as he touched it. Cold.

It was a side of beef, hanging from the ceiling.

Taking in a breath of the room's arctic-like air, and feeling more confident, he pushed forward to what he guessed was the open freezer.

It was a good thing he held his hands out like bumpers, because both his feet tripped over something—*probably another side of beef on the ground, only defrosted*—and he cartwheeled forward. He would have hit the hard floor face first, but his palms and elbows took the fall, and banged loudly.

Electric jolts of agony shot up from his elbows.

He breathed out a puff of frothy air, relieved that only his elbows absorbed the landing, and not his head. Then he gasped.

Just in front of him was a small object. At first, he thought it was another piece of meat that had fallen to the floor, only smaller. He still couldn't see anything in this white soup.

He reached out with a finger and touched it, retreating back instantly, as if the object had snapped at him.

It was warm, and furry. Not what he expected.

Panicked, thinking it might be Monsieur, he unhooked his feet from what had tripped him up and scurried forward on his elbows to get a closer look.

"Mon-sewer?" he begged, his voice cracking. He didn't want it to be true.

"Yip-yip-yip," shrieked a reply from the murk.

Al caught a flash of movement in front of him, then over him, and then behind him—a frightened sounding yip trailing behind, and then exiting the door both the dog and Al had entered.

He tried to turn toward the escaping animal to get a glimpse, to confirm his hope. He still couldn't see past his knees. But he was pretty sure it was Monsieur. He is all right.

The chill of the floor and the frosty air all around started to seep into him, making him shiver.

He had almost forgotten about the soft furry thing he had thought was Monsieur, but now confirmed it wasn't.

Then he was jolted with the thought that what had he touched wasn't the dog, but something else entirely.

He turned back with trepidation to see and was rocked once more.

It was a dead rat. Worse yet, half a dead rat. Its head was cleaved off.

Al shrank back in revulsion, pushing himself up so that he was again standing. More like wobbling.

Rubbing feeling back into his legs and hands, he tried to get his mind around what a still warm beheaded rat was doing inside the near-frozen butcher's area.

Scurrying sounds and an unmistakable squeak yanked his head up toward the open freezer.

Like a thunderbolt, Al exploded from the floor.

He wasn't much of a runner, but he was quite sure that it took him less than a second to find the exit, and close the solid door behind him. This was despite his tripping again over the body of the dead butcher—his mind didn't even offer an alternative to it being anything other than a fallen side of beef.

Al remained in front of the butcher's door, bent over puffing, his lungs gasping for air.

When he heard a muddled whimper below him, his heart practically leapt out of his body, thinking it must be another rat. But right away Al could see it was the toy poodle. It rubbed up against him, acting like it had done nothing wrong.

Then he saw the blood.

He reached down and scooped up the animal, and noticed that the little guy's paw was bleeding, although not badly. He did a quick wrap, using one of the plastic bags he carried to pick up any of the feces his boarders left during their walk. He'd have to clean up the dog's wound tonight and cover it. And less savory, he'd have to explain to the owner what had happened when she visited tomorrow.

"Come on, you little monster. Quit complaining."

He connected the leash to Monsieur's collar and ushered the pack back in the direction of the spa.

He was so focused on the dogs, he didn't even think to report the rats and the open freezer until the next day. It wouldn't have mattered if he had. A few minutes after Al and the dogs departed, an unsuspecting member of the kitchen crew tasked with getting a few more select cuts of meat for a specialty restaurant would open the sealed butcher's door and find a terrifying surprise.

09

Crew Mess

Flavio Petrovich from Romania—as it said on his name-badge—was headed to the crew mess carrying with him a giant attitude and an even larger headache.

He had just finished his shift, after being stuck training the world's dumbest person: *Chichi Vega from Chile*. Chichi had zero experience in the dining room, while Flavio had years of it. Naturally, the powers that be stuck them together for the rest of this itinerary, and maybe the rest of his contract. And to make matters worse, Chichi spent most of her time gabbing with the guests, instead of doing her job. She'd "Ooh" and "Ahh" at the guests' stories about rats and birds, while Flavio had to do his job and hers.

He had no appetite, but knew if he didn't eat, his migraine would get much worse. With his head down, seething with anger, he marched to the mess.

It was late. And as expected, the only sounds he heard were the echoes of his rapid footfalls, marching with him down the giant hallway. It was his preferred time to eat: long after the MDR shut down and most of the crew had already eaten and moved on to either their next shifts or their bunks to get some needed sleep before their shifts started again. Eating now meant that he missed out on many of the food options offered to the crew during the prime time. And there were quite a few, although not as many as what was offered their guests above. It was okay though, as Flavio didn't care for most of the offerings by this head chef, who was English. Flavio did not care for British food, and cared for this chef even less. He often stated flatly to his fellow crew, "How many culinary schools do you hear coming from London versus Paris?"

Eating late did have its benefits, though: there were fewer crew members around, which meant it was quiet. And after a day of noisy guests and dealing with Chichi from Chile, he could use some quiet time. It also gave him the chance to watch what he wanted on the satellite TV without having to haggle with the others over what should be on. One thing he always found interesting on this ship was that the crew had far more options on their satellite TV then the guests had on their own, including the news. But tonight, he wasn't interested in the news. He just wanted to get a little spicy Thai food (there was always an offering of Thai food, no matter the time of day), eat in quiet, and then return to his cabin and get some sleep. He was exhausted.

He considered what the captain announced to the crew, about many of their fellow crew not making it onto the ship because of flight cancellations and other oddities. Flavio felt pretty sure this was just some bullshit excuse the cruise line used to take advantage of workers like him, who were already working extra shifts. He was always telling others how the cruise line was trying to screw him and his fellow workers.

He realized his headache was really killing him. He might have to take his food back to his room and eat in the dark.

Flavio pushed through the door marked "Pub," which led to a combo pub and lounge area with comfy chairs and a giant flat-screened TV. It was a great place to get a drink, if he did that, and hang out with friends—he didn't have many. The beer was cheap: about a euro versus the eight euros the ship charged their guests. At least this was one way the ship didn't take advantage of its crew.

As Flavio stepped inside, he immediately saw something odd: there were dozens of crew here, even though it was so late. Usually there were only one or two, at the most. All were clustered around the flat-screened TV on the wall. Also odd was that they weren't watching the usual American soap opera or what they called "Reality TV." They were all watching the news.

He gazed at the screen showing Fox News with several people arguing about something he couldn't really hear over the crew's chatter, while a crawl of news points slid across the bottom of the screen...

"Animal attacks continue throughout Europe: four confirmed killed in Paris dog attacks... Rats attack city of Malaga, Spain..." Report after report spoke about animal attacks, over several places in Europe.

He hmphed in disinterest, and then turned back to the mess entrance to get his Thai chicken. The animal attacks were a concern, but not a big one to him because he and the others were on this ship for the next two weeks, headed to America and then the Caribbean, not Europe—where all the attacks were occurring. Now if they had this problem on the ship, then it might draw his interest.

When Flavio entered the crew mess he felt his anger grow even more. The trays that were supposed to hold assortments of food were empty. Other than a bowl of fruit and some desiccated Danishes, there was nothing. He saw a skinny dark-skinned man wearing the white uniform of a sous chef shoot him a glance before returning to his busy work.

"Hey, what am I supposed to eat?" Flavio was almost surprised to hear he was yelling at the man, who kept his back to him, clanging pans and pots. "I'm talking to you. Do I look like some monkey? You must think so if I have only bananas and other fruit to eat."

The skinny man finally acknowledged Flavio, but he kept his back to him. "You miss dinner time. We all closed up. Come back in morning."

There was a commotion in the pub area, probably some numbskulls fighting it out over what channel to watch.

He was too tired to fight with this man, not that it would make any difference nor get him his food. He'd go up to one of the main galleys and grab some of the food offered to the guests. Crew weren't supposed to do that, but the kitchens were supposed to feed him too. The ship's worry, not his.

Flavio pushed back through the crew mess entry and halted in the doorway, momentarily stunned.

Rather than the futile brawl he'd expected, he was shocked to see that the men and women who'd been sitting in chairs passively gawking at the TV were now spasmodically dashing around the lounge, like some wild version of musical chairs—without the music—attempting to get away from... What were those things?

Rats?

He hated rats.

They were dirty and disgusting animals. They brought disease and filth with them, and they most certainly didn't belong on his ship.

He withdrew a knife—he always kept a steak knife sheathed to his body—and held it in a reverse defensive grip.

Flavio blinked back his headache and marched toward the melee. He'd kill every last one of these things if he had to. Then, he'd get his meal.

DAY THREE

THE CAPTAIN'S MORNING ADDRESS BLARED, JUST OUTSIDE THE CABIN. NOT WANTING TO MISS IT, I RACED TO OPEN THE DOOR.

THESE WERE HIS WORDS, MORE OR LESS.

"GOOD MORNING, GUESTS OF THE INTREPID. THIS IS YOUR FRIENDLY CAPTAIN, JÖRGEN CHRISTIANSEN, COMING TO YOU FROM THE BRIDGE.

"WE ARE PRESENTLY LOCATED AT 36 DEGREES, 30 MINUTES NORTH BY 4 DEGREES, 30 MINUTES WEST AND ON A SOUTHWESTERLY COURSE AT TEN KNOTS. AS WE SLICE THROUGH THE OCEAN, JUST OFF THE SPANISH COAST TO OUR NORTH, WE WILL PASS BY FUENGIROLA SHORTLY. AT THIS CURRENT PACE, WE WILL ARRIVE AT THE BARBARY COAST TOMORROW AS SCHEDULED.

"TODAY SHOULD BE A CALM DAY AT SEA, WITH THE CURRENT TEMPERATURE OF TEN DEGREES CELSIUS OR FIFTY DEGREES FAHRENHEIT. AS WE ATTEMPT TO GET AHEAD OF THE CLOUD LAYERS WHICH SEEM TO BE KEEPING OUR TEMPERATURES DOWN A LITTLE, PLEASE ENJOY ALL THE ACTIVITIES IN ALL OUR LOUNGES. AND TO CELEBRATE OUR FIRST DAY AT SEA, TEQUILA SHOTS WILL BE ON SALE ALL DAY LONG FOR ONLY $5—I MIGHT HAVE ONE OF THOSE WITH YOU... JUST KIDDING.

"HAVE A FANTASTIC DAY ON THE HAPPIEST SHIP ON THE OCEAN, THE INTREPID, REGAL EUROPEAN'S SHINING STAR OF THE SEAS."

10

All Access Tour

The All Access Tour was supposed to have taken place near the last day of their cruise, but it ended up being pushed up to the second day for reasons unknown. Only later would they realize the tour would save their lives.

Last night, while eating, Ted confided in TJ that there were only three activities on this cruise which interested him: his time with her, the periods of ocean-churning inspiration while writing on their balcony, and the All Access Tour. The tour offered an exclusive look inside the bowels of the ship, a behind-the-scenes peek into what made a cruise ship tick. And only a few people were given this opportunity, if it was even offered during a cruise; because of security concerns, the tour was considered a privilege that did not come cheap. On this ship, participants would have to pony up $160 US, per person. Ted would have gladly paid more.

After they finished their room service, a call on their house phone informed them that the tour would take place at "9 AM sharp, tomorrow," their two spots were reserved, and it was gratis to them.

Anxious for the superficial respite before bed, they argued over the reasons for the free passes. Was it a gift from the captain, "because the captain is your biggest fan" as TJ loved to chide? Or was it additional compensation, as Ted argued, for his giving a lecture in a couple of days? They'd ask the captain to settle this dispute when they saw him at tomorrow's dinner.

Neither of them slept well that night. Ted spent more mental time puzzling over trivial matters—any excuse to avoid their larger worries. Before he settled into a fitful sleep, he wondered why he was so excited about the tour. He wasn't particularly interested in ships, or cruising. It was only because of his agent, and later, his wife's insistence that he even agreed to go on this cruise.

When the "restricted" doorway opened into another world occupied only by the ship's crew, Ted hearkened back to a childhood memory when he gazed into the glass ant farm, a thin layer of soil between two panes in a wooden frame. He remembered the thrill he had, with face pressed against the glass, knowing that he was witnessing the buzz of activity usually unseen by mere humans above ground. He felt the same sudden excitement now witnessing the unseen buzz of crew activity—the ship's worker ants.

Almost immediately, the apocalyptic worries of the outside world were forgotten, or at least pushed aside for later. They were replaced by the surge of questions he and his fellow tour-takers hurled at Stephanie, their All Access Tour director, about all that went into this working ship.

The efficiency of it all was the most surprising.

Then he saw the first kink in the ship's machinery.

Just off the main "highway," what they called I-95, they were supposed to turn to the food-storage area. It was on their tour itinerary and Ted was anxious to see it. But as they approached, Stephanie announced that they had to skip the food-storage areas for now because of a "hazard concern."

This struck Ted as something odd to say, and he wasn't alone, as he saw his wife cock her brow and flash him a glance that said, "That was a bullshit excuse." Their mutual supposition was vindicated when their group was rushed past the hallway which led to the various food-storage areas and Ted caught a glance that screamed "Problem!"

It was just a glimpse, but it was enough. An area halfway down the food-storage hallway was blocked with yellow tape, like a crime scene. The partially closed doorway to a room oozed a white mist that obstructed the view inside. If he had had more time, maybe he could have seen inside. But the oddest part of the immediately visible scene was the bloody boot prints.

At least that's what it looked like to him: boot prints leading away from the foggy entrance. Maybe that was just Ted's macabre sensibility. TJ always joked to him and their friends that she needed to sleep with one eye open after reading his first end-of-the-world book. Besides, it was just a glimpse.

Several steps past the suspicious hallway, Ted glanced over to TJ to see if she noticed the same thing he did, to confirm his own questions. But her pert features were entirely focused on their tour guide, who was now describing the recycling they did and how the ship used all the funds they derived from recycling to give back to the crew for new equipment for their living room and other leisure areas.

She must not have noticed what he did, as TJ seemed absorbed in the tour and what Stephanie was saying. Not bloody boot prints.

Ted immediately discounted what he thought he saw in his glimpse. And normally that would be that. But nothing was normal right now, no matter how much he wanted to not deal with it.

He gazed at TJ, now completely ignoring the tour. At least she finally found something to focus on other than the bizarre animal behavior currently going on outside of their micro-managed environment.

Ted must have become so absorbed in watching and thinking about his wife, he was startled to find that Stephanie was leading them down a small hallway of luxury cabins, with very regal placards: Princess Suite, Prince Suite, Queen Suite, and so on. They abruptly stopped at a plain entrance, whose placard simply proclaimed, "Bridge."

Ted had completely lost track of what deck they were on. He shot a glance back to where they had been and then forward again to see if he could catch a room number or something that would indicate where they were. Then, when his attention fell back to his wife, he noticed something odd.

TJ was no longer focused on Stephanie, who was speaking to the other three people in their tour group. Instead, TJ appeared to be looking past their group to Ted's right, at something or someone down a connecting hallway that he couldn't see. Then she mouthed something.

Ted inched up closer until the subject of her attention was visible past the edge of the connecting hallway's wall. It was a bald officer with four stripes, and he was mouthing his own silent words, back to Ted's wife.

Ted must have been staring—all too overtly—at this odd spectacle, because both the officer and TJ stopped and turned to him. Ted's cheeks flared heat, feeling like he was the one caught doing something he shouldn't. The officer offered up a warm and practiced smile.

As if on cue, Stephanie addressed their group now. "And I'm pleased to welcome the ship's staff captain, Jean Pierre. He is the second in command of the whole ship and we are privileged to have him, rather than one of the second officers, give you a tour of the bridge."

All the heads of their group now turned then to the staff captain, offering a golf-clap. Jean Pierre still held Ted's glare, for a long an uncomfortable moment, before finally turning his attention to the group. He thanked them all for coming, and for Stephanie's contribution to the All Access Tour. Then he told them they were going to be given a special treat and warned them to be quiet while they entered into the designated public area of the bridge, as the officers were on duty working. Finally, before turning to the door, he told them that the captain would join them in a couple of minutes as well.

He opened the narrow door, and one by one, their group crossed the bridge's thick threshold.

"Mr. Williams?" Jean Pierre whispered, just before Ted stepped through.

"The captain would like to speak to you personally right now. Could you please walk to your left"—he pointed in that direction—"and join him in his ready room? It's the first door on that side of the bridge."

Ted stammered, not sure how to respond, "Ah, I don't want you or the captain to make any special arrangements for me." Ted could feel the eyes of the other tour passengers and his wife on him.

"It's no trouble," the staff captain said.

Ted nodded and stepped through the metal doorway into a new world known as the bridge.

It was a vast room that felt surprisingly dark, because it was almost completely lit by the outside light pouring through the giant window-panels. Those slanted up and away, and spanned the 180-degree arc of the semi-circular chamber. Curiously, five of the most forward of the thick-looking panels had human-sized windshield wipers.

Ted's imagination immediately played scenes of the wiper-blades furiously beating back a tempest. He'd gotten lost again in his thoughts, and looked back to his group on the right. TJ was now whispering amiably in Jean Pierre's ear, cupped so that only Jean Pierre could hear her.

He turned toward the other direction, as he was instructed, and marched up to a line meant to block out the public. Beyond it, the only door on a wall. It was open and an older man with one more stripe than the staff captain beckoned him forward into the tiny room.

Ted stepped past the roped area.

"Mr. Williams." The captain, distinguished in his highly starched uniform with his crown of impeccable white hair, offered his hand. "Please come in for just a moment."

Ted proceeded forward, with his own hand extended. But he couldn't ignore the feeling he was just called to the principal's office for something he did wrong. He felt "off" and not entirely himself today.

The captain clasped Ted's hand and shook firmly. "Mr. Williams. I'm Jörgen Christiansen, captain of the Intrepid. Welcome."

When Ted entered, the captain immediately closed the door and drew the shades. Ted felt his heart start to beat faster.

"Please excuse the theatrics," the captain continued, "but I wanted to ask you something, privately. And I would ask that you don't mention our conversation to anyone, other than your wife, of course." His face was stern and focused.

Ted was definitely taken aback, and now wasn't sure what to say without knowing what the captain wanted. "Please tell me how I can help, Captain, and call me Ted." The captain cocked his head and flashed just the slightest look of confusion, as if he had perhaps expected someone different, before regaining his composure.

"Very well ... Ted. I have just been made aware of a very serious problem that affects everyone on board this ship and I think you might be able to help."

Ted's mind instantly recalled the bloody footprints from the misty room. "Should I sit down?" Ted asked.

"No, I don't want to keep you from the group. I'll be quick. I wanted to know if what you wrote in your book, Madness, is actually possible, or if it's all just a well-crafted story entirely made up from your imagination."

Before the captain spoke, Ted seriously thought that he was going to ask for the ship's wine back, or to tell them that the cruise line was sorry that their bag didn't make it, or something entirely trivial. But to be asked whether or not what they were experiencing was some sort of apocalyptic event, just like what he had written about in his second-to-last book, was the last thing he expected. And it terrified him to his core. This was no longer just his own supposition. It was real. His heart raced like an express train.

"I-Ah... I honestly don't know." He couldn't think of what else to say. He was wondering this very thing, but he hadn't come to any conclusion. It had seemed too impossible. But the very fact that this obviously sane man, who captained a ship carrying nearly two thousand people, was asking the same question he was asking himself was hard to comprehend. He felt dizzy, and drew in rapid puffs of air. He thought he might have a full-on panic attack.

There was a knock on the door, and then it opened a crack and the staff captain stuck his head in the door. "Sorry to bother you, sir, but Doctor Chettle has the autopsy results for you."

"Thanks, Staff Captain. I'll be right there."

Jean Pierre nodded once and closed the door, sealing Ted and the captain back in.

"Again, keep all of this between us. There appears to be an uncanny similarity between what you've written about and what is going on outside of this ship. I need to know what we have to look forward to in other ports, and I wanted to know if my concerns were valid, or not.

"Please consider all of this, and if it's okay, I'd like to call on you again during the cruise, if needed. Further, if you have any information that you feel might impact this cruise or anyone on it, would you please contact our staff captain or me?" He handed Ted a business card.

Ted almost missed grabbing it: he thought he saw two cards. He needed to get outside. Fast.

"This has my contact number on the bridge. Call it from any of the ship phones and they'll put you through to the staff captain or to me." Ted slid it into his pocket, without looking at it.

The captain opened the door and offered his hand again.

Ted quickly shook back, whispering, "Thank you, Captain," and rushed past him, in his attempt to beeline it outside. He didn't even think to talk to TJ, who was still on the bridge with the rest of their tour. He had to get to fresh air.

As Ted brushed past the security posted outside the bridge hatch and turned to the exit, all the enjoyment he had felt during the tour was forgotten. It was at that moment he knew they were all in big trouble.

11

Eloise

Eloise Carmichael made her money the old-fashioned way: she married it. The rest of the story, as Paul Harvey used to say, was that she had outlived three previous husbands, all of whom died of "mysterious causes."

It wasn't that she was some sort of black widow who purposely sought out wealthy potential husbands, with the plan to kill them for their money. At least the premeditated planning part wasn't true. She just got bored with them quickly. And divorce wasn't an option, with prenuptials and all. So she found an easier solution each time.

Months after her last husband's death, a cloud of questions stirred up by his siblings clung to Eloise like flies to a dead body. Frustrated at their persistent haranguing and their constantly calling the police on her, she'd had enough. So she sold her last husband's mansion and sought greener pastures in Paris.

It wasn't that she was interested in French men. Though she did love their beautiful-sounding words—like songs—when they whispered their desires to her, she just didn't want to have to learn how to speak it back. She was too damned old to learn another language. Yet

Paris was where Eloise believed her next husband would be found.

She had read about the few *arrondissements* where wealthy English ex-pats often lived. So she set her sights on their Parisian haunts and within twenty days, she had already found a suitable candidate: Sir Edgar Carmichael—the title part was an extra bonus. One month later, they were married.

Like the others, just as quickly as they had wed, Eloise became tired of poor ol' Edgar. It would be during their honeymoon that she would seek out Number Four's "accident."

It was purely a stroke of luck that Edgar told her of his love for transatlantic cruises and suggested that option for their honeymoon. Eloise didn't care for cruising, but she thought the open sea would present her with ample opportunities for Edgar's demise; after all, they were going to be in the middle of the fricking Atlantic Ocean.

While planning their honeymoon, Eloise immediately discovered a behavior that just wouldn't work for her: Edgar was cheap, even insisting that to get what she wanted, she'd have to spend some of her own money. It was one more reason why he'd have to go.

When he first offered to buy her a transatlantic cruise, Eloise suggested the QE2 because it fulfilled her one non-negotiable: the ship had to have an onboard kennel, so she could take her "baby" with them. The second requirement, although not an absolute, was only natural for newlyweds with substantial means: they should also have the best cabin on the ship. But Edgar became furious when the agent told him it would cost him 45,000 euros per person for their Grand Duplex suite on the QE2.

When she thought her intractable demands might scuttle the whole thing, and thus her opportunities, she went along with his recommendations of Regal European, as they were the only other one with kennel services. She pressed for RE's best cabin, even though Edgar made her pay for her share—she'd get it back from him one way or another. So for the bargain price of 10,000 euros each, his agent booked the Royal Suite for Eloise, Edgar, and Monsieur, her toy French poodle.

Once it was settled, she got to work on her plans to find the most dangerous place on the ship, or on one of their excursions. Everything was falling into place, until just before they checked into their suite on the Intrepid.

It was her little Monsieur. She was concerned because he was not acting himself lately. After their flight from Paris, just before going through customs in Malaga, Monsieur actually growled at her. She had been anxious to check on him since then and decided to do so now, before they got ready for dinner. She left Edgar at their cabin for his daily nap and set off to find the kennels.

After getting directions from one of the better-looking younger officers—she only spoke to the senior crew members and rarely dealt with the peons on the ship—she was told to take the aft elevators. She glared at the officer for this.

It was the third cruise she had been on and it bugged her to no end why they just didn't call this "the rear" part of the ship. If you had to explain that the aft actually meant rear, why the hell not just say "rear" for the guests?

She felt her temperature start to boil a little when she exited onto deck 1, only partially accessible to guests.

The deep thrumming of the ship's engines rumbled underneath her, adding to the already unsteady feel of walking with heels on a moving ship—another reason she didn't care for cruises. Now, she almost felt dirty, just thinking about how close she was to the ship's mechanical parts.

Finally, she found the Regal Pet Spa. *At least that sounds better than "Kennels."*

She pushed open the door.

Regardless of where she was, whenever she entered a room Eloise expected that all men's heads should snap to her attention. To aid in this proper response, she had donned her stilettos to announce both her approach and arrival. And to complement this effect she wore an ensemble so tight-fitting, she looked vacuum-sealed in it. All were designed to reveal her God-given—albeit often enhanced by top plastic surgeons—assets.

It was therefore almost an affront to her whole persona when the spa's only human occupant, a small dark-skinned man, didn't even acknowledge her entrance. Further adding to her indignity, as she waited an intolerable amount of time, the man paid her no more attention than he would to a warm breeze. He was purposely ignoring her. She even slammed the door of the kennel to demand his consideration. Nothing.

But the sting of this personal injury quickly faded when she heard the growling and barking from the farthest kennel. The bark's high cadence was very familiar to her. And so when the realization hit her like a punch to her liposuctioned gut, she knew it was her Monsieur.

She clip-clopped over to the small man, who was outfitted in standard worker clothes, not epauletted like an officer. She actually didn't care about that right now. This man, regardless of his lowly status, was trying to calm her dog. However, it became instantly obvious to her that he didn't know what he was doing.

"You're just scaring him more," she whined, pushing him aside and positioning herself in front of her pup's enclosure.

Her indignation swelled to epic proportions when she saw that Monsieur's front paw was wrapped in some sort of bandage. That meant her baby had been injured on Regal European's ship, and most likely under the supervision of this little man.

Then she nearly fell backward, the shock rocking her whole body. Instead of seeing her normally well-mannered Monsieur, there was a terrifyingly wild animal behind the windowed enclosure. His face was scrunched up in an angry scowl; his lips and cheeks were drawn back to reveal a surprising number of nightmarishly pointed teeth; and his eyes flared a ferocious red, like blazing rubies. She shuddered.

"Monsieur?" she begged, hoping to coax her beloved puppy to come out of this horrid looking one. "It's Mommy."

Monsieur growled a violent-sounding warning, like he was possessed by some feral animal. It was not the loving pooch she'd known for the last five years, who had comforted her through the trauma of her last three husbands' passings.

Eloise shot up, pulling down her skirt, which had hiked up too far, and preened over a rogue lock of her hair. "What did you do to my dog?" she barked at the little man.

"Ah, Mrs. Carmichael," Al stuttered. "Ah, this was how I found Mon-sewer this morning." He wanted desperately to avoid bringing up last night's events. "Have you noticed any behavioral problems before this trip?"

As if slapped, she recoiled, her own anger boiling over at this man's insolence. Still, his words rang true. Monsieur had been confused before they left Paris and then he acted a little aggressive yesterday morning when he was checked onto the plane. Maybe her baby was just scared of traveling. She knew she would often get tired and cranky after waking up from a long day of travel, like now. It's probably worse for an animal traveling in a cage, something she would otherwise never do to her

Monsieur. Perhaps this man wasn't to blame after all, though he would have to explain what happened to his foot. Still, she was sure he didn't know how to calm her pup.

She'd try what always worked when he was frightened.

"Leave us alone for just a moment," she said to the man. When she spoke to Monsieur, her voice went up an octave and down a few decibels. "Monsieur's mommy knows how to settle him down."

The worker, whose name tag listed an unpronounceable name and indicated he was from Mauritius, nodded and walked back to the front of the room and sat down at a small desk she hadn't even noticed when she pounced on him from the door. She knelt back down and tried to relieve her tiny boy's anguish, talking to him in baby talk as she normally did.

Monsieur emitted a long rolling growl, punctuated by a sliver of saliva hanging from its mouth.

A better idea struck her like a thunderbolt, and she almost shuddered at her own brilliance.

A guilty flash at the little dark man confirmed he wasn't looking her way. Feeling safe, Eloise opened her Hermès and yanked out a prescription pill bottle from her own stash of narcotics. She kept an ample supply for just about every occasion. Her doctor had given her these particular babies for her anxiety—she'd been having more of it lately, although she didn't know why.

She pulled out two large, white capsules.

She was allowed to have two of these at any one time. So one, for a dog maybe one tenth her weight, should more than do the trick. *Okay, maybe Monsieur is more like a twelfth of my weight, but who's counting?*

She flashed a glance once more at the little man and when she was sure she was alone in her next crime, she tossed one tablet into her mouth, then opened the door to Monsieur's enclosure just enough to thrust her hand inside. She kept her eyes glued to the man and blindly held her hand out for Monsieur, insisting he take the second tablet out of her palm, the way he'd usually take treats from her. When she felt the tablet drop out, she attempted to withdraw her hand—and Monsieur bit her.

She yelped, clicked the door closed, and bolted upright, clutching her injured hand. She gave a deep scowl at her dog for adding to her indignity. With her throbbing hand held at her side, she clamped down on it with her other, so the man couldn't see it.

"Are you all right?" He was bounding in her direction.

"Yes!" she blurted.

She glanced back down at Monsieur because he'd finally stopped growling. At first she was shocked to see the droplets of her own blood on and around the pill. A trail led to and pooled under her hands. Her dog's next action disgusted her.

Monsieur busied himself licking up her blood like some sugary treat, and with the blood, he ingested the pill. The sight turned her stomach. Holding back her nausea, she felt some measure of relief knowing her mission was accomplished. That downer should calm him pretty quickly.

She turned back to the man, keeping her body between her hand and him. "And I think Monsieur will be fine pretty soon, too."

With her back to him, she snatched a silk handkerchief from her purse and tightly wrapped the wound. She wondered if she needed medical attention, or if just a band-aid—*perhaps many band-aids*—would suffice. *No-no, a band-aid would not look right with this evening's special gown*, she thought. It was her fondest hopes that the gown alone would be enough to stop Edgar's heart. That wouldn't happen if her hands were covered in band-aids. Presentation was everything to her.

When she returned her attention back to the little man, she noticed that he was staring at her ass—at least he had a pulse, which is something he couldn't say about her Edgar—and then, startled at his own dalliance, returned his own gaze up to her eye level.

She sashayed past him and strutted to the door. "Thank you... Ahh ..." She acted out a harsh squint in the direction of his name tag, but wasn't going to even try to figure out what to call the man.

"Al is my name, Mrs. Carmichael," he said with a very sweet grin. *He is kind of cute, in a small-man sort of way.*

Eloise snickered at this and his chosen nickname.

"Thank you, Al." She gave him a genuine smile and paraded out the door, knowing where his eyes were now. Her smile grew even larger.

She hesitated after the door closed behind her, holding up her throbbing hand. The damned thing hurt a lot now, and it was still bleeding. She couldn't very well go to dinner bleeding all over the place. She caught a glimpse of the Regal Medical sign, conveniently located right next door to the Pet Spa. Perhaps the doctor had a skin-colored bandage. Then she remembered she had some white gloves she could wear over the bandage.

She didn't want anything to spoil her grand entrance tonight.

12

T.D. Bonaventure

T.D. Bonaventure, as he was known to his millions of readers, asked everyone at the captain's table to refer to him as Ted, and to his wife, Theresa Jean, as TJ.

Captain Christiansen still couldn't get over the disparity between "Ted" and "T.D." He had presumed someone different. Although T.D.'s stories dealt with one apocalypse or another, his writing style was literary, almost like poetry. And he often injected British idioms into his prose, which had led Jörgen to believe that T.D. was British, perhaps even belonging to the aristocracy, as he remembered reading something about a Bonaventure family in a British historical novel his wife had once given him. When he briefly met Ted on the bridge, and more so now, he could see he was completely mistaken.

His image of the aristocratic Mr. Bonaventure clashed greatly with the real-life Ted, in spite of Ted's handlebar mustache. Besides using a name some would consider uncivilized, instead of his given name of Theodore, he spoke with the coarse parlance of a common American, attaching primitive colloquial phrases to otherwise well-thought-out sentences. Yet, in spite of the clash with his assumed persona, Jörgen actually liked him better as "Ted." He was far more real.

"I'm so glad you've chosen to join us. I've been looking forward to speaking with you about your books."

Captain Christiansen spoke with jovial animation. Ted wondered if it was the same man he had met earlier on the bridge. But he reasoned that the captain was just keeping up appearances, and was attempting to play down what they both knew were growing problems closing in fast. Ted feigned a smile, trying to play along too. "Thank you, Captain. It's an honor for us to be invited to your table."

Being in the giant dining hall was already pushing Ted's limits. But sitting at the center of this fishbowl was almost unbearable. It took almost a bottle of the gifted wine to ply his nerves to a manageable enough level and get to dinner, albeit late. He'd need another bottle to make it through this.

His stomach was already in knots over reliving the events leading to their cruise. Ted felt his nerves ramp up even more now, eager to deflect the attention from himself. Before he considered the implications he blurted, "I'm curious, Captain, were you able to get most of your crew and guests on board before you had to depart early?"

This was the one conversation Jörgen had hoped to avoid while at the dinner table. His turn to deflect. "First, Mr. Bonaventure—"

"—Ted, please, Captain. Besides, you know Bonaventure is just my nom de plume. My British roots are pretty far removed from the Ted you see here."

"Yes, of course, Ted. I just wanted to thank you and your wife for your assistance in alerting the guests and some of my crew, so they could get on board before... we had a bigger problem."

"And thank you, Captain." TJ interrupted, "for the wine." She held up her glass of the wine served at their table, the same wine as their cabin gift.

Ted noticed that she was enjoying the wine as much as he was.

"It's my honor, Mrs. Williams." The captain raised his glass with a smile.

"Oh please, call me TJ. Everyone does."

"Theresa Jean sounds much better," Jean Pierre interjected, with a wider smile.

"Just TJ, please." She flashed a sloppy grin in return.

Ted noticed once more the familiar comfort they had with each other, and that they held one another's gazes for longer than normal.

"If you don't mind," the captain continued, "I'll call you Theresa Jean, which sounds far lovelier to me, too." He offered his own grin to her, but Ted found it to be more practiced, expected.

"To answer your question, Mr... Sorry, Ted. We have a total of 738 guests on board, and we had bookings for 1325. We're short 195 crew, but because of the lower guest number, we're in good shape. The good news is you can have seconds of everything!" The captain announced this with laughter. Again, practiced.

Ted caught the staff captain mouthing something to TJ. Ted glared at her, and she flashed him the look of a Cheshire cat with a canary still in its mouth. It was not like his wife to flirt with another man, except for her job, and certainly not in Ted's presence. But this was more than flirting. They knew each other and yet both were pretending otherwise. It was one more puzzle he did not want to have to solve.

"Excuse me Mr. Bonaventure?" Zeka, the ship's cruise director chimed in, interrupting his mental meanderings.

"Please, just Ted."

"Oh, ah yes, Ted. In your first novel, *Bugs*, how did you come up with the story of insects taking over the world?"

"Didn't you know?" TJ said with laughter in her voice. "He's actually an entomologist."

"Retired," Ted cut in.

"Yeah, he studied the mating rituals of praying mantis, or is that manti"—she flashed her sultry grin and raised her glass in his direction. "Anyway, he studied praying manti and other interesting shi... stuff."

"Of course, a praying mantis ate its mate... after." He clicked a smile and raised his glass.

"Touché, dear," TJ said clinking his glass.

"And what do you do Theresa Jean?" Zeka asked.

"Just TJ."

"Oh, don't you know," Ted said in his fake British voice, "My wife is a secret agent for the US government." He offered a smirk, exaggerated a look upward, while twirling his mustache.

"No, really?" asked Zeka.

TJ leaned forward and said, "But if I told you, I'd have to kill you."

There was a break in the table's conversation as food was being served. But it also seemed that an invisible bubble separating them from the rest of the guests had been pierced. At that moment, the din of the main dining room or MDR flooded their ears. The MDR's dinner guests were abnormally loud in their conversations. And there was little doubt about what they were discussing.

Although earlier the captain had publicly announced that they had set sail without problems, at their table he had just let on—loud enough that many around them could hear—that several of his crew and several hundred guests had not made it on board.

Ted was sure that this, along with what they had witnessed earlier in Malaga, was the subject of the nervous chatter rumbling around the room.

Many heads were glued to their phones, mouths reporting what their eyes saw. Because of the ship's proximity to the coast, many still had Internet or texting capabilities by connecting to nearby cell towers, in addition to those who ponied up for the ship's high-priced Internet service. Besides the stories around the Internet, word was bound to spread with communications from worried friends and family back home.

Ted's eyes wandered from table to table and took in the uneasy faces. It was like worry had taken on a palpable presence of its own, as it floated from group to group, like some dark cloud that rained down disquiet upon each table, and then moved on to the next one.

The person with the phone at each table, after sharing their news to their table mates, then shot dark glances in Ted's direction at the captain's table to see if they shared in their same worry.

Then everything changed.

Another presence commanded the attention of all those with eyesight at the MDR.

It was Eloise Carmichael.

A very attractive woman with long black hair strutted along the port-side walkway running through the MDR, an elderly man in tow. Even though it was the first formal night, it was not unexpected to see all manner of formal and wildly informal dress every night of the cruise. But formal nights often brought out the most outlandish. This woman's dress, or lack of one, was what drew everyone's gaze. Men and women, guests and crew, all gaped at what they saw.

Every curve was visible through her sheer gown, which looked as if she had delicate white lace flourishes painted directly onto her arms, shoulders, breasts, torso, groin, and legs, all of which conspicuously covered just barely more than a sheer negligee might. As she approached their table, it appeared to Ted that the dress's long skirt and train—also nude-colored—hid everything from her hips down. But everything else above this was all her.

TJ's elbow found Ted's gut, in a not too subtle chide. "You're staring, dear," she huffed.

"Everyone is staring, dear," Ted chortled.

"Good God Almighty, what is that?" quipped Urban, one of the captain's first officers, who was known among his fellow crew members for his often prudish comments about guests and their poor taste in clothing.

"That would be Eloise Carmichael, and her fourth husband," announced Zeka.

"I'm sure she married this one for love," TJ offered sarcastically.

There were a couple of snickers, but Zeka ignored the comment and continued, seemingly more mesmerized than the others. "I have that same dress. J. Lo wore it to the '13 Golden Globes. Hers and probably this one are by Zhair Murad. Mine was a knock-off from China. Besides, I don't look like that."

Most of the dining hall gawked at Mrs. Carmichael as she paraded to a table for two in the middle of the two-story hall, only one table away from the captain's.

"Fourth husband? That's a lot of divorces in a short time. She doesn't look that old," Ted mused out loud.

"The other three died of quote *mysterious causes* end quote," said Jean Pierre, who seemed more interested in Ted's wife than Mrs. Carmichael, now directly behind them. Ted looked at Jean Pierre and then around to the Carmichaels' table.

Carmichael made eye contact with them, flashed a big smile, and waved a white-gloved hand in their direction.

She paused while her husband waited for her to sit, but she changed course and headed in their direction, leaving her husband waiting for her.

"Oh look, dear, she's coming over to meet you," TJ continued to tease her husband.

"More likely Captain Christiansen," he responded, but he felt his panic increase as he watched her advance and stop directly in front of him.

"Mr. Bonaventure," she said through an exaggerated smile accentuated by oversized lips. She daintily offered that white-gloved hand. "I'm a huge fan. I'm Eloise—"

"Mrs. Carmichael," Ted said in a somewhat British accent. He stood and accepted her hand, although he was unsure if he was supposed to give a peck on a knuckle or shake it. The dilemma and the pause made him immensely uncomfortable. He hadn't even wanted to come to the damned dinner, preferring the anonymity of room service. Their checked bag arrived and with it their formal clothes. Without any more excuses, TJ insisted, and so they came and he was thrust into this situation. But then something caught his eye.

"Mrs. Carmichael? I'm sorry, but I think your hand is bleeding." Ted released her. The back of one of her gloved hands looked padded, like it was full of wads of cotton balls. On the top of the padding was a moist semi-circle of red, apparently from a wound that had bled through. *That explains the gloves.*

"Ah, thank you, Mr. Bonaventure," Eloise said, covering her injured hand with her other, shrinking back from him. She stared past her hands for a moment, seemingly befuddled. She snapped back to attention. "I better go back to the doctor," she announced. "Captain," she nodded in Jörgen's direction.

"Mr. Bonaventure. Until later, I hope." She turned and left, following the same parade route she had arrived on.

This time was not for show. She hurried, not even waiting for her husband who attempted unsuccessfully to catch up.

"See, Mr. Bonaventure, your fans even bleed for you," TJ snickered.

"Before you sit down, Ted, would you offer a toast?" boomed the captain.

Ted, already completely out of sorts, was now mortified to see he'd not only drawn his table's eyes, but those of the entirety of the dining room.

TJ leaned toward him, whispering just loud enough for him to hear. "And don't fuck it up." She smiled, knowing it was probably exactly what he needed to hear.

He just glared at her. But his glare turned into a winsome smile. His wife always knew which buttons of his to push at the right time.

Ted reached down to grab his wine and noticed a flute of champagne at each of their place-settings. He hesitated only a moment before raising his, waiting for everyone from their table and the dining room to follow. A character from one of his books was in a similar situation—if that was even possible. And from it he offered this toast:

"May the wind be at our backs and the seas ahead be calm as we sail on to our next port of adventure."

"Cheers," the table said in unison, followed by the entire dining room.

All clinked their glasses, sipped their champagne, and the MDR's chatter built back up. Finally, Ted sat down, shrinking into the more comfortable confines of his own chair.

"Captain," TJ asked, her voice almost inaudible through the din, "Do you think Mount Etna's eruption will affect our itinerary?"

"In a way, it already has, Theresa Jean." Captain Christiansen sipped a coffee. He was about to say something more, when the head waiter handed him a note.

At first, the captain's stately poker-like mug held. The distinct lines of his ruddy features were like deeply chiseled navigational marks carved over forty years of working on ships. Then they did a course correction, only for a moment. But others were watching. So they steered back to their normal intensity.

He grabbed the shoulder of his staff captain, and when he stood up he whispered something that changed Jean Pierre's demeanor in an instant.

"I'm sorry, but I have to leave you, but we have a few things we must attend to. I'll be in contact with you shortly," he said to Ted. "Theresa Jean and Ted." He smiled and nodded to both of them. "Thank you for your enjoyable company."

He still acted like there was nothing wrong in the world, yet he hurried to a back exit. The staff captain followed, but hesitated as he passed by TJ, casually thrusting his hand out into TJ's. "Charmed, Theresa Jean... Ted." He then bounded quietly after the captain.

While Ted and the MDR watched them leave, TJ glanced down into her palm. In it was a crib note: "Tomorrow @ 6:30 A.M."

13

Jaga

"Taufan?" Jaga whispered, fearful of letting anyone outside his quarters hear him.

"Taufan?" the young man called again, rummaging through the belongings around his bunk.

He stood back up and glared at his bunk area, scratching his disheveled hair, forcing himself to think of what he must have missed.

"Jaga, what are you doing?" boomed his best friend, who had quietly entered and snuck up from behind.

Although startled, Jaga was also relieved that it was just Yakobus and not someone else. Then, Jaga's features drooped, like a slice of cheese on a hot sandwich. He leaned over to his friend's ear. "Yakobus, I can't find Taufan anywhere. He's not in his box."

Yakobus nodded calmly, and quickly stepped over to the open door of their shared quarters, closing it tight. Putting an ear to the door to make sure what they said would not be heard, he whispered, "Could he have gotten out?"

"I don't know." Jaga moaned while trying to massage the worry from his temples.

They both knew Jaga would be fired for hiding his pet ferret on board. Their superior, the assistant chief of housekeeping, was okay with the infraction, if it was kept quiet and no one else outside of his roommates knew about it. If their secret left their inner circle or if Taufan happened to spring free to another area of the ship, Jaga's years with Regal European would end abruptly.

His roommates would never break Jaga's confidence, not only because they too loved Taufan, but because they believed the little guy brought them luck. They also felt sorry for him. Besides being small for a ferret—not that ferrets were big to begin with—Taufan often shivered when scared. It was both pitiful and cute at the same time. Taufan apparently had a much lower than normal body temperature and pulse rate, compared to a typical ferret. So he often shook as a reflex to the outside temperature. Jaga had even hand-stitched a little covering out of athletic socks to keep him warm. Although it looked ridiculous, his roommates agreed the ferret-suit was perfect for Taufan.

Jaga first noticed Taufan was missing when he found the empty sock covering on his bed. When Jaga noticed it was somewhat torn, he became alarmed and started his search.

At night Taufan normally slept with him under the covers. And when Jaga arose, before he left for the day to start his duties, he would put Taufan in a giant shoe box, with holes poked into it for air. Inside was a small rolled-up towel, which acted as a bed, and even a little litter compartment, separate from Taufan's sleeping area, for him to do his business. At night Jaga left the box open and Taufan would crawl in and use the ferret-bathroom or he'd crawl up and say "hello" to his roommates, or just prowl around the room. Usually when Jaga woke up, Taufan was by his side, often snuggled into his neck. But during the day, he stayed in his box. No exceptions.

Today, when Jaga had returned, Taufan was gone and his box's top was askew.

There were previous occasions where Jaga had thought that Taufan had broken free from his box. Items under his bed, where the box lay, were moved and the box top was not quite on right. Yet he had never caught Taufan outside of his box during the day, until now.

Yakobus pulled Taufan's box from under his bed and poked around underneath with his flashlight.

"I already searched there," Jaga snapped.

Yakobus shot back a glare and then took a long breath and said in a soft tone, "Jaga, I'm just trying to help. You might have forgotten something."

Jaga hung his head, feeling sorrow for his momentary spike of anger directed at his friend. It was obvious Yakobus had his best interests in mind. Mostly he just missed his little friend.

The door crashed open and Asep bounded through, like the big, bumbling fool that he was.

Yakobus and Jaga both spun on their heels, their eyes meeting Asep's, who halted mid-motion. This was the roommate they liked the least. Worse, Asep was assigned to several of the concierge class rooms on deck 8 of the ship and always reminded his roomies of this.

"What's going on, brothers?" Asep asked, eying each suspiciously from under his flawlessly coiffed hair, which hung just above his eyes. He sported a crooked smile, perfectly chiseled into his olive features, which had never shown a blemish. He was working on a dark stubble, even though he had shaved a second time at noon.

Asep was always calling them 'brothers' even though they had no direct relation—that they knew of.

Jaga hesitated answering, intent on measuring his reply so as to not reveal too much. So Yakobus jumped in. "Jaga has lost something. I was trying to help him find it."

"It wasn't that silly rat of yours, was it?" Asep was always calling Taufan a rat.

"Have you seen Taufan?" Jaga pleaded.

Asep looked over his shoulder first, apparently making sure no one was listening, then back to his roomies. "I came in here about twenty minutes ago to get something I had forgotten. Anyways"—he always started his stories with *anyways*—"sometimes, when no one's here, I would say 'Hi' to your rat. He's my buddy too, you know."

Jaga nodded, now understanding why Taufan's box top and some of his own belongings had been moved at various times.

"Anyways, when I came back to the room twenty minutes ago, I visited with Taufan. But he jumped out of his box and bit me." He held out his hand to lend support to his story.

"Did he escape?" Jaga wasn't interested in Asep's superficial wound.

"Well, no. Anyways, I closed the door right away, as you had asked, and he ran around the room, all crazy-like. Anyways, he stopped on our desk." Asep pointed to the common desk they all used. "And I was standing there." He pointed to where Yakobus was standing now, in front of an open locker.

Asep paused, like he was trying to gather how to explain what he was going to say next. "Anyways, your rat just stared at me and his eyes were red, and... well, I swear he growled at me."

"Ferrets don't growl," Jaga snapped back.

"Anyways, he made weird noises—it sounded like a growl, *okay*. And then he ran at me and then jumped for me. His mouth was open and I swear to you he was going for my face..."

"What happened, pretty-boy?" Yakobus prodded, impatient to conclude the story. Asep loved to draw out a story forever, especially if it concerned his "perfect olive complexion." Besides, they all had to get back to work soon and certainly couldn't be standing around here all day long listening to another one of Asep's stories.

"Anyways, Taufan tried to attack me—I swear—and I just reacted. So I fell to the floor." Asep demonstrated, collapsing down to his hands and knees.

"Anyways, Taufan missed me and landed inside the locker there." Again Asep pointed to where Yakobus was standing.

"You opened this locker?" Yakobus asked, looking at the closed locker.

"No! It was open when I got here. Catur must have left it open. Anyways, Taufan had landed inside Catur's locker. And you know Catur is a pig and so Taufan couldn't get out because he was trapped in all of Catur's stuff. So I spun around and slammed the locker door shut while he was flailing around inside." Asep demonstrated Taufan's movements, convulsively waving his hands and arms, like someone having a seizure.

"You left him in there?" asked Jaga, somewhat incredulous about Asep's whole tall tale.

"That's why I came back here again, I wanted you to know that I—" Asep glared at Yakobus, who was opening the locker door. "Don't do th—"

Yakobus yelped as Taufan leapt out of the locker past Yakobus and made a beeline for the entrance to their quarters, which Asep had left open.

Asep reached for the entrance door, just one second too slow. As the door seemed to shut in slow motion, they all watched the flash of Taufan whipping around the door frame's base and down the hallway, out of sight.

They stood silently for a moment, unsure what to do next.

Jaga leapt for the door, opened it, swept through, and ran after Taufan, anxious to save his ferret and his job.

14

Al

The speed with which Al had lost control of his boarders, and therefore his career, was mind-numbing.

After a quick nap, he was woken in his room by a call from the hotel captain, "We're getting complaints on decks 2 through 4 about some full-on ruckus involving dogs."

Al could hear them long before he stepped into the Regal European Pet Spa. Inside, the barking was so loud he had to cover his ears. He hollered at the guests. "Hey-hey-hey. What's all the barking about?" It was a rhetorical question, because he knew exactly what was upsetting all the animals.

He marched down the spa's walkway, passing each pet-suite. If he had looked through each floor-to-ceiling glass door, he'd have seen each resident scurrying around its space, barking its discontent at the last suite at the end of the walkway: The Presidential Pup Suite.

Al halted in front of this double suite, which looked even bigger because of the diminutive size of its occupant. He just glared at the pup.

Not acting its size, the white toy poodle stood resolutely behind the clear glass, with all the bluster of an animal ten times its weight. It snarled erratically through its teeth. Then, upon seeing Al, it focused an ascending growl at him, as if seething with pure hatred. Its eyes were a crimsoned fury. Its gnarling rumble crescendoed and, like a coiled-up spring releasing, it leapt at the door. Ignoring any tenderness it must have felt from the injured paw—there were three stitches under those bandages—it pummeled the glass boundary with its front paws and jaws.

Al could do nothing but gawk at the poodle, driven mad by something absolutely mysterious.

The poodle's behavior had him completely flummoxed. After its owner had left, the dog had almost immediately fallen asleep in its bed, without so much as a whimper. And he figured the poodle had finally settled down.

Then this morning, when Al came in to clean the suites, Monsieur's personality rapidly changed. First it was confused, bumping into the walls and barking at the air. Then, it became outright hostile. When Al attempted to take the animals for their morning walk he had to muzzle the poodle and leave it to stew about its behavior. It wasn't his first time dealing with an aggressive dog. And so he assumed this pampered pooch was no different.

Al had learned long ago that he had to act quickly so as to wrestle the behavior out of the animal before there was a chance it would bite him or any of the others. It was simple: he'd quickly muzzle the offending dog, and that dog would learn its boundaries. Dogs were smart and pretty quickly figured out what was acceptable and what was not. An Aggressive would settle down soon after that. Once its behavior was more passive, he'd remove the muzzle as a reward. If it didn't play nice at that point, he'd muzzle it again. With the more combative breeds such as pit bulls or chows, he'd sometimes have to muzzle the animal as many as three times before it had learned its place. With Monsieur, it had already been four, and was about to be five. It was only then that he started to doubt whether this behavioral modification technique was going work at all with this boarder.

Al pulled the clipboard out of its sleeve, just off the door, and reread Monsieur's details. Maybe he'd missed something.

He hadn't.

Then he considered the injury to its paw. He'd thought the dog had cut it on one of the many sharp objects in the butcher's area, but maybe it was something else. A horrid thought hit him: what if it had been bitten by one of the rats and the rat was rabid?

Although the dog now displayed many of the signs common to rabies, there was the problem of incubation period. From his veterinary training, he knew the typical period from exposure to onset of clinical signs was weeks, not twenty-four hours or less. No, it had to be a behavioral issue. Al made a decision.

He flipped a switch on the wall, and the Presidential Suite's glass door went milky-white. Its snarling occupant disappeared from his sight. He wasn't sure how the door worked—something having to do with electrical poles and filaments—but it seemed to mostly silence the animal's tirade. Rather than growling, it seemed to busy itself, probably with one of its many toys.

Al turned and walked back toward the front of the spa, flipping each of the suite's door switches as he passed, until he reached the first door. The spa's din rapidly became muted, and then blinked out. It was time for their walk, and Al thought it would do them good to get out and walk out their agitation. He'd muzzle and leave the poodle once again, for punishment. One last shot with that one.

One by one he pulled out each dog and attached their leashes to the master harness, making them sit and stay by the door. Although two of the dogs acted confused, they all behaved. When it was time to deal with the poodle, he flipped the light/door switch. His mouth drooped open and his jaw went slack.

The double suite was utterly destroyed: the bedding ripped to shreds, the toys similarly disemboweled, pictures from the walls knocked down and torn, and finally, bloody paw prints everywhere. The little dog stood transfixed by itself in a cracked mirror on the opposite wall, foaming spittle pooling below it.

Al shook his head once and regained his composure. Now was the time to muzzle the dog, while it was preoccupied. Al acted quickly, but the dog was quicker.

He swished the door open and took three rapid steps to the dog, who was still glowering at its mirror image. It appeared frozen but for its rapidly heaving chest. With his left hand, he reached for the dog's collar, and with his right he moved to slip on the muzzle. But before his left touched the collar, the animal snapped its head back and sank two of his canines into Al, who reacted by dropping the muzzle. Monsieur then dashed out the door, toward freedom. Al leapt for the crazed animal, futilely attempting to get a hand on it. But the dog was gone.

Al scuttled out of the suite on elbows and knees, just as Monsieur hopped on top of the giant German shepherd named Max, the same dog who had stomped on Monsieur last night.

Max, like Al, watched in sheer disbelief as the toy poodle, who was maybe a twentieth the size of the shepherd, sank its itty-bitties into the massive shepherd's neck. The shepherd shrieked and then clawed at the air and flung its head and body sideways to detach the small ratlike dog. Monsieur flew several feet before sliding to a stop against a wall. But it wasn't dissuaded. The poodle righted itself and leapt into the pack of dogs, chomping at anything near its mouth.

All the dogs were panicked now, snarling and barking at the pint-sized terror. But size didn't seem to matter in this crazy world. Little Monsieur viciously targeted the next dog in the group, a gray schnauzer with white legs. Once again, the smaller but far more ferocious dog had no trouble overpowering the larger one.

Al was panicked himself, as he raced to break up the melee. The little dog was drawing blood, lots of it. And the other dogs were going crazy trying to get away from the little devil. All the dogs were going to be seriously injured if he couldn't stop this. And... he glanced down at his throbbing hand and saw that he was gushing blood everywhere from a larger than expected gash.

E loise Carmichael stumbled on the last step of the stairwell, nearly falling over before one of her five-inch heels caught the sheer material, partially tearing the train of her $20,000 dress.

She righted herself and inspected the damage, pulling the train's folds forward and contorting at an odd angle. From what she could see, she assessed it was only a small, unnoticeable tear. Most eyes shouldn't be on that part of her dress anyway.

She stood erect and automatically preened her hair, certain some of the strands must be out of place. She stared forward at nothing. She felt lost and now, thinking about it, she'd completely forgotten why she was on this deck in the first place.

Her eyes searched for some sign and she found herself before the deck 1 elevators. Both sets of doors were framed by a golden metallic material, polished to a nearly mirror sheen. Eloise now saw her own reflection. Better do a systems check, as husband number two or three—she couldn't remember which one—used to say.

She scrutinized her face. After her second most recent facelift, she looked pretty good. Her fingers patted at her throat, causing some small tremors in the little wattle that hung below her chin. She would need to have them work on that soon, but otherwise...

Passable.

She touched at the ends of her hair, which had held well throughout the evening.

Passable.

Next, she examined her figure, wonderfully accentuated by the dress. She stood up straighter still and held her hands below her bust, pushing up and letting go: the dress didn't have any bra inside to lift and support, although, after the $30,000 augmentation by her plastic surgeon, her puppies held firm.

More than passable.

Just then, she caught a glimpse of her hand, her clutch dangling from her wrist. It throbbed worse than before and now a large red stain glared back at her.

She reached into her clutch, considered the four pills she'd had earlier, hesitated, then yanked out another three Valium and dry-swallowed them. She was tired of the pain.

It then occurred to her that this was one of the reasons why she was down on deck 1: to see the doctor again. But there was another reason, and it was related to her hand. *What was it?*

She couldn't seem to hold her thoughts as the night dragged on. Maybe it was the alcohol or the Valium or that she was second-guessing herself about killing Edgar. She just felt off tonight.

Then, she remembered: her dog bit her. That's why she was bleeding... *And, what?*

She was going to see if Monsieur was okay. That's also why she went to deck 1. *And what?*

To tell the little man... *Al something... That's it!* She was going to give Al a piece of her mind for letting her dog get injured and go crazy.

She was startled by the clip-clop of her own heels on the hard floor, surprised both by the clatter it caused—it was the only guest floor in all the ship, besides the outside decks, or the dance floors, that wasn't carpeted—and by not remembering that she had started to walk.

And I'm here because why again?

She had forgotten already.

Eloise found herself standing—no, swaying—in front of the Regal European Pet Suites door, scowling at it, as if it were alive and she was daring it to talk back to her. If it did, she'd rip the door's head off... *but that's silly because it doesn't have a head. What the hell is wrong with me?*

She turned the doorknob and pushed open the door, expecting to find that silly little man on the floor again, but instead the giant mug of a German shepherd was right there at face level. Its dirty paws punched against her clavicle, knocking her backward onto her keister. Husband Number Two, the first Brit she'd married, always called her rear her keister. And so there she was, tumbling hard onto her keister.

Her world crept into slow motion as the massive mutt leapt over her, screeching and whining, as if in pain. The other dogs immediately followed, jumping over her, en masse. She had been falling slowly, but these dogs were moving like the wind, treating her like she was the stationary center of some cruel dog-trick, as part of some dog show: the "watch the dogs jump over the flailing lady on the floor" routine.

For a moment, she thought the lights had gone out. But then she realized the dogs had blotted out the ceiling lights above as they passed over her field of vision.

The horde bounded past her, trailing a single long leash, and then down a side hallway, which she could swear hadn't been there before, opening into the crew-only area.

Another much smaller dog sprang out of the room. Like the others, this dog bounded over her. The realization of which dog this was struck her like a cold slap across her face: it was her little baby, her Monsieur—*that's why she was here, to check on her little Monsieur!*

The cruel dog show continued as Monsieur bounded down the same side hall, less than a dozen steps behind the others.

"Monsieur? Are you all right, my baby?" she called out to her white toy poodle, covered in red splashes. He didn't even stop to acknowledge her, instead chasing the other dogs while growling viciously.

She watched the pack scamper into an opening and then veer into a wide hallway out of sight, their yelping and cries of fear following them. Several crew members braced themselves against the hallway wall, trying to avoid the frantic animals. Little Monsieur furiously scratched his way around the same corner, growling behind them, seemingly determined to close the distance.

Adding to her insult, Al was out of the pet spa next, leaping over her. "So sorry, Mrs. Carmichael," he said, while dashing into the crew area. "I'll get Mon-sewer," he huffed, before he disappeared out of sight.

It was her husband's fault that they chose this discount cruise line over the QE2, because he was too damned cheap. He was the reason she was lying there on the ground, in her favorite gown. Her chest filled up with air like a giant dirigible until it reached its limit and she let loose with a roaring scream, as she had never done before. It was an exhalation of all the built-up frustration and anger, and something more primal that she neither understood nor cared about. She knew one thing: she was more determined than ever to kill her damned husband, and she wanted to do it now.

She attempted to jump up, but something was holding her legs to the floor. This incensed her even more. She thrust out her legs much harder this time, pulling with all her might on the hall railing until she felt something give. It was just a little at first, as when a stuck zipper lets go and then slides all the way down to open effortlessly, like a knife through butter. In this case, there was a rude ripping sound. But she was standing.

Eloise attempted to move forward, but her ankles felt restrained and she was falling forward, a return run to the floor. Before she tumbled, she grabbed the railing, with both hands this time, dropping her purse in the process. She then glanced down her legs and saw that the lower part of her dress at her waist had ripped completely off, and it was still wrapped around her ankles. A thought flashed in her mind—she should have worn underwear. But that wasn't important now. Her legs just needed to be free.

She scissor-kicked the fabric away and then stood upright. Seeing that nothing else was keeping her from her needed chore, she thrust forward, high heels clacking.

A few guests, walking up or down the aft stairwell from decks 6 through 2, swore that a half-naked woman in high heels, somewhat conspicuously covered in white lace, was running up the stairs between 10 and 11 PM, growling the name Edgar.

But most who heard this story attributed it to that evening's two-for-one Long Island ice tea special.

DAY FOUR

THE CAPTAIN'S MORNING ADDRESS BLARED ONCE AGAIN RIGHT AT SIX O'CLOCK. THIS TIME I WAS READY AND I TURNED THE VOLUME CONTROL TO THE MAX SETTING ON THE LITTLE SPEAKER BOX, WHICH WE HAD GUESSED EARLIER WAS THE SHIP'S INTERCOM SYSTEM FOR DELIVERY OF THESE KINDS OF MESSAGES.

"GOOD MORNING, INTREPID," THE BOX ANNOUNCED, "THIS IS YOUR FRIENDLY CAPTAIN, JÖRGEN CHRISTIANSEN, COMING TO YOU FROM THE BRIDGE.
"WE ARE PRESENTLY AT A HEADING OF 36 DEGREES, 8 MINUTES, 44 SECONDS NORTH AND 5 DEGREES, 21 MINUTES, 47 SECONDS WEST, OR MORE COLLOQUIALLY, WE'VE ARRIVED AT THE PORT OF GIBRALTAR, WHICH THE CUTE AND LOVABLE BARBARY APES CALL HOME. WE'LL START THE DISEMBARKATION PROCESS IN THIRTY MINUTES ON THE STARBOARD SIDE OF DECK 1.
"IT'S A COOL 9 DEGREES CELSIUS OR 48 DEGREES FAHRENHEIT OUT THERE TODAY. SO BRING YOUR JACKETS AND DRESS WARMLY. THEN DRINK A PINT FOR ME AT ONE OF THE MANY FINE PUBS THE TOWN HAS TO OFFER. BUT DON'T STAY TOO LONG, BECAUSE WE WILL BE PULLING OUT OF THIS PORT AT 4 PM AND HEADED OUT TO SEA, AND WE DON'T WANT YOU TO HAVE TO SWIM AFTER US."

I REMEMBER HEARING A COUPLE OF LAUGHS IN THE BACKGROUND. WE SNICKERED, TOO. IT WAS THE LAST TIME I REMEMBER LAUGHING WITH TJ.

"HAVE A FANTASTIC DAY, AND WE'LL SEE YOU BACK ON THE GRANDEST SHIP ON THE OCEAN, THE INTREPID, REGAL EUROPEAN'S SHINING STAR OF THE SEAS."

15

TJ

TJ adjusted her compression shorts and started a morning run that she would never finish.

The ship's outdoor trek stretched one quarter-mile around the main pool, the most popular area on the ship at midday—at least on sea days—when the sun's rays would normally have warmed the sea air to a satisfying 22 degrees centigrade. That was when the weather was normal. Nothing seemed normal in the last few days, least of all the weather.

It was downright cool out. The sun, a bare ghost in the sky, appeared more distant today, as if it were embarrassed to be seen. TJ rubbed warmth into her arms.

Menacing clouds undulated above and around her. They weren't the typical storm clouds, heavy with water and ready to burst. She tossed a glance behind her to confirm they weren't the plumes of smoke from the ship's single giant smokestack blowing onto its decks. They weren't. She peered then to her sides and saw that these clouds were everywhere: out to sea, around the port, blanketing the sky, covering the top of the Rock of Gibraltar, overlooking the town.

These clouds were also astringent, rather than water vapor, biting at her lungs, causing her to involuntarily gasp. The smell gave it away: it was sulfur. She instantly flashed to their time at Yellowstone when she labored to breathe the foul air.

She also hadn't noticed, until now, that a gray layer of dust coated the track, the chairs, maybe even the people. It muted the color out of everything, like death.

TJ ignored these unpleasantries and focused her attention on the near-empty running track before her.

Even without the weather anomalies, she knew early morning above deck was usually a ghost town. And during days at port, like today, even those hardy few who would otherwise be up here were most likely already queued up and waiting to leave the ship. Because of her husband's phobia, she and he would be the last to leave. To be honest, she preferred avoiding the crowds too.

Only a few walking dead stumbled about the track. In her previous cruises, those usually using the track at this time of day were the ancient folk barely able to walk, or the excessively obese. The obese were the most common, fooling themselves into believing that walking a few steps around a rubberized track constituted exercise. Most barely expended a dozen calories in the process of trudging their ballooning bodies around the small oval, just before heading inside to one of the fifteen restaurants, ready to start the first of their half-dozen daily ten-thousand-calorie meals. The gluttony of a cruise ship often got to her, especially when she worked so hard to keep her own weight off.

She sprang forward, her muscles instantly feeling tight from the cold. She should have worn warm-ups.

As if on an obstacle course, where the obstacles were moving in slow motion, she darted around multiple targets, each seemingly tasked with slowing her down: a fat man wearing a straw hat and muscle shirt that said "Grand Cayman"; a beach ball-shaped woman wearing overly stretched-out running shorts, hiked up to just below her mountainous breasts; and then there was an elderly couple, walking hand in hand. A juxtaposed reflexive image hit TJ just then, a brick wall that blunted her energy.

After gliding past the couple, she stopped and stared back at them, rubbing her watering eyes. She wasn't sure if it was the lack of sleep, bad dreams, or just the growing feeling of utter terror: these two looked *exactly* like the couple they had seen at Alcazaba two days ago, and then more prominently in recurring images from horrific nightmares.

This same couple was getting pulled to pieces by wild seagulls. She'd always wake up when one bird started snacking on an eyeball.

TJ shook the nightmare away. That's all it was, she reasoned with herself.

She watched the old couple hobble by, their heavily lined faces carrying their own share of worry. Upon closer inspection, she realized they weren't the same couple she had seen. And she was merely reflecting her own worry on them. Their lines were softer, and looked less like concern and more like contentment. Their facial creases folded into their smiles. It was joy they exuded, buttressed by a mutual understanding and an unflappable peace. No doubt all of this was born from their many years together. Oh, they looked physically feeble, but they were undoubtedly strong in their resolution, as if they could deal with anything, as long as they were together.

What the hell is going on with me, and with the world?

Although she was prone to psychologically analyze people—her job demanded this—she never personalized her targets, not that this couple was a target. She approached everything from a fair and analytical view. But lately, she'd felt very... *Emotional!*

She shook her head in disbelief at her own obtuse thoughts. *Were not the events of the last two days enough to make anyone emotional?* She reasoned.

Like one of Rodin's marbles in his sculpture garden, she remained a statue, contemplating the old couple's life and her own. Now she had become the obstacle in the middle of the track to the oncoming zombies. Her eyes remained fixed on the backs of the old couple, until they disappeared around the bend of the jogging track.

Worries about her mom sprang up again. She'd always looked after her mother, ever since her father's violent death, before she left for school. Last night they had talked for a couple of minutes—at ten bucks per minute she kept it short—and she sounded fine, but she still worried about her.

TJ jumped to attention as if she'd been defibrillated. She was here for two reasons.

A quick twist of the wrist to check the time. Her watch said it was 6:28 AM. She'd still make her rendezvous, but the run was out of the question now.

She jogged a few dozen more steps before finding the stairwell Jean Pierre had told her about, a little farther forward, "just past where the jogging track turns..."

She ducked into an alcove, underneath an outdoor stairwell that led to another sun deck, if she remembered the ship's map correctly. This area wasn't viewable by anyone else, unless they walked up on her, while she waited for him.

Less than two minutes later, Jean Pierre—also dressed in running gear—jogged down the same track. He looked nervous, checking both sides, to see if anyone—guest or crew—saw him. He even wore a hat, pulled low on his head so that he was less conspicuous, what with his polished dome being so recognizable.

Just before the alcove, Jean Pierre stopped and reached behind a towering steel beam to stretch a cord out and across the walkway, connecting it to a concealed hook behind another beam on the other side. It clicked home, effectively blocking anyone from walking their way and ensuring that they wouldn't be interrupted.

Jean Pierre immediately saw her turned away from him, behind the stairwell.

He stood before her while she was straightening her little jogging outfit and flashed him an embarrassed smile.

"We don't have much time before the captain needs me back. I'm sure you can guess we've been a bit busy up there."

"No problem. What do you have for me?" she said with a smile and a wink.

I t was a jarring screech. If anyone was around him, on another balcony or in another cabin, they would have no doubt compared it to nails on a chalkboard. On a normal cruise, to Ted, this would have sounded like music.

Other than yesterday's All Access Tour, this was the other activity Ted had longed for.

The veins on his head bulged as he dragged the heavy table closer to the balcony railing, until it clinked metal to glass, announcing it had reached the balcony's limit. Next, he pushed the mesh chair closer to the table. Both were now ready to accept him. He then ducked into their cabin to retrieve and lay out the rest of what was needed: his iPad tablet, the Internet passcode in an envelope, a pot of coffee (ordered the moment they had awoken), creamer and a cup, and finally his iPhone containing some notes he'd dictated to himself earlier.

Except for the briny air and clatter from the port, this setup was not unlike what he had at home where he'd do his writing in the morning. He'd envisioned doing quite a bit of writing at this very spot while on this trip. He had imagined the inspiration that would be fostered by gazing out across the water as the ship's screws churned up the seas, leaving a white foamy wake. Even parked at one of the two ports on their itinerary, he had looked forward to his creative juices flowing, unleashing a flurry of words.

There would be none of that today.

He needed to know more about what was going on in the world and to do that, he needed more information. From all he had witnessed or heard, buttressed by the knowledge he had gained while researching his second-to-last book, Ted thought he might know some of what was going on. He hadn't let on to the captain, when Christiansen asked if he thought that the story of Madness could be coming to life. His answer was "I don't know." But he thought he did know.

And if he was correct, what that might mean for their lives and the lives of everyone on this planet absolutely terrified him.

His wife kept insisting on talking to him about the animal attacks, but that was the last thing he wanted to do. Talking about it would only make it real. Similarly, his fictional tales, floating around in his conscious brain and his subconscious nightmares, became real—at least to his readers—only after he wrote them down. That was fiction.

This was not.

If he was being honest with himself, he'd have to admit that part of this research effort was to avoid dealing with the consequences of making this real. But he knew it was also wise to double check his information before panicking the whole ship. So he'd excused himself from discussing this with TJ once more this morning when she brought it up, until after completing his research review. But he really didn't need to, because the more he thought about the whole concept of *Madness* and the research behind it, the surer he became that he was correct.

He was just going through the motions now.

First, he'd check his email, and procrastinate even more.

He logged into the ship's WiFi network, another freebie because of his upcoming lecture on the ship; he would never have paid the twenty dollars per day they charged for this service. He paused before clicking open his email program app and instead opened a browser and pulled up Google News. On a hunch, he typed "animal attack" in the search box, and tapped the ENTER key.

There were hundreds of stories, and he scanned through several of them.

"Good morning!" blared Captain Christiansen's voice from the loudspeaker.

Ted shuddered and then reflexively examined his watch. It was 6:45 AM.

"We should be letting all of you loose in a few minutes. You're welcome to proceed in that direction.

"I would ask that you return a little earlier than planned. We'd like you back on board by 3 PM. This is one hour earlier than we expected. Again, 3PM is now the time you must be on the ship.

"Have a wonderful day in Gibraltar, before you return to the most wonderful ship in the Mediterranean, Regal European's Intrepid."

Ted considered the captain's rosy message for a second, then returned his gaze to his tablet's screen and refined his search to "animal attack Gibraltar."

The first story in the results demanded his attention and so he opened it and felt an electric shiver crawl up his spine with each word he consumed. On a hunch, he refreshed his search and a new article popped up which he opened in a new tab. Halfway through the article, he slapped his iPad and keyboard closed, grabbed his key-card, and dashed out of the room.

He had to see the captain, and he had to see the captain now.

16

Bollocks

"Hey, little guy. What's your name?" asked Boris, a Brit with a pale face that resembled a plastic bag stuffed with dinner rolls. He offered the visitor a wide grin.

Boris carefully balanced a plate loaded with six chocolate croissants stacked up like some monument to the God of Chocolate Gluttony. In fact, they were a favorite of his wife of ten years—one of many surprises he'd planned to bring her during their anniversary cruise. He shot a quick glance at the monument, glad he hadn't attempted to make it bigger with one or two more on top of the pile. He didn't want to lose the whole lot and spoil his surprise.

He hesitated for just a second, and then carefully plucked a small morsel from the chocolate tower to offer up to his new friend.

He didn't want to scare the little bugger away, so he clenched his teeth and carefully bent his knees to get closer to the ferret, who seemed to be patiently waiting for its prize. Boris feared that he might not be able to get back up if he crouched down any farther—his knees weren't used to many, if any, ups-and-downs and he'd already accumulated some extra pounds since their holiday had begun. So he struggled to push back up, tensing the muscles in his face. As if on cue, both his knees buckled. The plate of pastries tumbled toward the ground and so did he.

Boris attempted to slow his fall, using his right elbow against the bright colored carpet and his right shoulder against the wall.

He came to rest in the middle of the hallway, like a jackknifed tractor-trailer blocking a large roadway. Thankfully this roadway had no traffic, minimizing his embarrassment. Unfortunately, his load—the appetizing morning snacks he'd secured for his wife—was now spilled all over the carpet.

Not one of his finer moments.

"Bollocks!" Boris grumbled under his breath, mad that he'd tasked his already shaky knees too much. "I hope you're happy, mate." He scowled at the ferret, who just stared at him with its creepy red eyes.

Funny, Boris thought. He didn't remember ferrets having red eyes. His brother in Camden had a ferret, and its eyes were brown, not red like this one.

A moment of panic set in as Boris realized that he really was utterly alone, as everyone was trying to get off and see the sights in Gibraltar. His wife would not come to his aid, and the ship's crew might not come across him on the floor for a while. He glanced past the ferret, down the hall, and then tried to turn his body around so he could look the other direction, but he couldn't twist far enough.

"Double-bollocks!" He looked back at the ferret. It had moved closer to him. With Boris' own face almost ground level, the ferret was literally staring at him red eye to bloodshot eye.

Still, the ferret didn't move, as if it was considering its options.

"You know it's rude to stare, mate? Here, take this morsel." He shook the piece of Danish he still clutched in his right hand. Maybe he should save it, since it was the only piece of Danish that hadn't touched the carpet. He glared back at the glorious chocolate croissants scattered over the carpet, taunting him. The five-second rule had long since expired.

He glanced back at the ferret, who was sniffing him, like a blooming dog. It opened its little mouth—he was glad it was little because it was filled with lots of ferocious-looking teeth. Just then it looked like the little guy was planning to take a chunk out of his nose. Instead, the ferret reared back on its hind legs and peered over Boris' head as if it saw a better offer behind him. Then the little thing hissed, turned and quickly scurried away.

At the end of the hall, the ferret turned back and looked once more at the silly human dumped all over the hall, hissed again, and then disappeared out of sight, where the hallway veered off to the right.

This was all very strange behavior for a ferret, not that Boris was any expert. Although at this point he recalled when one of the neighbor's dogs once stuck its wet nose up against the front window to inspect his brother's ferret, which was running around the living room while they were watching the telly. His ferret—named Charles, after the Prince of England—hissed at the dog, just like this one did.

He had a horrific thought, which he knew was incongruent with reality: what if a dog was behind him? That was, of course, ridiculous because pets weren't allowed on cruise ships. Though he was also remembering something his wife had said on the day they boarded. It was right before the craziness with the rats happened, she said, "Look there, Boris, among all the hand luggage: there be pups in those crates."

The three-tone chime of the ship's intercom rang out loudly, startling him.

"We are all clear to Gibraltar, and we'll be releasing everybody in a few minutes on deck 1. Please have your sea-pass ready as you visit the land of the Barbary apes."

The rumble of the ship's engines had stopped some time ago, after they had made port—and yet, it sounded like there was a rumble, almost like a growl. But this wasn't coming from below him. It was coming from the hallway behind him.

The skin on the back of his neck crawled and became prickly. He let go of the bit of croissant that he'd been holding this whole time, and threw his arms around his head in an attempt to roll around in the other direction, knowing he couldn't just turn his head. He grunted at the effort and felt a shot of pain pierce his hobbled knee. He waited for the pain to subside, his face contorted—the rolls in his cheeks sucked in as if they had been eaten—and then he opened his eyes.

The pain had made him forget for a moment why he went to such effort to turn around, but when his eyes opened, they instantly focused only a few meters ahead, fluttering several times to bat away any foggy obstructions. He could see that his situation was much worse than he had thought.

A little white toy poodle, covered in blood, like some miniature hound from hell, stood a few feet away from him. Its eyes glared an angry red, and then it leapt at him.

"Oh, bollocks."

"I need to see the captain, please," Ted pleaded as he bounded down the hall, toward the bridge.

A Brazilian member of their security stood between Ted and the entrance to the bridge.

"I'm sorry, but the captain is very busy right now. If you want to see him, please go to Guest Services. They will arrange a tour fo—"

"—Look..." Ted cut the man off and took another step closer, almost in his face. "I appreciate what you're doing, but I really need to see Captain Christiansen *now*." Ted looked down and patted his pocket for the captain's business card, only remembering at that instant he'd been given one and could have called ahead first. But Ted was in such a hurry to personally share what he'd learned with the captain... He looked up and realized his stance appeared too aggressive to the security guard, who had adjusted his posture. He risked landing himself in the ship's brig, assuming they had one—not surprisingly, that wasn't part of the ship's tour. He took a step back and said, "Tell him it's Ted Williams, or maybe you should say, T.D. Bonaventure. He asked me to contact him if I found something. Please!"

The man wasn't moving.

Better the brig than to do nothing.

"Tell him *every* passenger on this ship may die if he doesn't act right now!"

The guard's eyes grew wide, and without hesitation, he yanked out his radio, mumbling some words in Portuguese, and then in English, he blurted, "Code Alpha! I repeat, Code Alpha!" The Brazilian fixed a stern gaze upon Ted, but it was masking the concern that he had just encountered a madman. The guard thrust a palm into Ted's chest and shoved him backward, away from the entrance and back down the hallway.

Ted knew he pushed it too far, but continued his pleas, while being forcibly moved backward, farther away from the bridge entrance and the captain. Several more reverse steps down the halfway, Ted backed into a human wall of very substantial proportions. The wall clasped him on the shoulder, and a hand like a vise clamped down uncomfortably hard.

"Come with us, sir," said the booming voice that belonged to the hand, thick with a harsh Slavic overtone.

Ted felt something hard press against his side. A quick downward glance confirmed it: a stun gun.

He regretted his decision altogether now, wondering if he could get out of this. "I'm sorry, I have the captain's business card. I'll go back to my room and call him directly."

The two guards continued to firmly pull him down the hall, one step at a time, not answering or even acknowledging his new request. In fact, the Slavic guard squeezed harder, if that was possible. Discomfort was fast turning into pain.

"Captain Christiansen knows me and will want the information I have. Please, I'm begging you. Let me go back to my room and I'll call him."

They nearly had him out of the hallway and into the aft stairwell.

"Ted? Is that you?" the captain called down the hall.

They all stopped and gazed forward.

"Captain. Oh, thank God. I need to talk to you," Ted bleated.

"Code Blue, gentlemen. I repeat, Code Blue," Jörgen bellowed.

The giant Slavic security officer opened up his mitt, releasing Ted. The Brazilian moved out of the way. "We're sorry, sir. We were just following orders." His voice had turned timid.

"It's all right." Ted pushed past the Brazilian and dashed back toward the captain.

Overhead, the loudspeakers announced that passengers could now start leaving the ship and enjoy the warm hospitality of Gibraltar.

Ted was face to face with Jörgen, the two guards trailing not far behind him. "Captain, please tell your security not to let anyone off the ship. They're not safe in Gibraltar."

Jörgen shot Ted one glance. It was quick, but for a man who seemed to rely on his crew and making quick decisions, Jörgen only needed a second for this one. To the guards behind Ted, he barked, "Tell Patel to hold up the passengers until further notice from me."

The Brazilian, who must have been senior of the two guards, repeated the message on his radio.

"Please come in and tell me why we're going to ruin our passengers' day in Gibraltar."

17

The Barbary Apes

Over three hundred Barbary macaques of Gibraltar represented the sum total of the wild monkey population on the entire European continent. Only today would the town realize how wild they'd become.

Because they were tailless, they were often referred to as "apes." The Spaniards called them *monos* or monkeys, which was technically a more correct identification. Regardless of their label, for years they'd been favorites of visitors, who reveled in the monkeys' acumen for stealing bags belonging to selfie-focused tourists from park benches and unattended food plates from tables at nearby cafes.

For the most part though, the Barbary apes stayed out of the town, choosing to remain at the Gibraltar Nature Reserve as the star attraction. And other than some occasional petty theft and a few cases of minor property damage, the *monos* had been good neighbors. They didn't fear humans, learned through their daily intermingling, and were never considered a menace. Yesterday, that all changed.

One of the apes attacked a tourist. Then, another attacked and killed a British pub-owner. This morning, there was another attack. And because it was still too early for the rumor mill to fan the flames of worry, residents and tourists continued their activities as if nothing had happened.

It wasn't until the *Intrepid*, Regal European's shining star of the seas, pulled into Gibraltar's port and announced its arrival with its throaty horn that all the apes appeared to go crazy.

Each ape, having ten times the strength of a human, easily tore through people and property, without pause. Most bit wildly at anything with a pulse: store owners, just starting their day; residents and pets enjoying a walk during the morning coolness; and visitors, eager to consume their first espresso at a street-side cafe. Most of the town's occupants seemed unaware of the approaching ape mob until a wave of screams hit their ears.

When the apes entered the more populated areas, some stopped to take larger chunks out of their victims or just tore at limbs, which came off easily. Although they acted crazed and independent from one another, all the apes seemed to be charging through town in one direction: toward the port and the only cruise ship currently docked there.

The mass of apes wasn't yet visible through Captain Jörgen Christiansen's binoculars, as he scanned for some visual vindication to his decision. Moments ago, he had made the announcement to cancel this port of call, explaining to his frustrated guests that it was just too dangerous, and that they'd be leaving port shortly. Ted, who had just left the bridge, made far too compelling an argument. Still, Jörgen scanned the farthest reaches of the town with his binoculars, both wanting and not wanting to find visual verification. And while his crew busied themselves, they anxiously glared at their captain's head and awaited his next order.

"Do we still have the refueling ship available?" Jörgen barked at Jean Pierre, who was standing patiently beside him. The staff captain hadn't agreed, but backed the captain's decision.

The refueling ship was still tied to a berth on the other side of them. They had waved it off earlier, with their plan to refuel in the Canaries. But that was before Ted's report and their decision to leave.

"Yes, sir." Jean Pierre snapped to attention, repeating the information they had already discussed. "They only have heavy fuel and it's heated higher than your preferences. And I have confirmed your calculations with the chief engineer that we're already 20% over needed heavy fuel until the Bahamas."

"JP"—the captain rarely used first names, much less nicknames on the bridge, without titles—"I fear we might need more fuel than we're guessing. Please fill us to capacity. If I'm wrong, we can replace with MGO before we pull into US waters, and still satisfy their environmental standards."

"Aye, Captain," Jean Pierre confirmed, and then quickly turned and picked up the outside phone line to the harbor master. He wasn't sure what the captain was thinking, but he trusted his judgment.

Captain Christiansen didn't know what lay ahead, but he was going to ensure they had more supplies than they needed. He had learned this back in 2005 when twenty-eight hurricanes hit during the season, cutting off supplies and stranding them at one or another of their ports while they waited for a refueling ship. Generally, he kept his ship's fuel supply at 20% over the calculated maximum needed amount for their long route, in case he had a problem with a supplier. This afforded enough leeway to move to the next port and refuel there. It wasn't hurricane season, but with everything going on, a voice inside told him he'd need every drop he could get right now.

Jörgen watched from the swing deck with controlled nervousness as the refueling barge sidled up to their ship's port side, while remaining tied to the berth. It only had to move a few meters before it was in position. It was maybe half the length of the *Intrepid*, but only a couple of decks above water level. It was completely full of heavy fuel, something akin to crude oil. He kept one eye on his crew and the tanker's two crew members racing to connect the giant hoses; with the other he gazed at the digital fuel gauges, mentally pushing them upward. Deep down, in the pit of his stomach, an apprehensive worry burned like fire. A part of him felt sure they had very little time left.

Nigel James blew warmth onto his hands and vigorously rubbed them together in a vain attempt to get feeling back to his digits. It wasn't the abnormal temperatures outside; the pipe fittings were ice cold. Touching them seemed to leach the coldness directly through the thin material of his gloves. Then almost instantly the reverse happened, as the heated fuel cascaded through their barge into the ship. He felt the fittings change from cold to warm and then to hot. Now he started to sweat and stepped back to wait until he was told they were done. He looked at his mate manning the controls, who nodded at him. Then Nigel gave thumbs up to the two crew from the cruise ship, who were already stepping inside their hatch, eyes wide, like they were worried they were going to get docked pay for cavorting with sludge-sloppers like him. Most crew from cruise ships were cordial. The *Intrepid's* was not, which was very strange.

Nigel glanced up at the top decks of the sparkling cruise ship, admiring its recently painted hull. Several decks had lines of balconies, some with passengers—no doubt on holiday—luxuriating. His eyes scanned for a pretty female until he found one in a sumptuous bathrobe. Then he imagined himself in that very room with that pretty lassie. He remained fixed in her direction, not so much as leering, but watching his mind play out the narrative of his daydream...

They had just made love before having their morning cafe out on the balcony. He could almost taste its bitterness and the smooth sweetness of the milk stirred into it. He'd have had several by this point, while he planned his day with his super-model girlfriend: where they'd go, what they'd buy at the store—

"Nigel, is our seal still strong?" his mate hollered from behind him, rudely interrupting his reverie.

He hated this job, but he needed to keep it. So he bit his tongue and didn't tell him what he could do with the bloody seal. Nigel shot a glance at it. "Looks good here."

He furtively glanced back up to the balconies, searching for the woman. She was gone. There were more passengers now on their balconies, all looking over Gibraltar. Many were pointing at the town.

"As if there was anything that interesting in this bloody town but a few bloody monkeys on a hill," he snickered.

A scream drew his attention to a passenger more forward from where he'd been gawking. He squinted and found the screaming passenger also pointing with one hand, her other clutching her mouth. Beside her, an elderly man was gazing through binoculars. Nigel heard a muffled, "Oh my God."

He now turned his attention in the same direction that she was pointing.

"Perhaps the Rolex she wanted was no longer in the window of her favorite store," he grumbled.

But there was something going on in town. Some sort of commotion. He wished he had some binoculars too. But he was close enough that it didn't take long for him to figure it out.

Not far away from them, just outside the port, was a street lined with outdoor restaurants. Nigel had daydreamed plenty about drinking unlimited pints of Guinness out there, instead of drinking a local brew at a pub much farther inland for about a fifth of the price. Outside each of these restaurants were little tables and chairs, which would be soon bustling with visitors from this ship and at least one other that was due to arrive later. There were only a few people there now, but they weren't sitting. They were moving away from the street, slowly at first. Then, they darted inside as several objects moved down the street, mostly ignoring the restaurants. One of the objects, a brown and gray blur, dashed inside and then moments later bolted back outside, carrying what looked like a rolled-up towel that sprayed liquid.

It was still very hard to make out at this distance with the naked eye.

"Hey, what is that?" Nigel called out to his mate.

"Don't know," was the reply.

Another scream. This time, more of a screech, not as distant. And he could just barely make out the objects now: the brown-gray objects were actually those blooming monkeys. And that one monkey that had come out of the restaurant wasn't holding a rolled-up towel.

It was holding up someone's severed arm, like a macabre trophy. Now it was swinging it in the air, while it cried out to the other monkeys.

They all seemed to be headed to the cruise liner terminal... in his direction.

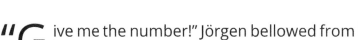

"Give me the number!" Jörgen bellowed from behind his binoculars. He did his own calculations on the port-side swing deck of the bridge, while glancing at the pandemonium in town drawing perilously closer.

"Ninety-two percent," Jessica snapped back, her eyes glued to one of the many large tilted computer screens in the middle of the bridge.

"That's good. Cut loose and let's get out of here." Jörgen scanned his entire port side before his gaze fell on the two barge workers, who appeared to be watching not their stations, but instead the town. Then one of them reacted abruptly and ran toward his bow, slipping down into an open hatch below. Both workers were needed to disconnect so that they could leave.

He wondered if they had waited just a minute too long.

Nigel looked back up and noticed the *Intrepid's* captain was outside, gazing down at him, before turning and ducking inside his bridge. Nigel glanced back for his mate, but he was gone too. Probably went down below deck.

The two Regal European crew members who had made a hasty retreat earlier were back outside, yelling orders at him. "Disconnect! We need to leave *now!*"

Nigel was about to panic and bail: jump into the water and swim away. He then imagined how cold that water would be; he hated the cold. Then he reasoned that maybe he and his mate could get away in the barge and he'd be dry, if only he could do what they asked and disconnect.

More screaming, again from the balconies above. This time he ignored them all and examined the connected hose.

There was a blur to his left side for just a second, and then it was gone. Nigel looked over in that direction and saw two monkeys crawling on the tie line connecting the barge to the dock. The monkeys were headed for them. They couldn't leave until they were disconnected, and he couldn't disconnect until the flow had stopped. Nigel made a quick decision and darted to the outside control panel, where his no-good friend should have been.

He punched the emergency stop button and dashed back to the hose coupled to the big cruise ship. One of the crew from the ship was already trying to pull it off, but it was too soon. The man had to wait until the pressure was equalized, which wasn't going to be for another moment or two. He desperately clawed at the fittings, shooting a glance at Nigel, just as Nigel pulled up to him. His eyes were wild with terror. And he was bleeding.

"The apes. We've got to go!" he yelled. Letting go of the coupling, he leapt up to the hatch at the same time as a monkey jumped up to greet him.

Nigel watched in disbelief as the monkey attacked the worker, who was trying to escape into the ship. He couldn't help the guy. He had to disconnect now, if there was any chance of leaving. He lunged for and unclasped the coupling and it burst off, spraying black oil everywhere. He had pulled it off too early, but he didn't have the luxury of waiting any longer. Part of the nozzle still held to the fitting. So he yanked once to pull it free and lost his footing on the oil already covering the deck.

All of his one-hundred-fifteen kilos tumbled hard onto the deck of the barge, his head hitting harder, and his vision exploded in fireworks.

He lay there for what was probably only a couple of seconds, but seemed like forever, as he tried to clear the daze that held him. He watched a monkey viciously bite and tear at the Intrepid crew member above. His crewmate, already behind a sealed door, stared through the porthole.

Then Nigel saw people above him, on those nice balconies, looking down at him.

One passenger was smoking a cigar.

What an idiot, Nigel thought. *Didn't your ship tell you it's against the rules to smoke?*

He watched the passenger move over him, unable to tell which was moving: the cruise ship or his own barge. Then he saw the cigar do somersaults in the air, seemingly on a wire, guided right at him. While he heard more cries and screams, Nigel gazed incredulously as the cigar bounced off his chest and landed on the deck's oily surface beside him.

Nigel knew he still had a minute or two to abandon ship, as the heavy oil shouldn't explode like the MGO. But it would burn very hot.

He attempted to right himself, but he couldn't get a foothold. The oil looked a lot like black blood.

He felt a rush of heat and knew that the oil was already catching. He'd forgotten that heated oil burned quicker, and their oil was heated high. This was usually good for them because heated oil took up more room, which meant they could sell less of it for the same amount per liter and make more money. It wasn't good now. The boat's owner's money-grubbing ways were going to get him killed.

With all his effort, he found himself standing hunched over, head craned up sideways like Quasimodo, glaring at the cruise ship as its bow passed by him. He knew what he needed to do to save himself. Only five feet separated him and the barge's edge, and therefore the water. He put one foot in front of the other, slowly at first, then a little quicker, even though a searing pain swept up his legs—his pants must be on fire.

Three feet.

His hands started to burn.

Two feet.

A blanket of heat covered his arms.

One foot.

A blaring screech hit him at the same time as a large brown object, sending him back onto the smoldering deck.

As Nigel's face started to singe, a gruesome ape, mouth agape, screeched at him. Before it sank its giant fangs into his face, he noticed its eyes. They were red like blood.

18

Ted

For Ted, the unfolding of the last two days' events was akin to watching a painter throw together a watercolor canvas on one of those PBS shows. But this version was even more excruciating.

The artist always started with a blank white canvas; what it would become was only known by the artist. First came the foundational colors: splashes of blues, browns, and blacks. Even after all of these were applied, the canvas revealed nothing to the audience. The blurry mess could have been anything, or nothing at all.

As the artist added flourishes to specific locations on the canvas, images started to take shape. On one corner, mountains burst upward out of the browns. On the other, low cloud formations billowed from the blue skies. And among the darkest portions of the canvas, a single boat emerged from the murk, like a ghost.

Each of these disparate images had its own story, which should belong to separate canvases. Or so it seemed. Of course, it was obvious to the audience that they must be somehow related, because of their single but most crucial connection: They were attached to the same canvas.

The animal attacks and the volcanoes were seemingly unrelated anecdotes splashed upon the same grand cataclysmic landscape taking shape before the eyes of the world. It should have been obvious to all that they were related. But Ted suspected few if any were connecting these anecdotes. He was instantly overwhelmed by a fear that by the time the world's audience perceived this connection, it would be too late.

Near the end of the PBS show, the television show painter would toss a few quick strokes of his brush onto the canvas and instantly connect all the images into one: land, sky, and sea all seamlessly woven together into one symbiotic mosaic. Only then did the reason or theme of the painting become obvious. Those final flourishes were all that was missing to provide that ah-ha moment.

Ted was trying to speed up the process to get to that ah-ha moment so that he could understand why the animal attacks were connected to the volcanoes. If he did, maybe he could help to save his wife, his ship, maybe even humanity.

He sat heavily on the small couch of his cabin, facing the open slider and shrinking view of Gibraltar. His head was back and his eyes closed while he considered this real-life apocalyptic canvas that he and all his shipmates had found themselves splashed upon.

Something had caused animals to go all wonky in Spain and other parts of Europe. And whatever was doing this drove those animals into attacking other warm-blooded creatures. He was pretty sure he knew the root cause of their madness. After all, he had based a fictional book on this. But something had to instigate this mass bout of rage with the animals. Some sort of inciter.

In his book, it was a virus created by an insane anarchist. He doubted this real-life story had a human antagonist behind this. He wasn't sure what logic was driving his thinking, but he believed this had to be natural and caused by the volcanic eruptions, he just didn't know why. If he was at all correct, what would become of them was terrifying. And would this disease of madness remain only in Europe or spread elsewhere? And if he could even solve this part of the puzzle, would there be any way to stop it? The possibilities of more than half of all animals in the world being afflicted were too scary to even consider right now.

Ted sat up, still holding his binoculars, but he hesitated to raise them to his face, fearful that seeing it would make it real. TJ and he had traveled to Gibraltar once before, as part of a tour of Spain. He had been looking forward to seeing Gibraltar again, in spite of the large ship-spawned crowds: the majesty of its "Rock," easily accessible by tram; the humor of its infamous residents, the Barbary apes; and its uniquely British feel, bursting with pubs serving Guinness on tap along with more tasteful twists to traditional British food, or what they'd call *flavour*.

Ted and TJ swore that they'd come back again. After the hordes had disembarked the ship, they'd take a little time to stroll its cobbled streets, enjoy some of its food and imbibe a pint, or two. That wasn't going to happen now, and perhaps not ever again.

He considered the magnitude of this epidemic, with the numbers growing daily: three days ago, a couple; two days ago, several more; yesterday, an explosion of them. Today, the international news blogs and TV stations were abuzz about the animal attacks in Europe.

He considered two primary commonalities: the animals seemed crazy and their eyes were red. From as far north as Iceland to as far south as Egypt, and from Portugal in the west to Turkey in the east, birds, dogs, cats, and rats (and monkeys) were going mad.

From *Le Figaro* in Paris, yesterday:

"Packs of dogs roaming the Latin Quarter attacked other dogs and people. Seven deaths have been reported."

From *La Vanguardia* in Barcelona, a few hours ago:

"Twenty-five people were treated for injuries sustained from what several victims reported as 'rabid cats, with red eyes.'"

From *EL PAÍS* in Madrid, two days ago:

"Five people at a Hertz rental car parking lot were mauled by a German shepherd. Two died on the scene."

And finally, from the *Dario Sur* in Malaga, yesterday:

"Fifteen people were attacked by seagulls in the Alcazaba castle area. An elderly couple was found dead at the scene."

These last two prompted Ted to look specifically for stories from the next few scheduled ports. So far, there were no reports of attacks in the Canaries, although he had read a few mentions about recent earthquakes and worries about one of its active volcanoes erupting. But in Gibraltar, he found one small news story on a local blog site. It was the one that had prompted him to warn the captain. Then a minute later, it was backed up by a UK paper.

"British tourist mauled and nearly killed by one of Gibraltar's infamous Barbary apes."

In a way, he wasn't too surprised, and this alone didn't cause him worry. Frankly, he always wondered why more people weren't injured by those monkeys, whose evil charms and proclivity to steal from unattended bags earned them favor among the tourists. If one of them wanted to get violent, there wasn't much that could be done to stop them. And at least once before, several of the more "aggressive" monkeys were relocated to a wildlife park off Gibraltar.

But it was the report that had popped up in the UK's Daily Harold that made him grow cold.

"Molly Adams of Lancashire was expected to make a full recovery after having her nose reattached. She couldn't offer comment, because of heavy sedation. However, one of her

nurses had reported that Ms. Adams kept screaming about 'their evil red eyes.'"

That's when he knew the captain couldn't risk exposing the passengers of the Intrepid to more potential animal attacks. Christiansen seemed unsurprised by Ted's reporting and responded with conviction, immediately canceling disembarkation and sealing up the ship. Now they were sailing out of port after topping off their fuel.

Ted felt good about this, but he knew to his bones that this was just one more vignette of this apocalyptic canvas unfolding all over Europe, and perhaps elsewhere. He hoped that he would be proven wrong, even though it would mean that he alone was the reason for everyone missing out on Gibraltar.

Please be wrong.

But he knew in his gut he wasn't.

The whole time he had been back at their room he hesitated to look upon Gibraltar as it faded in the distance. He just didn't want to confirm his thinking. Finally, Ted brought the binocular lenses up to his eyes, which were assaulted with both the surreal and horrific.

There were several fires burning, including a scary black blaze at the port they'd just left. Stores were damaged, cars had crashed, and in between each were glimpses of monkeys jumping onto people, running after others, and killing still others on the ground. A startling bright red-orange light burst filled his field of view, as if he had pointed his binoculars directly at the sun.

Ted jumped, his heart skipping several beats. A deep thumping boom shuddered his suite's back slider and their living area mirror.

Ted gulped back his surprise and watched in awe as a rolling ball of black smoke and fire spun upward. Something big had just blown up in the harbor.

Their cabin door opened and then slammed shut and TJ strolled in, her arms full of plates of food and two Stellas.

He had wondered what had happened to TJ as she had been gone the entire time Ted had done his research, convinced the captain to leave Gibraltar, refueled, and then returned to his cabin. It had been hours since she had left for a run. He even started to fear that she had somehow left the ship, even though the captain had confirmed no one had. He was immediately relieved to see her.

"I heard what you did and figured we needed some sustenance," she said, her face grim.

She seemed unaware of the explosion, or the monkey attacks, but she was aware of his efforts to convince the captain to avoid Gibraltar—or was she?

"How did you hear?" he asked, laying the binoculars down on the vanity.

She set the plates and beers down on the coffee table and wrapped her arms around him.

She hugged him hard, and then released him, her face painted with a bright coat of anxiousness.

"We need to talk."

19

The Talk

They had closed the slider, sealing themselves in, and talked for more than an hour. It was a tough talk. TJ first admitted to him the truth about their cruise: it wasn't part of his book tour. It had all been set up by the Bureau because of her job, not his writing.

She didn't tell him the entire purpose of the cruise or the number of times she was meeting up with Jean Pierre. She couldn't yet.

He suspected some of this, but he had to admit he was a little disappointed. Yet none of that really mattered. Regardless of the reasons behind their trip, or TJ's long disappearances, or the secrets, both they and the ship had far greater concerns.

He told her everything he knew, and as he did, he became more and more convinced that he had predicted the crazy animal crisis they were experiencing today. He felt the need to hold back some of the details, because he didn't want to scare her too much, but she needed to know what was basically happening, and talking about it out loud helped him to see if there were holes in his theory. To TJ's credit, she accepted everything in a very measured manner, treating every point logically and not emotionally as he expected. It was after all an animal apocalypse, and she was frightened of animals.

"So why volcanoes? I mean, what do they have to do with the spread of this disease that makes animals crazy?" she asked.

"I don't know. I haven't figured that part out yet. But they have to be connected."

"But you think most animals that came in contact with the discharge from a volcano could be affected?" TJ took a final swig of her Stella Artois. She wished she'd plunked down another twenty for two more.

Ted was tapping away on his iPad, almost as if he was ignoring his wife's question. "Yes, I believe so, if my theory is correct," he said without looking up. Finally, after a minute of silent scrutiny of his screen, Ted looked at his wife. "Um, sorry. I just had a thought. I wondered where the trade winds would blow the discharge from the Iceland and Mount Etna volcanoes." He swung his tablet around to show TJ. "This is a picture of the ash cloud over eleven days during the 2010 eruption, and remember this was just from the one volcano, from Iceland."

"That's all of Europe," her eyes followed the progressive lines of the ash cloud. "...half of Asia, and part of the US."

"And again, that's just one volcano..."

"The Canaries look like they may be in the covered area. Did you check to see if there were any reports in La Palma?"

"There was nothing as of a few minutes ago." Ted rose from the couch and stretched. They'd been sitting the entire time. "I need to take a bathroom break and I think I hear our room steward. I'll drop our dishes outside for him."

"Cool, do you mind if I do some searching?" TJ pulled the iPad onto her lap. "And see if you can get him to bring us some more beer."

"Sure, on both." Ted gathered up the tray of dishes and their two empties. He padded to the door, balancing the tray in one hand and opening the heavy door with the other. A whoosh of wind whined through the cabin. It was a wind-tunnel blaring from their back slider—they'd cracked it open a few minutes earlier to get some air movement—through the open front door. Ted let the door close with a deep thump, forgetting for a panicked moment whether he had his key on him. Then he remembered it was in his back pocket.

He looked in both directions and didn't see Jaga's cart of supplies, so he leaned over and set the tray down by the door. He'd call room service for the beers and ask that they pick it up. His head snapped to his right toward a rapid motion, and he froze, still holding the tray.

"Hey there," he said to what he at first thought might be a very large rat, and then he realized it was a ferret. He figured someone must have brought it on board and it got free.

He froze.

The ferret didn't move, and just gazed at him with blood-red eyes.

Ted was still bent over. His face and neck were completely exposed to this animal, if it attacked. His heart beat a countdown to what he thought would be the ferret's eventual strike.

Ted's fingers softly glided across the tray's surface where he remembered seeing a metal fork, which he could use as a weapon. He felt his chest pound, as he remained frozen. Nothing else on him moved, other than the tips of his fingers, brushing slowly across the tray. When his hand found the fork, the ferret popped up onto its haunches and made sniffing sounds with its nose.

Ted thought that was the signal, and he waited for it, freezing in place and bracing for imminent impact. Instead, the ferret lowered itself to the carpet and then raced past him, down the hallway. It turned right and dashed down another corridor.

He let out a long series of puffs and lifted himself up, clutching the fork in his left hand. Then he considered the ferret's behavior.

He had been sure the ferret would go all honey-badger on him when he first saw the red eyes, but then he realized the animal wasn't crazed, like the other animals. It was thinking, considering. The mad animals seemed to lack all reason: they just attacked.

"Mr. Williams?" asked their room steward, Jaga, "can I get you something?"

Ted was startled, completely lost in his thoughts and what he thought was going to be his violent end. "Ah, hi! No, we're good, thanks." He turned, slid the key into the door, and let himself inside their cabin. With a *whoosh* and a *thunk*, the door slammed behind him.

"Thought you dropped into a black hole. Come here and look at this." TJ pointed to the iPad. "Never mind, I'll just tell you about it. There are still no reports about animal attacks in the Canaries, at least not recently. However, there were a rash of attacks in the 1700s. There's a book on Google, a history of the Canaries, and it talks about one period—which by the way was days after a volcanic eruption—where, and I quote, 'a dark period fell over the islands, where people and animals were said to have gone crazy.' Coincidence or harbinger?"

Ted had found his place back on the couch, while he listened to TJ's findings. "Good find. By the way, do you know anything about the typical eye color of a ferret?"

She looked at him like he was the one who had gone crazy, especially with what he held in his hand. "Ah, no. And what's with the fork?"

148

He glanced down and saw that he was still unconsciously clutching the damned fork he had been about to brandish at the ferret.

He hesitated and then decided to tell her about the ferret he'd encountered when a double pulse-tone reverberated throughout the cabin.

It felt to them like the dreaded phone call often received in the middle of the night, carrying with it the news of a family member's illness or death. Both TJ and Ted glowered at the phone, feeling their chests leap and their stomachs turn over at once. It rang again, but neither of them budged.

Being closest to the phone, TJ finally picked it up.

"Hello?" she answered, her face steely and serious. "Oh hello, Jean Pierre," she said, now much friendlier.

She nodded, looking down at the desk, where the phone was located. "Ted too?" She looked over to him. "Both of us?" Once again, she looked away. "Okay, thank you. We'll see you shortly."

20

Taufan, the Ferret

Taufan finally zeroed in on the source of the scent it had first gotten wind of.

The ferret had never been outside of the three-meter by two-meter chamber its owner shared with the other roommates, so every square meter of the ship was new to it.

Taufan didn't understand what was going on, and certainly couldn't comprehend why. It was a ferret, after all. It only knew that it was confused, lonely, and very hungry, all at once. These feelings were as foreign as the hectares of ship it'd already explored. Until today, it'd only experienced its little belly being filled when it wanted food, and the love of its owner and its owner's roommates.

Now it had felt the pain of hunger all day long and was unable to find any food. Twice, it thought it had a chance of getting fed. Earlier, a big man tried to feed it, but a larger animal chased it away. And then a man looked like he might offer it something on a tray, but then Taufan smelled something far more appetizing.

A crew member had left a restricted doorway open. And through that doorway, down a stairwell, is where it caught wind of the glorious smells of fish. Lots of fish, along with other foreign but equally tasty aromas. Taufan wasn't finicky. It only knew the taste of fish, and it was so hungry right now. Even the humans it raced by looked like food, though it had never thought of its owner and his roommates as food before. It was then that Taufan became frantic. It burst into the vast main galley where all the food was being prepared for the ship's guests.

Because the ship was missing half of its kitchen staff, and dinner was still expected on time, many of the kitchen crew found themselves working two jobs. And amid the craziness of everyone racing around the kitchen, no one even noticed the small ferret scurrying inside and then working its way toward the aromas it'd been attracted to the whole time: the fish prep area.

Taufan had only experienced cooked fish, from the tidbits that Jaga and his roommates would bring it each day from their own dinners. Jaga was a fish fan himself and therefore so was Taufan. But the smell of fresh salmon was almost too much for the starving ferret. Like a guided missile, Taufan rocketed as fast as its little legs would accelerate it to its target, working its way around all impediments with ease.

It hopped onto a bucket beside a haphazardly abandoned cleaning cart and followed the makeshift staircase up the cart and onto a counter, bringing it belly-level with the kitchen crew. It remained unnoticed.

Without pausing, it scurried up several pots to a long shelving unit that stretched across the many stainless-steel food prep areas, almost the entire length of the kitchen. At the end of this shelf was the fish prep area.

The kitchen crew took great pride in making sure that they followed rigorous safety procedures for handling food. That way there was no chance of contaminations, which could lead to infections or outbreaks. But with the short staff of this cruise, including the loss of their safety officer (who never made it back from Malaga), mistakes were being made. Those mistakes were like dominoes, which started a cascading effect of failures that not only allowed a ferret to find its prize, but something much worse.

A bucket of dirty water, left by one of the short-handed cleaning crew who had to run to clean up a mess in the auxiliary galley, was precariously perched on the edge of the same shelf that Taufan was scampering over. This type of infraction was absolutely unheard of on cruise ships, especially those run by Regal European. During normal times, food would be discarded immediately if there was any chance that it touched the same place this bucket did. Again, these weren't normal times.

At the moment Taufan brushed past the bucket, which was partially blocking his route, a large ocean swell caused the ship to roll in the same direction, and the bucket started a long tumble to the floor. One-third of the way down, it hit another cart, also carelessly parked below. Because of the surge, this cart had also started to roll toward the opposite side of the main kitchen walkway and the produce prep area. The bucket struck in such a way that most of the blackish water—a disgusting combination of old fish parts, slop from the floor, and other sludgy unmentionables, all ripe with bacteria—splashed outward toward the table of leafy greens.

Just before this, Samuel Yusif from Somalia, standing behind one of the prep tables, carefully adjusted his yellow scarf, earned from his two earlier contracts. He scanned his area for the green tub he absolutely needed for his next step. It was gone. He had already chopped up everything that would need to go into the special tub, which would be used to transport the greens to an area occupied by other yellow scarves to prepare that evening's salads. Normally, the tub was brought back to him by another crew member, usually one of the green scarves. But several of the greens hadn't made it on board in Malaga. He hmphed under his breath, knowing he'd have to find the darn tub himself.

Leaving his area, Samuel barely acknowledged the sound of the crashing bucket behind him; he had just spotted one of his missing tubs and was focused on grabbing that and getting rid of his greens before his supervisor yelled at him for taking too long. As Samuel grabbed the tub, the falling bucket splashed its blackish contaminated water all over his freshly chopped lettuce, and then bounced unnoticed under his prep table.

When Samuel returned and scooped his chopped greens into the tub, he never even noticed the little specks of food particles and dirt that peppered his lettuce. The wet floor was odd, but that only sharpened his focus on not slipping and dropping his Romaine.

He quickly walked his tub over to the salad preparers who were waiting for it. They then assembled the leafy greens with other freshly prepped ingredients into each bowl. Another yellow scarf added the freshly made croutons. Each was beautifully presented, as always. Only one of the yellow scarves noticed what looked like pepper flecks, but she didn't think to mention it, as their new head chef was always trying new things.

Flavio breezed in from the service elevator, turned the corner into the main kitchen aisle, and pulled his cart over to the salad prep table. Immediately, without a spoken word, the yellow scarves loaded it with the freshly prepared salads. When his cart was full, he swung it around and pushed it quickly back toward the elevator.

As he turned the corner, directly past the smelly fish prep area, he witnessed what he thought he'd never see in a clean kitchen: an odd-sized rat was gorging himself on one of the large planks of fresh salmon. He hated rats and thought he'd already taken care of the ship's rat problem. This pissed him off.

He looked to his left and right and didn't see anyone in that area. So he decided to take matters into his own hands. He was tired of this ongoing issue.

Flavio withdrew a steak knife from his sheath; in his position, he always needed a knife, and the steak knives were versatile and plentiful. It didn't have the balance of the throwing knives he carried back home or his Morakniv carbon knives that he kept in his cabin, but it would do.

In the rat's direction, he hollered, "Hey rat!"

Taufan glanced up at the yelling human, while it frantically chewed a mouth full of delightful salmon.

The waiter paused just a moment—knife poised to be released—as he considered this odd-looking thing: its body was longer than a normal rat and the ones he encountered yesterday. But like the others, its eyes were as red as Ukrainian rubies. The red eyes were just too much to take. That momentary pause was all the creature needed.

Flavio let loose the knife. It had the perfect speed and arc, and it was on target. But it hit right when the long rat had jumped from the table. The knife clattered off the surface, cleaving away an additional piece of the ruined plank of salmon.

He *humphed* a momentary frustration at his miss before putting his weight again into the cart. Hungry diners were waiting for their salads. Somebody else would have to kill this rat. He reached under the cart and grabbed a replacement steak knife and sheathed it. He'd have to remember to sharpen this one. He hated dull knives.

Just before he entered the elevator, he spotted the senior assistant chef, Jon. Just the man to whom he needed to report this egregious infraction.

"Hey, Jon." His Romanian accent and limited English vocabulary kept him from expressing the indignities he wanted to articulate, but his mind screamed them. *How could you allow a rat to even exist in this kitchen, which up to now has been pristine? How could planks of fresh salmon be left unattended? And how could you allow a galley that was so well run go to shit?*

Flavio already hated this assistant chef because he was English, just like the head chef—he really hated English food. But this was all too much to stomach.

He had served more contracts than this fool, and from the staff captain on down, he was very well respected among his crew because of his skill and work ethic. Still, the assistant chef was his superior.

When he had Jon's attention, he spat out, "You have a rat eating the salmon planks, and no one is there to see it. You need to take better care of your kitchen."

He didn't wait for a reply.

As he pushed the deck 6 button, which would lead right into the MDR, he watched with both disgust and a little delight as the strange-looking rat scurried around the kitchen, chased by Jon and two yellow scarves.

21

The Rabid Toy Poodle

"It was a blooming rabid toy poodle, I tell you!"

Boris sat up from his infirmary bed, cheeks rosy with agitation. "The thing is vicious. And it had red eyes, like a little devil." He pointed to his eyes and clenched his teeth to make himself look scarier. "You've got to warn the captain."

"Settle down, Mr. Thompson. We'll tell everyone who needs to be told. Let's make sure you're fine first." Dr. Chettle turned to his nurse, and whispered the order to take Mr. Thompson's temperature once more.

Her last reading was 97.02, which was far below normal. He assumed that she didn't do it right the first time. She'd never served on a ship before, and at this moment he couldn't remember her qualifications. *But she should be able to take a damned temperature.* At least he thought so.

He suspected that Boris Thompson was in fact fine, other than very superficial puncture wounds from three dog bites and a few minor abrasions from the carpet, which broke his fall. There was very little tissue damage from the punctures, which hadn't penetrated more than a couple of millimeters of epidermis. Infection was the biggest worry. Thompson's blood pressure was slightly elevated, but this was normal considering his current level of agitation and his weight. They'd already cleaned and bandaged him up fairly quickly. Mr. Thompson could be released once Chettle had an accurate temperature for his records.

More concerning to Dr. Chettle was that this was the third dog bite he'd treated in the last twenty-four hours, and it was only the third day of the cruise. So he'd tell his superiors about this incident, and even include Mr. Thompson's colorful commentary. Not because he believed in the story of a rabid toy poodle; he believed that Al was not taking care of business at the pet spa. If Al allowed a toy poodle to escape, imagine what would happen if he didn't keep the kennel's larger dogs contained, especially next door to the ship's clinic?

In truth, Dr. Chettle despised having a dog kennel on the ship, and was so blinded by the chance to catch his colleague in a mistake, he missed any connection between dog bites and the several cases of rat bites on the ship, including those on the body of their butcher, who died from a trip and fall accident.

He tapped out a couple more notes on his tablet and then attached the file to an email he had already started. He read it over again, changed "second" to "third," and then sent it to the staff captain. He looked back up to Mr. Thompson, who was sitting up again and slinging animated words at his nurse.

"No, your bloody thermometer is not broken. My temperature is naturally low, so what? You're wasting time. You need to warn the captain, and he needs to warn the crew and passengers about this crazy dog. We're not safe!"

"I think he went this way," said Yakobus, who knelt by a pallet of crushed cardboard and pointed down the throat of a junction off the I-95 hallway.

Jaga and Catur stopped short behind him and looked around, pretending to have a good reason to be there, one that didn't involve chasing after their illegal ferret. Whenever a ship's officer would approach, they tried to act normal. Any crew member ranked lower than an officer wouldn't care what they were doing loitering along I-95. They had been looking for Taufan for hours now, and when they heard that a "really long rat is loose in the kitchen," they came running. They picked up Taufan's trail on I-95. And then they lost it.

I-95 was the busiest and longest thoroughfare on the ship, stretching from bow to stern. And because it was used by all crew to trans-navigate the ship to get to their shifts and transport supplies outside the scrutiny of guests, Taufan could be anywhere now.

An engineering second officer strolled past them for a second time, glancing at the curious room attendants, who seemed out of place.

"Sir," they all said in unison.

"And I think you should report the missing clothes to the laundry," Yakobus hollered at Jaga, much too loudly, acting as if they were caught in mid-conversation when the officer passed.

When the second officer was no longer visible and out of earshot, Jaga knelt down to where Yakobus had been pointing and saw the droppings, plus something else: a fish bone. This had to be from Taufan, when that nutty ferret reportedly raided the salmon in the kitchen. Jaga couldn't blame his buddy for going after fresh salmon. *I'd have done the same if I was in his shoes... I mean, paws.*

"Hey guys," warned Catur. He had popped up like a tower, and like Yakobus beside him, he was facing straight down the long hallway junction toward the vast provisions areas. Both wore looks of shocked anxiety.

Fifty feet away, in front of a pallet of bottled waters, was a pack of dogs barking and scratching at the containers. Some of the offending bottles had burst and still sprayed water like fountains. All the dogs appeared crazy, consumed by some rabies-like frenzy. And Jaga could see the object of their fury.

In the middle of the pallet, surrounded by the water bottles on all sides, was a small man cradling himself, and rocking back and forth. Beneath the pallet was little Taufan, attempting to shrink into the dark recesses to evade the dogs. The dogs didn't see him.

"What do we do?" To Catur's shock, he watched Jaga already tentatively walking on the balls of his feet, approaching the pack of wild dogs.

Jaga hugged a wall and quietly stepped closer to the pack, attempting to look small and not make any noise that might attract their attention. He had no idea what he would do when he got there, but hoped he'd figure something out before the dogs attacked him.

He halted halfway to the snarling pack. Before him was the crumpled form of a man lying behind a box of bundled papers waiting to be deposited at their next port. Jaga reared backward a couple of steps, almost losing his footing. The man appeared lifeless; his skin color matched his gray work clothes. A puddle of blood expanded slowly from his neck and sought escape under the box. The man appeared to have tried to hold together his mangled neck in a failed attempt to stay alive. Bloody bite marks spotted his body, and gory paw prints made it clear; the dogs were the killers. It must have just happened.

"Oh my God," Catur yelped, having just left Yakobus behind and caught up to Jaga, and now seeing the body. He said this much too loudly.

The pack of dogs abruptly halted their ravenous clawing and barking and turned its collective attention away from Taufan to the trio.

"Oh crap," Catur yelped once again.

Jaga wanted to kill him, but instantly knew they would be next.

A crazed little poodle scurried around the edge of the pack, and despite its tiny size issued a terrifying, high-pitched screech.

Jaga sucked up a scream when he realized the chase was over. There was no way they would be able to run away from this pack. He made a quick decision and leapt out to the middle of the hall, and then ran toward the pack, waving his arms and screaming the vilest swear words he knew in Indonesian at the top of his lungs.

Catur stood dumbfounded as he watched his friend Jaga charge the pack of crazed dogs in an attempt to divert their attention from them to him alone.

The dogs—all but the poodle were leashed together—charged after Jaga, with the toy poodle trailing. Both Jaga and dogs were converging quickly, with barely a second or two separating them. Just before they crashed into each other, Jaga dove into one of the wide-open refrigerators.

The pack of dogs didn't see this coming and attempted to change course immediately, but their feet—slick from the blood and the water-bottle attack—slid across the hard floor. Each attempted to regain its footing, some doing somersaults and others flailing at the air. But no amount of effort on their part could stop their momentum. Finally, they stopped.

They spasmodically righted themselves and bounded, as one tangled group, for the open space of the refrigerator. Jaga, unseen inside, seemed insane himself as he yelled more Indo curses at the oncoming pack, which bounded through the door almost at the same time.

There were multiple crashing sounds, followed by breaking glass, barking, and chaos. Then Jaga burst out of the refrigerator. He pivoted quickly and pushed with a grunt at the massive sliding door. It clicked closed just as the muffled sounds of the dogs pounded and scratched on the other side.

Jaga, practically hyperventilating, searched around the walls for something and made a small sound of satisfaction. He lumbered to the other side of the closed refrigerator, took down the notice about an upcoming crew party, flipped it around, and with his Sharpie wrote "Don't open! Crazy dogs!" on the back and slid the notice into the handle: a warning to the next person who might be tempted to open this refrigerator.

Jaga then mustered the last of his strength and sprinted to the pallet of ruined water bottles. Finally, Catur and Yakobus caught up. They checked on the rocking man and helped him out of his faltering water-bottle containment. "Are you okay?" they asked.

"Come here, Taufan," Jaga called into the dark space under the sloshing, dripping mass of eviscerated water bottles. Yakobus and Catur quietly plodded behind him and the three listened, hoping Jaga's pleas would be rewarded.

A barely audible squeak blurted back in reply, and moments later a soaking wet Taufan waddled over to them and leapt into Jaga's arms.

None of them reveled in their joy at finding their little friend and not dying in the process. Rather, they turned and left the area quickly. All three averted their eyes when they walked past the dead body. They would head back up to their room and put Taufan back, safe and unseen, into his bed. Only then would they report the dead body and the locked-up dogs.

They turned back onto I-95, Jaga cradling Taufan while his friends draped their arms around him, heaping praise upon him for his heroics.

A few seconds later, the warning sign Jaga had made slipped off the door and fell to the floor, note-side down.

22

Edgar

E dgar trudged through the bedroom to close the slider, but left it slightly ajar. It had been open the whole cruise, despite the cool temperatures. He liked it cold, and she didn't mind. But in her state now, it seemed right to close out the cold.

He'd checked the one in the living room, and it remained shut behind the sheers and drapes, which were fully closed. She wanted it that way, having no interest in seeing the outside.

After making sure that their cabin was secure, he sauntered back into their bedroom and paused at their bed, studying her and wondering what he should do next. More accurately, what he should do about her.

Eloise had come home last night after a late-night bender. He was in their lavatory dealing with an upset stomach after that evening's meal. He heard her clumsily rumble through their cabin, yelling his name, and then she was quiet. A few minutes later, when he exited the loo, he found her face down on their bed in much the same state she was in right now. He had turned her over once, just to make sure she was breathing. She was. She'd had been passed out for hours now. For this, he was glad.

At this moment, he had the best of both worlds: she was unconscious, which was far better than her annoying conscious self, and she was almost completely naked, and he did enjoy looking at her body. What was not to appreciate after she'd spent so much money attempting to perfect it? And if he was being truthful, her looks were what attracted him to her in the first place.

He harkened back to when they met, and she had come on to him.

He had not been with a beautiful woman since secondary school. After he graduated from college, he'd married a respectable woman of fine lineage; it was Martha who he had faithfully been with the entire time, until her death last year. Martha may have been homely on the outside, but her beauty was deeper and evidenced by her kindness to others. Eloise was the opposite.

He rehashed the images from that night when he first saw her at a pub he and a few of his friends frequented, near his Parisian home. She was wearing a bright red dress that was quite revealing and clung to her curves. He could also see she'd had way too much to drink. She staggered toward him and then halted a few feet away, wobbling such that she had to steady herself on a bar stool. She was searching for something in her designer clutch and then pulled out what looked like car keys. He remembered thinking, *You're not going to try and drive in that state, are you?* He couldn't let her do it. He excused himself from his mates and approached her as she was trying to figure out which of the three keys went to her car.

He insisted that he drive her home. She responded with measured resistance, but almost immediately agreed and dropped the keys into his open hand. He had put an arm around her when she almost flopped over, just to steady her, until they reached her Mercedes. But before he could drive her, she'd passed out in the passenger seat. Without an address—her little purse held only a wad of euros—he carried her to his home across the street and placed her in one of his five guest bedrooms. The next morning, he woke to find her in his bed.

The rest was a blur: the sex, the whirlwind romance, the small wedding—she wanted it small—and now the cruise/honeymoon. But the more he got to know his new wife, the more he realized he simply didn't like her. Oh, she was beautiful on the outside. But something was very wrong with her, like a delicate red apple with a spoiled core; you didn't know it was bad until you bit into it. It was only after the wedding that her true self came out, and the sex stopped immediately. He suspected then that her whole purpose was to get to his money, which was funny because she seemed to have lots of it herself.

And now he found himself on this cruise, married to a woman he didn't love, and didn't even really like. Other than her being great in the sack—before she put a stop to it, anyway—and being movie-star beautiful, she had nothing he wanted anymore. He no longer wanted to be with her. He had insisted on a prenuptial agreement, and that was good, because he decided then and there, while staring at her unconscious body, that when this cruise was over he'd tell her he wanted a divorce. She could keep what she had and he'd keep what he had.

He glanced at her beautiful body, lying peacefully in their bed. She was so arousing though, and he was an old man, not likely to ever have a woman who looked like this, unless he paid for it. He felt himself tighten up, and a wicked thought grew in him. This was probably his last opportunity to lie with her. She sure wasn't going to have him when she was conscious.

That little part of him that was still good, that last part that she hadn't yet destroyed, protested. *This is wrong!*

He considered her once more: drool ran from the corners of her mouth toward her ears; her healthy chest—only her nipples were covered by the fine flowered embellishments of her damaged dress—was now heaving up and down rapidly; her lower half—where the dress was torn completely off—lay fully exposed and beckoned him.

He decided to do it.

He dropped his trousers and quietly walked around to the front of their king-sized bed. Her legs were bent at the knees, draped over the edge of the bed. Her thighs waited. He pushed his large, tangled comb-over to the other side of his head, and then parted her legs. He pulled her closer to him and mounted her.

At one point, he thought he heard her moan. Otherwise, she slept through it all.

DAY FOUR Cont.

LA PALMA, SPAIN

IN 1971, CUMBRE VIEJA, ON THE ISLAND OF LA PALMA AT THE WESTERN TIP OF THE CANARY ISLAND ARCHIPELAGO, ERUPTED FOR THE SEVENTH TIME IN SIX HUNDRED YEARS. COMPARED TO SOME OF ITS PREVIOUS ERUPTIONS, THIS ONE WASN'T VERY LARGE AND DIDN'T LAST VERY LONG. THE ERUPTION IMMEDIATELY PRIOR TO THIS ONE, IN 1949, LASTED THIRTY-SEVEN DAYS AND SHOT LAVA THIRTY METERS INTO THE AIR. BUT EVEN THAT ONE WAS SMALL IN COMPARISON TO THE ONE IMMEDIATELY PRIOR TO IT IN 1712. AND STILL THESE WERE NOT CONSIDERED "MAJOR" ERUPTIONS.

WITH EACH YEAR THAT PASSED WITHOUT A MAJOR ERUPTION, TOP SEISMOLOGISTS WARNED, "THE BIG ONE IS COMING." PAPERS WERE WRITTEN, BUT MOST VOICES ONLY RECEIVED PEER REVIEW AND NOT THE ATTENTION OF WORLDWIDE MEDIA, EVEN THOUGH THE POSSIBILITIES OF A GIANT ERUPTION WERE GREAT. AND THE EFFECTS OF SUCH AN ERUPTION WOULD BE MONUMENTAL... "APOCALYPTIC," SOME WOULD EVEN SAY.

UNLIKE THE THREATS FROM MOST VOLCANIC ERUPTIONS, WHERE BLACK ASH, PYROCLASTIC CLOUDS, OR EVEN MOLTEN LAVA WERE THE PRIMARY CONCERNS, CUMBRE VIEJA POSED

A MUCH GREATER THREAT TO ITS NEIGHBORING CANARY ISLANDS AND EVERY COASTAL TOWN ON ALL SIDES OF THE VAST ATLANTIC SEABOARD: A GIANT TSUNAMI.

A MASSIVE SLAB OF ROCK, TWICE THE VOLUME OF THE ISLE OF MAN, HUNG FROM THE NEARLY TWO-THOUSAND-METER-HIGH MOUNTAIN, BARELY CLINGING TO ITS ROCKY BASE BY ITS NAIL-THIN ROCK ANCHORS. EACH YEAR, THOSE ANCHORS WERE WEAKENED FURTHER. BECAUSE OF THE SLAB'S ENORMOUS SIZE, EXPERTS SAID THAT THE NEXT LARGE ERUPTION WOULD MOST LIKELY DISLODGE IT, CAUSING IT TO SLIDE INTO THE OCEAN. THE ENERGY FORCE CREATED BY THIS WAS PEGGED BY ONE SOURCE TO BE THE EQUIVALENT TO SIX MONTHS OF ALL THE POWER GENERATED BY ALL OF AMERICA'S POWER STATIONS. THE RESULT WOULD BE A MASSIVE TSUNAMI, LARGER THAN ANYTHING EVER RECORDED.

ESTIMATES VARIED WILDLY. ONE SAID THAT THE RESULTING INITIAL WAVE COULD ATTAIN A LOCAL HEIGHT OF 600 METERS AND PEAK AT 1600 METERS, OR ONE MILE HIGH. THE MOUNTAIN-SIZED WAVE WOULD TRAVEL AS FAST AS 450 MILES PER HOUR, OR NEARLY THE SPEED OF A COMMERCIAL JET AIRCRAFT.

A WAVE THIS SIZE WOULD FLOOD THE COASTLINES OF AFRICA IN AN HOUR; THE BRITISH ISLES WOULD BE DELUGED IN THREE TO FOUR HOURS; AND EVEN NORTH AMERICAN COASTS WOULD BE SWAMPED IN SIX.

THE DEVASTATION WOULD BE UNIMAGINABLE.

AT 5:40 PM, THE UNIMAGINABLE HAPPENED.

23

Bridge Trouble

It was the second time in a few hours that Ted had been up on the bridge. Neither visit was pleasurable.

"Please wait here," said the first officer, Jessica, who ushered them to the entrance of the ready room.

They stood with their backs to a wall, ready room on their left, active part of the bridge on their right, and quietly watched the bridge crew do its thing during what was probably one of the most stressful times any of them had ever experienced. The nervousness was palpable and hung like humidity during a hurricane.

During his previous visit to the bridge, as part of the All Access Tour, Ted had not spent more than a moment to really take in the bridge, even though that was the tour's purpose. Now, while they waited for the captain, he studied all that was going on around him.

The *Intrepid's* bridge was an expansive mélange of old and new, hierarchical and exclusive, functional and symbolic. This was demonstrated by all the systems and the personnel working on it. Each member of the bridge crew proudly wore two bars or more on their shoulders, signifying the bridge's obvious importance. And yet, its purpose was somewhat archaic. He remembered hearing one surprising fact from the tour: 95% of all ship functions, including all maneuvering, could be handled by Ivan, the operations room chief, and his crew, three decks below. There were other seemingly anachronistic elements in this "modern" bridge.

A captain's chair stood up high and resolute in the middle of the room, giving the captain a 180-degree view of everything outside the ship. Of course, there were no other chairs, because no one sat while on duty, least of all the captain, who seemed to spend most time eyeing a monitor farthest back, and away from the most forward view of the ship.

Eating up a lot of the floor space were maybe a dozen bulky platforms, each rising to chest level, each with a tilted computer screen blinking multitudes of data relevant only to the five crew members bustling around them. One per each crew member would have been sufficient, as surely each of these had the same conning and ECDIS software and would have been connected to the same computing power available to those in the operations room

Finally, a vestigial remnant from the past lay in front of them: a gigantic back-lit table, which would have held navigational maps on an older ship, took up a large portion of the bridge on the port side, where they waited. Instead of paper maps—replaced by the ECDIS system—there were now permanently fixed schematics of many of *Intrepid's* deck plans. Different from the public deck plans displayed on every deck, these revealed protected details like locations of restricted hatches. As an afterthought, in the middle of the table was a large to-scale-model of their ship, encased in a glass display.

Ted and TJ couldn't hear what exactly was being said, but they could tell that the crew members were treating each decision like it was one that concerned life or death for them and everyone on board.

The first officer who asked them to wait was a young woman with model-like features, including Icelandic-blonde hair that starkly showed off the three bars on her pressed white uniform. She couldn't have been more than thirty and looked like the youngest of the bridge crew. She leaned into the captain's ear and said something, no doubt concerning them. The captain flashed a glance their way, nodded and said something more to the first officer, who proceeded to another area of the bridge and glared at two computer screens with a feigned indifference, as if this were her normal day.

The captain's shoulders were pointed in their direction, but his head was focused on Jean Pierre, the staff captain, to whom he barked off some orders. Jean Pierre's bald head spun around, searching for someone or something, before he responded subserviently.

The captain nodded back and barked something more, before finally walking in their direction. Ted thought that Christiansen looked like he was carrying the weight of the world on his shoulders.

"Thank you for coming, my friends. Please join me in my ready room." He thrust his left arm out, toward the door. TJ opened it and the three of them walked in.

"Time is precious right now, and I'm sorry to lay my burdens upon you, our guests. But I suspect you know why you're here. So, I'll cut to the proverbial chase. Thanks to your warning, Ted, we avoided a catastrophe in Gibraltar, but our problems have just begun."

The monkey had worked its way up and over the metal railing of the crew's outside cigarette break area on deck 4. Because its hands and feet were slick from the fresh blood, it slid down almost an entire deck before regaining some traction on an opening in the metal. It didn't hesitate, as it was overwhelmed by a hunger for more. It had to have more.

A human voice called out, catching its attention. A man appeared just above and called out again to someone behind him.

The monkey didn't need any more prodding. Nails and digits scratched up the side of metal and glass, its rapid clattering over the ship's surfaces mirroring its frantic desire. It scurried up one of the windows framing the Windjammer Cafe. On the other side of the thick glass, ten-year-old Ashley Brown watched with wonderment, a giant spoon of ice cream shoved in her mouth, while her eyes tracked the monkey as it slipped by the window and pulled itself up to the next deck.

One foot slipped, and so it took a moment to regain its footing and glance back up. The back of its prey's head was still in sight, so it leapt the last five feet. But the man stepped away just before the monkey could sink its claws and teeth into his skull. Instead, it clutched air and started to fall.

With nothing to stop its progression downward, the monkey flailed in the air, skittering and bouncing off Ashley Brown's window—she dared not blink for fear of missing it pop up again. She needn't have bothered... With one final reach before its unobstructed plunge into the ocean below, it frantically stretched out one bloody hand and hooked itself on a deck 8 balcony. It yanked itself up like a shot over the railing, smashing back-first into the large balcony's arranged set of table and chairs.

An old man sleeping on a lounger outside rose to a sitting position, unsure what awful noise had woken him. His wide eyes glared at the balcony's shadows, floppy comb-over having come un-flopped, dangling in place on the side of his head. From behind an overturned table in the corner of their balcony, something flailed and banged against metal. It rose onto its hind legs. A furry beast, almost invisible in the dark shadows, its red eyes glaring like stoplights, fixed... on him.

He planted his feet on the balcony's non-slip surface, sprang up, and darted as fast as his legs would take him. He shot through the drawn curtains, over several of his wife's discarded pumps strewn over their bedroom, past his buck-naked wife still sleeping off her Valium hangover. He bounded through the bedroom door, pulling it closed behind him, not daring to look back. The door weakly rebounded off the frame, and came to rest slightly ajar. He skittered through to the reception area, where he turned the corner and scurried to their suite's exit. Almost there.

He clawed at the door handle, frantically attempting to push it down and simultaneously pull the door open, but he missed. Off balance, he stumbled to his knees.

A whimper burst from his lips as he bolted up again, grabbed the handle with both hands, twisted and yanked at the surprisingly heavy door. It sprang open. He thought he might make it.

He lunged for the opening's safety just as an immovable weight piled on top of him, driving him into the entry foyer's welcome mat. His head was smashed hard into the "te" of "Royal Suite." He lifted and turned his head to scream, but the beast shoved his face back into the floor and simultaneously sank its teeth painfully into his left scapula. Out of one eye, he could see a room attendant turn a corner, only a few feet from their suite entrance, and then stop in front of another cabin. The attendant opened the door and slipped inside, but never turned his way. The old man tried again to lift his head, perhaps his last chance to plead for assistance. But he couldn't, under the weight of the beast's foot. He groaned, "Help!" but it didn't come out much louder than a dull crackle.

The door of the same cabin popped back open and the attendant's hand wedged a towel underneath it to hold it open.

The old man felt the beast leap off him and watched it bound toward the partially opened cabin. It hopped inside, its foot tangling in and dislodging the hand towel, causing the door to flop closed. He heard a muffled scream and then a pounding against the door.

The old man managed to push with his right arm and move his damaged body backward out of the path of the door. Parts of him felt broken, but he thought he might actually survive this ordeal, if he could just get the door closed.

With one final effort, he spun around and pushed himself up to a sitting position, dislodging himself from the door, which swung quickly and slammed with a thud. After some time collecting himself, he felt the back of his shirt become wetter and he feared he wouldn't have long. He stood, his legs wobbly and unsure. He bent forward, forcing himself to stagger in the direction of the reception area, his feet scraping over the carpet. Once in their bedroom, he halted at the foot of the bed, his eyesight now foggy. He hesitated, while swaying from side to side, ready to topple. He knew he needed to wake his drugged-out wife, and risk her getting him to the ship's doctor, although he suspected she might not.

Finally, he grabbed her bare leg and aggressively shook while he groaned her name. She woke abruptly, screeched at him once, and then everything went black.

24

The Captain

"The animal attacks are not just in Europe; we've had several here on this ship. And there have been casualties: we've lost three crew members and two more of our crew have been bitten, along with three guests. This havoc has been wreaked upon us by rats, dogs, and a Barbary ape, and that's just in the last two days."

Ted and TJ were seated in two of the eight cushy leather chairs surrounding the cherry wood conference table, which had undoubtedly never witnessed a discussion like this one before. They listened attentively. TJ's mouth uncontrollably drooped open.

"Were their eyes red?" Ted asked, seemingly unfazed by the captain's revelation.

TJ's hand clenched his under the table, with almost viselike compression. Her mind then registered her husband's question and she reflexively nodded her head, even though she did not want to hear the captain's answer.

"Yes, I believe so," he responded, while examining his tablet. "There are at least two reports of this: one regarding the dogs and one for the rats. In both, witnesses stated the attacking animals had 'red eyes.'"

"Did any of your reports include a ferret?"

Both the captain and TJ looked at Ted.

"No, why?" the captain asked.

"I saw a ferret outside of our door, just before your first officer called us."

"You weren't bitten, were you? Wait, why didn't you mention this?" TJ huffed.

Ted winced a little as she squeezed harder. "No, I wasn't bitten." He tried to pull his hand away, but she wouldn't let go. "The ferret wasn't aggressive, like the other animals. It seemed more... confused and... hungry."

He softly laid his other hand on top of their mutually clenched ones. "I didn't mention it because I was still processing this, and I didn't want you to freak out at the prospect of a potentially wild animal on board this ship. I feel pretty sure now that this particular animal is not a threat. But I am sorry for not telling you."

"And yet it had red eyes, like the animals who've been attacking people?"

"Yes, and that's what's puzzling. It seems obvious that the animals affected by whatever this is exhibit not only the red eyes but also a crazed desire to kill and feed on flesh. This ferret's behavior was thankfully aberrant to that of the others. Or it means something entirely different."

"Couldn't it mean the mad, aggressive tendencies will pass?" TJ was fishing in a very small pool of hope that most animals in the world were not trying to kill them. Ted wished he could cast his line into that same pool.

"I just don't know. But we also have to consider that this tells us that not all infected animals exhibit the aggressiveness. The fact is, we don't know enough to say if we're at the beginning or at the end of this thing." Ted pulled off his ball cap and rubbed his temples.

Captain Christiansen sat down, finally. They noticed the uncharacteristic bags under his eyes, and his shoulders sagged. He laid his tablet on the table and asked, "What do you think is causing this and more importantly, is it contagious to humans?"

"I believe it's some combination of an infection most animals already have, along with something else that was caused and/or spread by the volcanic eruptions. I have no idea if there will be any effects on humans, but perhaps you should isolate those who have been bitten until we know more."

"That sounds like a fair suggestion. We'll do that." He tapped his forefinger on his table.

"Where are the animals, you know, the ones that attacked on the ship?" TJ sank deeper into her chair, her death-grip on Ted unyielding, and if possible, squeezing harder with each revelation. Ted's head turned back from her to the captain. He wanted to know this as well.

"The rats are all dead. One of our crew members killed them all, before they could do much more than bite a couple other crew. The monkey attack occurred outside the ship; we closed the hatch before it could come in. The dogs, on the other hand, are still loose somewhere on deck 1. The good news is that all the exits to that deck are being closely monitored. In theory, the dogs will be contained there. I'm convinced, we'll find and subdue them soon enough. So other than the ferret, there shouldn't be any more animals unaccounted for. I think we're safe, at least on this ship."

TJ's grip relaxed somewhat.

Ted continued to stroke her upper hand with his free one. "Any thoughts on what you'll do with the dogs when you catch them?"

TJ pulled that hand free. "You need to destroy them all!" she declared adamantly, pounding the table for emphasis.

"Remember, they belong to the passengers." The captain averted his eyes. "But that's probably what we'll do to avoid further infection." Jörgen and Jean Pierre had been discussing this very point earlier. Jörgen knew this to be the right answer, no matter how many times the ship would be sued for it. He was hoping for an alternative.

"But..." Ted smiled at TJ before returning his attention to the captain. "I'd like to get a look at one of them before you do—you know, after you catch one."

TJ firmly gripped Ted's hand again with both of hers and she tugged at him, so he was again facing her. Her face said it all. He had known his wife long enough to know she did not agree.

"Look, Ted, I understand your interest here, especially with all the research you did on this subject. But I don't like it. We don't know if this—whatever it is—is contagious. And until we do, then you should stay away from these animals even after they're captured."

The captain added from behind them, "Once they're found, they'll be contained at the pet spa, where they had been before they were accidentally released."

Ted nodded, and then looked deeply into TJ's agitated eyes. He squeezed her hands back, albeit tenderly. "Only after they are secure, I'll go see the pet spa guy—what's his name?"

"He goes by Al. He's already aware of your thoughts on the animal attacks outside of the ship. And I'll let you know when they've captured the dogs so you can go."

TJ nodded slightly. "Yes, that all sounds fine, Ted. But you're just a sci-fi author. You're not a vet or an epidemiologist from the CDC. Why do you need to take the risk to see them?" She was both angry and visibly shaken.

Several long moments passed in quiet.

"Your wife is probably correct. I'd rather not put either of you at any more risk. Al is a licensed vet. He will also thoroughly examine the dogs and report his findings to me. I'll make sure you get a copy. Additionally, you can talk to him, someplace outside of the pet spa. And again, that's only after we catch these things."

"Fine, just keep me in the loop then." He didn't want to push her anxiety about the animals any more than he already had.

Ted and TJ's gazes were now firmly fixed on the captain, who seemed more interested in the activities outside the ready room's windows. There appeared to be a commotion on the bridge. Abruptly he rose, pushed his chair away, and pulled open the door.

The quiet of the conference room—obviously well insulated from the bridge—was suddenly filled with the sounds of an agitated beehive of activity and a pulsating alarm.

The staff captain's large frame filled up the ready room's doorway. "Captain, La Palma has erupted and we have radar confirmation of a tsunami coming our way. ETA fifteen minutes."

As if this were the most natural thing and part of the normal course of events on the bridge, the captain replied, without any hesitation, "Sound the alarm. Get everyone to their cabins."

"Yes, sir," Jean Pierre replied, pivoted on his heels and then jogged over to Jessica, who was tapping away at a console in the middle of the bridge. Jean Pierre hollered a command that everyone on the bridge nodded to.

The captain turned to Ted and TJ. "I'd recommend that you two go back to your cabin as well. We've experienced rogue waves before and we'll be fine. But you'll be safer in your room." He quickly ushered them out of the conference room and through the bridge, stopping at a small desk built into a wall. On it was a nest of radios, connected to a charging station.

The captain grabbed one and handed it to Ted. "I want you to contact me if you think of something that might help." He opened the hatch and waited for them to file out. "I'll be in touch shortly. And thanks for your help."

"We will, Captain," Ted said, following TJ into the hall. They both turned to see a guard was posted by the closing hatch. Just before it shut they heard the first officer state, "Radar has the wave at over fifteen meters, and grow—"

Ted and TJ stared at each other and then started jogging down the hallway to the most forward stairwell and elevators. Their plan to take the stairs was jeopardized by the flood of passengers in semi-formal clothes, filing down for early dinner seating. Just then an elevator opened in front of them.

"Let's grab this," TJ said, pulling on Ted's arm as he was about to check the deck-plan to confirm which was the quickest route back to their cabin. "We'll take it down to six, walk aft and then up one to our deck."

"How have you already memorized the entire deck-plan?"

"I just don't want us to not be in the room when a fifty-plus-foot wave hits our ship."

They stepped into the elevator just as a double-horn sounded on the ship's intercom system. "This is a shipwide alert. Attention, we have a tsunami alert. In ten minutes, we expect a tsunami wave to hit this ship. To prevent any injuries, all passengers are instructed to go directly to their cabins and put on their life vests."

The elevator doors closed and the elevator started its descent.

"Attention. This is a shipwide al—"

The overheads flashed off, sending their tiny room into darkness, and the world around them abruptly stopped.

25

Chen Lee

C hen Lee stopped to blow her nose and then made sure she still looked good before continuing.

She wore his favorite traditional kimono with her hair put up precisely, held in place by black chopsticks with white pearl inlay. Underneath her kimono, she wore nothing at all.

She had no intention this time of giving him what he wanted. Instead, she was going to show him what he would be missing, and then maybe she'd stab him to death with one of her chopsticks. She was that mad right now.

Earlier today, she was speaking with Lana, a girlfriend who also worked in the spa part-time because of the staff shortages. Normally, she worked at the photo gallery. Chen found Lana in the crew mess and they got around to the subject of men. Lana gloated right away that she had been seeing the head of security, Robert Spillman, and that they were having sex all the time, and in fact, they had a rendezvous set today for four.

Chen was ready to tell Spillman it was over, when he left a message that he had a meeting at four, but could they meet in a new room at five instead?

The last thing she was going to do was participate in his sloppy seconds. She recalled all the times he had been conveniently unavailable over this past month. That's when she got real angry and decided to get even. She figured the best gotcha would be to show him what he would be giving up by sleeping around. She knew neither Lana nor any other woman could give him what she did. She worked at it. She couldn't wait to see his face. Just a few minutes more.

The new room—he was always changing rooms around—was a luxury suite on deck 8 that wasn't going to be used until the Canaries, when several maintenance crew were being added to help with some of the systems that hadn't been fixed yet while the ship was in dry-dock. That's what he told her.

Robert said he changed the location because he could no longer hide their meeting at the cabin they had been recently using on deck 2. Something about the ship's maintenance fixing everything and he could no longer disable the cameras. And that meant they might be caught if they didn't switch their meet locations. In his position as a first officer, he said, they couldn't be caught, or it would mean his job.

For this meeting, he told her that he had found a cabin which was just outside the view of all but one camera, and he would take care of that one. Robert gave explicit instructions to wait until right at 17:00 and then to ascend the outside forward crew stairwell and exit port side on deck 8, to cabin 8504.

She couldn't care less where it was. She knew he was interested in only one thing, and so was she. Before finding out about his infidelity, she had been happy to give him what he wanted because he promised her a life in America after this cruise was over. So she'd played the part of the demure geisha, even though she was Chinese, offering sexual favors in whatever form he desired. Then when they were married and she had her citizenship, she could do whatever she wanted. Even at the time, she knew he was using her, so she didn't think it was wrong to be using him too. But that had all changed now. She'd find another officer after him.

She tilted her watch—a gift from him—and saw it was time. She bounded up the crew stairwell, the hem of her kimono clutched tightly in both hands and held close to her body to shield her private parts from anyone who might walk underneath. No one was going to get a free show, least of all Spillman.

The stairwell lights blinked twice and then she was covered in darkness. She felt hot and had started to panic when the lights flashed again and remained on, but considerably dimmer than before. She continued up the stairs.

At the entrance to the hallway, she felt light-headed. Maybe she was coming down with a cold. She held her fingers to her forehead to see if she was running a fever. She was warmer than normal, but that was probably because of the kimono. Perspiration streamed down her neck and the small of her back, so she loosened the heavy garment to let in some air. She hated the damned thing, and him more.

The hallway had a murky feel from the orange glow of the backup emergency lights. The power must be out, probably part of Robert's plan. She marched forward, wanting this to be finished as quickly as possible.

When she found the cabin, it was as if something inside her snapped. The door was supposed to have been propped open by a room attendant, but it wasn't. Spillman had given her someone else's key-card, but he said it should be used only as a last resort. He didn't want evidence of her being there and so he'd have the door propped open. As she pulled out the stolen card, her anger completely overwhelmed her reason and she imagined slicing his face up with it.

She thrust the card into the door and yanked it out after a green light told her it was unlocked. She shoved the door open with a crash, her anger pouring out.

None of the lights were on. Nothing happened when she flipped on the light switch. This angered her more. Only the hallway light provided illumination enough to see partially into the room.

She jumped, startled by someone on the farther of the twin beds. He sounded like he was eating, but in a crazed sort of last-meal-like way. The small figure had his back to her and he was near the corner of the room, where the meager hallway light couldn't penetrate. He seemed oblivious to her.

At first, she was angry at Robert for screwing this up and sending her to the wrong room. She was going to apologize, but then felt the urge to take her aggression out on this person for being in her room.

She let go of the door, and simultaneously flipped on the light switch, already forgetting that she had tried this before and the power was out.

The door flopped closed loudly, its frame shuddering. With the hallway light cut off, the room fell back into complete blackness.

Behind the closed cabin door, a muffled high-pitched scream leaked out, and was immediately consumed by the carpet before it had a chance of being heard.

26

Robert Spillman

Robert Spillman's career problems were mounting, and to protect himself, he'd have to put the whole ship in jeopardy.

Captain Christiansen and Staff Captain Haddock were already suspicious of his disappearing one too many times. Then the damned maintenance guys fixed the cameras in such a way that he couldn't disable just the one camera. And then, to add insult to injury, he found out that the one area on deck 8 that he thought was a hole in their camera system wasn't a hole anymore, as the maintenance men also swapped out the nonfunctioning camera #387. Once again they had eyes on every corner of every hallway on the ship. And Chen Lee was going to be walking by 387 and into the cabin he had set aside for them in less than two minutes. A cabin that was supposed to be empty. He had to do something quick or they'd be caught.

Shift change wasn't for another two hours and now he only had one minute ten seconds, if she followed his instructions. Desperation was setting in, and so was his longing for her body; hers was far firmer than Lana's. He did the only thing he could think of: shut down a portion of the ship's power, and most of the cameras.

Oh shit! I'm going to Hell for this, he thought and then he pulled the lever.

The lights went out, and he waited for the emergencies to flash on. Then he shot out of the confines of environmental and dashed out and around to the entrance to the monitoring room, where he met Fish at the door.

"Fish, go check the breakers. I'll hold up here and check with the bridge," Spillman commanded, holding up his radio.

"Yes, sir," Fish said and dashed out of the room, heading down the path Spillman had just come from.

Robert smiled at his ruse. But he only had thirty seconds at the most. He reached underneath the work table and opened a panel revealing all the circuit boards. Next, he pulled out a folded piece of tin foil, unfolded it, and pressed it against the back of the main circuit board, which he knew controlled all the cameras. From what he understood, this would work. He'd been waiting to try this trick, but only when it was necessary, or when he was desperate. Like he was now.

He left the panel open and then stood up, waiting for the power to come back on. He had flipped a switch that only controlled two decks and shouldn't affect any of the other areas of the ship. At least that was what he remembered from his research.

If this didn't work, he was pretty sure he'd find a way out of this mess, just like he'd always done in the past. Even when he was fired from his department for watching porn videos in his patrol car, he worked his magic by having a friend change his employment record and remove the reason for his termination. That gave him the freedom to tell his next employer it was mutual. Most prospective employers wouldn't dig further. Certainly, Regal European didn't.

The bright overheads flashed back on and the emergency lights darkened. Almost immediately, the monitors flashed on. At the keyboard, he toggled to camera #387 and saw Chen walking to their meeting place. She was wearing the kimono he adored.

Then all the monitors flashed again and went dark. There were sparking noises inside the panel and the smell of something burning.

Quickly, Robert reached back into the panel to grab his foil, but it had melted to the circuit board, which was melting too. *Oops. Better think quick.*

He grabbed his walkie and hollered into it, "Attention, this is Security Chief Spillman. I need at least two security personnel to appear at the monitor station, on the double."

Just then Fish strolled in and said, "Sir, someone had flipped off the master power lever. I flipped it back..." He wrinkled his nose. "What's burning, sir?" he asked, but his superior didn't reply.

Three security guards arrived at the door and Spillman let them in.

"Okay, Fish, admit what you did and we'll go easy on you," Spillman demanded.

Fish shot him a confused glance. "Sir, what do you mean?"

"Don't play games with me. This is your last chance."

Fish swung around to see the guards come up behind him. That's when he got nervous. "Sir, I really don't know what you are talking about. But I assure you, whatever it is, I didn't do it." He thought maybe he was about to be busted for his card games with Deep and the other crew.

"So you didn't flip the master switch off and then pretend to switch it back on—"

"—what? Wait, you just asked me to check it out."

"And the whole time, you set up the monitors to crash? Why? Who's paying you to do this?"

The guards grabbed his arms to restrain him.

"What are you talking about? You saw I was here... Wait, you're trying to pin something on me, aren't you? What did I ever do to you?"

"Take him to the brig. We'll let Captain Christiansen sort this out.

"You," Spillman said to one of the guards. "You stay here. I'll be back in thirty minutes."

Spillman bounded out the monitor station's door and into the hall, where several other crew members had assembled and were nervously talking to each other.

"Go about your business!" he yelled at them, barely slowing.

He charged out a crew exit, turned two hallway corners and found himself in front of the cabin in less than a minute. He pulled out his keycard and opened the door to the cabin.

It was pitch dark; this time not even a flickering candle waited for him.

"Chen Lee, are you here?"

He flipped the switch and it didn't work. A scary thought flashed across his mind: what if his efforts caused power to go out in more than one area? The lights should have been on; only the cameras should have been disabled.

A crazed scream curdled his blood. It came from the back of the room and it was rushing in his direction.

He had pulled out his phone to engage the flashlight app on it. He flicked it on and caught a flash before he felt his eye explode.

27

The Bridge

"Bring us around to a heading of two-zero-nine point five. We're going to go straight into the wave at full speed," the captain announced.

"Can't we outrun it?" pleaded First Security Officer Wasano Agarwal, voice fluttering. He bit his lip before it quivered to hide his fear from the others. Even if he wasn't the most junior officer on the bridge, he would have been forgiven. The others were just as frightened. They merely hid it better.

"Afraid not," Jessica cut in. "It's traveling at over four hundred knots, and of course, our top speed is only twenty-five. And even if we could travel faster, there's no place to hide. No, we have to go directly into it."

She tapped away at her keyboard and then a window popped up on all of their display screens. Inside each of their pop-up windows were three numbers telling them all they needed to know at a glance: the wave's current height, now 29.58 M; the speed, 418.61 K; and finally the time to impact, 00:09:47:53. All three numbers fluctuated rapidly. The first two kept increasing. The last and largest number ticked down much too quickly for the crew's comfort.

Jean Pierre hung up one of the multiple phones on a wall at the back of the bridge, and then padded over to the captain while examining his tablet. "Engineering is preparing to give us full power on all engines so that we can slice through this bad dude. Also, the shipwide announcement has gone out and is being repeated every two minutes."

Wasano added, "I'm already getting reports from my security officers." His voice grew stronger, more resolute as he too stared at his tablet. "Passengers are proceeding to their rooms in an orderly fashion. There's at least one security posted at each stairwell on each deck to help whoever needs it."

Jean Pierre nodded to Wasano and then added, "Hotel captain reports that they've started the process of storing away glassware and other breakables. But he said there's not enough time to secure everything. There will be damage."

Urban Patel, the deck officer, added, "And shipwide, the crew are taping up windows and binding tables and chairs to limit damage and potential injury."

"I hope these are our biggest concerns," said the captain, voicing what they were all thinking. He scanned the bridge area. "And where the hell is Spillman?" he yelled at Wasano.

"He's still missing, sir. My men were looking for him before the tsunami alert sounded."

"Captain?" Jessica hollered, sounding very alarmed.

All eyes turned toward Jessica.

At first it wasn't immediately obvious to any of them since there was little lighting on the bridge. This enabled them unhampered views of their screens and everything beyond the bridge windows. The black screens should have been the biggest clues, followed by the absence of the muted illumination from the recessed lights.

The crew understood the problem at the same time... their electric power was out.

"Where's my power?" yelled the captain.

Jean Pierre had one of the ship's phones at his ear almost immediately. "You too? Merde! Call us as soon as you do.

"Sir," he hollered from the back of the bridge, "engineering reports loss of power as well. They have comms, with no controls. Chief Engineer Ivan Pavlychko has already given the order to set up for manual. That way, we'll have manual controls if computers remain offline, to steer through the tsunami. They'll report to us as soon as they're done.

"He also reported that the stabilizers will be stuck on until we get our power back. We may not have all the speed we need." Jean Pierre was stating the obvious to the captain as he glanced at the screen for the current speed, but it was still dead. Only seconds ago, they were doing just over fifteen knots. It felt like they were going faster, but still much too slow. If they didn't get more speed, the giant wave could capsize them.

The lights flashed once, and the crew held their collective breaths.

Then they flashed again, but remained on.

"That's emergency power, but we still have a shipwide outage," Jessica announced. More stating the obvious, but that was the protocol. Cold comfort, if any.

The windows in their screens appeared to be resetting, indicating their computers were rebooting, which meant they might regain helm controls. Each screen finally updated its numbers: 33.87 M, 423.18 K, 00:05:56:21

Jean Pierre wasn't a praying man, but at that moment he looked up to the sky he couldn't see and said a quick prayer for his ship, her crew, and her passengers. They would need some divine intervention if they were to make it through this one alive.

28

Ted & TJ

"Here it is." TJ's disembodied voice poured out of the dark opening in the elevator's ceiling above him. A few seconds later, a grunt and scraping sounds preceded a ladder unrolling from the hole, reaching its end a foot from the floor.

"Great find," Ted stated earnestly, as he quickly planted both feet and then his hands, carefully moving up two rungs at a time. "This looks pretty heavy-duty, like it might even hold me. How did you know?"

"I didn't, but I guessed they must have something up here, for emergencies." She smiled at him when he popped his head through the opening. "And it's an easy ladder up half a deck to 6."

"What do you suppose happens if the power comes back on?" Ted mumbled.

"I guess we'll be able to better see the elevator when it runs over us, then."

"Ha-ha. Not funny," Ted deadpanned.

The emergency lights inside the elevator shaft flickered, and the elevator under their feet shuddered, moved—and then stopped.

Then the lights flicked back on.

They exhaled and shot forward, scurrying up the ladder's rungs and into the recessed safety of the deck 6 doors before the elevator moved again. An easy release on the inside gave them their exit—Ted thought they were going to have to find an ax or something else to pry open the doors, like in the movies.

The alarm horns blared twice again, followed by the message about heading back to their rooms.

"What I don't understand is if their engines are running, and they provide the power needs of the ship, how can the power go out?" TJ asked.

"I was wondering the same thing too. How much time do we have?"

TJ glanced at her watch, her face instantly twisting in a grimace, before she glanced up at Ted. "Um, less than five minutes. Let's run."

*H*ugo from Philippines dashed up to the first refrigerator in the hallway and tugged on the handle, making sure it was properly sealed and didn't budge. It was secure.

He jogged to the next. This one held the spirits, wine, and beer. As he stopped in front of the huge door, one foot slid on a piece of paper. Realizing he was going to go down, he reached for the only solid surface available to stop his momentum: the door-latch handle. Immediately the door clicked and slid with his forward motion, opening the vast space before he and the door finally came to rest. His heart raced at his nearly catastrophic fall, which probably would have resulted in his breaking a bone and losing his contract, had he not been able to grab something. He let go of the latch and lay on the floor to collect himself.

He'd been running for the last five minutes in the vain attempt to make sure all the food and supplies were secure. *Who is going to make sure that I and my fellow crew members are secure?*

He'd lost track of time and wasn't sure how much time was left, but it felt like there couldn't be very much.

A wet blob from above him landed on his forehead with a splat.

Hugo slipped his fingers over the wetness, closing his eyes in the process, and rubbed it. *It's slimy.*

His vision instantly shot upward. The ceiling lights were blotted out by red and brown... and it was panting.

It was a large German shepherd spotted in red-brown, like dried blood, as if it had been in a dogfight. The dog was shivering, and there were other dogs behind it, connected to it.

"Hey there, dogs, what you are doing in the liquor su pplies... having a drink?" He smiled at his humor. Then his smile slid off his face when he remembered the staff captain's warning to the whole crew about crazy dogs on the ship.

Hugo spider-walked backward, his butt sliding. After a little distance, he pushed himself onto his knees. He kept his eyes on the dogs the whole time and tried to remember what had been said about them. Animals were going mad on the mainland, and they were to watch out for several dogs that attacked some of his fellow crew and passengers. He couldn't remember their breeds or how many. But when he was eye level with the shepherd, he remembered the most crucial trait. He remembered his skin crawling at the thought, just like it was now.

Their eyes were red. Red like the color of fresh blood.

"One minute, twenty seconds," TJ called out, as she stretched out each stride like a gazelle. Ted huffed and puffed behind her, his heavy footfalls clobbering the grotesque carpeting into submission. He sounded much heavier than someone who weighed two hundred pounds.

She held up, just before their cabin. Ted stopped beside her, hands on the wall, struggling for air. Clattering sounds pulled at their attention, where their hallway T'd and connected with an outside doorway. On the threshold were two feet, wiggling, and their owner was groaning.

Ted arrived first, leaning over the elderly woman, whose walker had skidded outside across an open deck. "Can I help you, ma'am?"

"Oh, aren't you sweet," she replied.

"I'll get your walker," said TJ, who slipped past them as Ted tried to attend to the woman.

"Are you injured?" he asked.

"Oh, mercy no. Just my pride is a little beat up, and my shins." Her voice was all Southern belle.

"Where is your cabin, ma'am?"

"Only two floors from here. Just wanted to see the giant wave."

Ted helped her to her feet and steadied her against the door frame. "Well, you're going to have to stay with us until this passes. There's not enough time to get you up two..."

Ted's voice trailed off as he fixated on his wife, who had just unhooked the elderly woman's walker from the railing and was gazing forward, toward the horizon. Her mouth was agape, as if her jaw no longer had the will to hold it closed. Her face tensed, her brow furrowed. He'd seen this look only two other times: when she was almost attacked by a pit bull, several years ago, and when they were almost attacked by the German shepherd, three days ago. She was terrified, and now so was he.

From the distance a deep rumble like a Cape Canaveral rocket launch tumbled through their hallway. The salt air felt motionless and heavy.

"Ted... Run!" she yelled.

Ted was already moving the elderly woman, slowly at first and then picking up speed. TJ blasted through the hatch and pulled it shut behind her. Before it clicked closed, the rumble outside had already built to a terrifying crescendo, and now the muffled roar vibrated under their feet.

TJ discarded the walker in the hall and caught up to them, grabbing the woman's free arm. The three of them pushed themselves the last few feet: the last leg of a three-legged race.

The three-member team from Tucson and someplace South fell over the finish line of their open cabin door just as the tsunami struck.

29

The Tsunami

"Withdraw the stabilizers," the captain stated in an almost matter-of-fact way. His eyes drilled forward. He no longer needed binoculars to see what was about to hit them.

Second Engineering Officer Niki Tesler, brought on the bridge because of *Intrepid's* power problems, touched the control that immediately withdrew the two mid-ship fins. "Done."

"We're at twenty-one-point-five knots, sir, and rising," declared Jean Pierre, while lowering his binoculars.

There was not much more they could do. The ship had been straightened and was headed in a perfectly perpendicular angle to the giant surge. All power from the ship's four engines pushed the ship's two screws to their limits. They hoped to coax them up to twenty-five knots, which was well past the ship's rated maximum. If they could only gather enough speed, they might be all right. Might.

Only minutes before, they had regained helm controls after Buzz found and corrected the electrical outage problem: some odd wiring problem with the alternators. And it was deliberate. But learning who the perpetrator was and what their criminal intentions were would have to wait for after. If there was an after.

The important thing was that they had control. And for the next few seconds, they could steer the ship precisely. That was, until the moment the wave reached them. Then their fate was in the hands of the sea and God.

That moment was now.

It took only milliseconds for the one-hundred-fifty-eight-foot wall of water to travel from bow to stern, but like an old reel-to-reel film, the individual images of this movie flashed by each actor one by one, as if slowed down to the speed of a slide presentation.

The captain glanced at their speed. He blinked once at the odd number.

"-190.2."

The controls were supposed to be reading the ship's speed compared to the water around them. Now it read the leading edge of the currents generated from the wave.

Jean Pierre blinked at the sea and sky becoming one, as if some leviathan of unfathomable size—too large to even see—had appeared from the depths and swallowed all in its path.

Their bow. Eaten.

Followed by their open forecastle. Gone.

Urban squinted at the bridge windows. He wanted to ask if they'd handle the force of the impact. Even if he had the time to ask the question, it would have been pointless: none of these officers, not even the captain, had ever experienced this before. Urban's vocal cords and oral cavity got as far as forming "W—" before the rumbling monster ate the bridge too.

Jessica flashed an image of her ten-year-old son, who was waiting for her with her husband back home in Iceland, after her contract was up in two months.

Niki reflexively shut her eyes, in anticipation of the water's impact.

It was so quick, none of them could even register its breaching the farthest port-side window of the bridge, left unlatched earlier by Urban when he didn't believe the frigid outside temperature reading, wanting to test it himself.

The immense pressure from the unstoppable surge buckled the window, cracked its hinged panel, and then broke free, shot inward along with thousands of gallons of salt water through a one-foot by three-foot opening. It stormed through the captain's ready room, destroying everything in its path, including the captain's favorite *Uffda* coffee mug. The to-scale model of the *Intrepid* broke free from its glass case, and rode the wave. With nowhere else to go, the water was diverted inward, a mini tidal wave that rocketed through the bridge, catching each of the officers mid-gape and sending them to the floor to scramble for traction.

And then it was all over.

Had this enormous swell hit land, its immeasurable power would have leveled anything standing in its way. Every structure would have been scrubbed away, without exception. But Regal European's *Intrepid*, just like a surfer diving into the full force of an oncoming curl, pierced the towering crush and came out the other side mostly whole.

The damage was still substantial.

The monster took with it all the ship's antennas and satellite dishes, disconnecting it from the rest of the world.

The single smokestack listed backward, like a giant scab about to come off, barely covering an open wound, which now bled its black exhaust from its exposed base.

Two of the three zip lines were torn from their moorings; their steel cables had been cast forward, driving their bulky connectors, with whip-like precision, through the pool area's glass windows and walls at nearly the speed of sound.

Her decks had been scoured of the few remaining tables, chairs and loungers left top-side, gobbled up like the leftovers from a Thanksgiving meal—the deck crew had stowed away the rest.

It was miraculous that there were only a few fatalities, and much of the credit was rightly given to the assistant safety officer's efforts to button up the ship. But it would take a day to do a head count before they knew the final number.

The fatalities seemed odd at first, but were clear upon closer examination: the occupants of two forward cabins failed to close their outside balcony sliders.

In one of the deluged cabins, the newlywed occupants had been too busy with their lovemaking to bother heeding the ship's multiple warnings. During one breathless moment, the new bride said, "What's that rumble?" To which her spouse quipped something about the power of his loins, but was interrupted by a large portion of the Atlantic crashing through their cabin. At least they'd drowned in each other's arms.

The other cabin, just starboard of the bridge, on deck 8, and therefore partially protected, sustained only minor water damage from a slider being left ajar. Its occupants were already under investigation by the FBI, but their whereabouts were unknown and no crew had been inside the cabin for the last two days.

Not until the next day would the horror of what was behind the door of cabin #8500 be seen and understood.

30

After Effects

The announcement blared through the ship's loudspeakers—at least those which were still functioning.

"Attention crew and guests. This is Staff Captain Jean Pierre." His Belgian accent was thicker than normal.

"The tsunami struck, but your ship, the Intrepid, fared quite well. Now you'll have something exciting to tell your grandchildren: the wave that hit us was almost fifty meters high, or over one hundred fifty feet.

"Although there was some damage, what concerns us most are your injuries. For everyone's safety, please stay in your rooms until further notice. All restaurants and guest areas are closed until we've had a chance to check on every passenger, and then assess the damage.

"If you have minor injuries and you can walk, please go directly to the Wayfarer Lounge on deck 6 and our medical staff will treat your cuts and bruises.

"If your injuries are more serious, please report these immediately from your cabin phone. Just dial zero. To assist us, please do not use your cabin phone for any other purpose. We have limited staff to attend to your calls. So again, please use the cabin phones only for extreme emergencies.

"Additionally, our crew will be making a room-by-room check to make sure everyone in your cabin is safe and uninjured. To assist us, if you're not going to the Wayfarer Lounge, please prop your cabin door open with one of your life preservers. That way, we'll know you're in your cabin. We will check on all the open cabins first.

"If your room is damaged and you feel you cannot stay there, you are also welcome to come to the Wayfarer Lounge on deck 6. Our crew will ask you about the damage to your room, and either schedule immediate repairs or get you placed into another room.

"For everyone else, please remain in your cabin until the morning, again with your cabin door propped open. There will be an announcement first thing tomorrow morning.

"Thank you!"

Right after the wave had passed, Al, the pet spa director, got a call from Hugo: his dogs had been found shivering in the giant refrigerated storage room that held the ship's liquor. He rushed over to find all the dogs, calm but confused. He carried each of them individually to the pet spa, mostly because they wouldn't respond to his commands, and some had sustained injuries. He breathed a hearty sigh of relief when he had them all behind their doors.

Two of them were pretty badly injured and had lost a fair amount of blood. He bandaged both and for one, he had to set up an IV. All the dogs were now heavily sedated. He was taking no further chances with their escaping or attacking one another.

Strangely, even though they had been exhibiting the aggressive signs of rabies earlier, none of the animals was aggressive now. If it was some strain of rabies, they'd still have been aggressive. Stranger still was their eyes.

Each of the dogs' irises appeared crimson-colored, like the blood vessels had exploded. He had only heard of this affliction in albinos, who have extremely low quantities of melanin, and cursed his computer because he couldn't connect to the ship's Internet to research it further. He was sure that it was related to their rabies-like behavior, which now appeared gone. The other odd symptoms could be explained away.

Before being sedated, each dog was confused. That symptom could be a result of the stress each had experienced, as could the labored breathing. Each dog, although sedated and unconscious, was breathing heavier than normal, as if its metabolism was working overtime.

His original theory that each had come down with some sort of virus was knocked out when his initial tests indicated their body temperatures were below normal. Without a fever, his virus-borne disease theory had to be thrown out.

Al opened a document and started typing up the details. Without access to the ship's intranet, he couldn't open a new incident report, which he'd eventually be required to fill out for corporate to explain what had happened, not that he could state that with any clarity or certainty at this point.

As he typed out a chronology of events, he was coming to believe that whatever aggressive tendencies had affected the dogs must have passed, in spite of the eyes and the confusion.

He wiped the sweat from his head with a towel. The air wasn't working—probably related to the tsunami—and it was starting to get hot in the pet spa.

Propping open the front door provided instant relief. Somewhere on the ship, there were windows and doors open to the outside, and this air was immediately cooling off deck 1. Lucky for him and everyone on board, the outside temperatures were cool enough that it did the job of their nonfunctional air conditioner systems.

When his radio called to him, he realized that he forgot to update the bridge regarding the dogs. They had asked him for updates on the hour.

He stepped back into the spa and snatched the unit from the charging stand. "This is the pet spa director. Hello, Staff Captain."

Jean Pierre's voice poured out in a fury. "Report on the dogs. We understand you have them. What's their status?"

"I am very sorry for not reporting sooner, sir. All dogs are sedated and stable in their rooms. Sir, I believe the trouble has passed. They are no longer showing aggressive behavior. When I retrieved them a couple of hours ago, they were confused, but certainly not aggressive. I believe the incidence of aggression is only temporary. I am typing all of this up in detail, but I cannot file an incident report because there is no connection with the ship's intranet."

"That's great news on the dogs, and better news on the Rage Virus."

"Rage Virus, sir?"

"That's what the news is calling it."

"I don't believe it's a virus, sir."

"Regardless, can I report to the captain that the danger is over?"

"I believe so."

"Thanks, Second Officer. Staff Captain out."

"**G**lenda Biggins, 82," as she announced proudly in their introductions, would not entertain having the medical crew look at her injuries, which she said were so minor, they didn't warrant anyone wasting any more time over one foolish old woman.

After having thrown the kindly Southerner into their room just as the wave hit, Ted and TJ stayed with her until the announcement, minutes later.

She preferred to go back to her cabin and wait for the crew to come by and check on her. She did not want to trouble them any longer. Ted and TJ escorted the slight woman back to her cabin and said their goodbyes. She thanked them profusely for saving her life and invited them to come visit her at her home on the beach in South Carolina. Again, she apologized for her silly exercise of attempting to gawk at the huge wave.

Ted didn't have the heart to tell the woman that her home on the coast of South Carolina was probably already gone, or at least severely damaged, one of the millions of tsunami casualties. He wasn't sure TJ had considered this, either. That was fodder for another day.

On their way back to their cabin, they came across one person after another who needed some sort of medical help. Surprisingly, none of the injuries were bad: only cuts and bruises. But there were quite a few people who appeared in some state of shock. Some couldn't remember their names and where they were, and some were almost completely non-responsive to Ted or TJ's questions or to those of the crew.

Each injured or confused person was escorted to the Wayfarer Lounge to be attended to by the ship's crew.

The medical staff shared with them that they too were encountering quite a few confused guests, but they attributed this to the stress and shock of the giant wave. The Williamses also heard, indirectly, about the young couple drowning in their cabin, because they hadn't closed their slider before the wave hit. But those were the only two deaths they'd heard of. And if that was the extent of the deaths and injuries, the Intrepid could consider herself very lucky indeed. Luckier still for everyone was the news from Jean Pierre.

He called the Williamses to report that the dogs had been found and were currently sedated at the pet spa. The vet was typing up a report on what he'd observed, but said that he thought that the dogs' aggressive tendencies had passed. He added that the vet believed the rage affliction was only temporary.

It was after one in the morning when both Ted and TJ finally lumbered back to their cabin. As they lay in their bed, they were filled with hope that they would wake up to a new tomorrow where the animal attacks were subsiding and volcanoes would stop erupting. They fell asleep almost as soon as their heads met their pillows, their thoughts turning into dreams, and then their dreams quickly turning into nightmares, which didn't end, even when they woke.

DAY FIVE

THE CAPTAIN'S MORNING ADDRESS BEGAN PROMPTLY AT 07:00. THAT AND THE BLARING TONE THAT PRECEDED IT WERE THE ONLY SIMILARITIES TO THE ADDRESSES OF PREVIOUS DAYS. EVERYTHING ELSE WAS DIFFERENT. GONE WAS THE JOVIAL BANTER OF A MAN WHO ENJOYED EVERY MOMENT OF THE JOB HE WAS DOING. HIS TONE WAS ALL BUSINESS NOW. I IMAGINE ANIMAL ATTACKS AND A TSUNAMI LEADING TO THE DEATHS OF PASSENGERS AND CREW MEMBERS WOULD DO THAT TO A CAPTAIN.

THE INTERNAL SPEAKER UNITS IN OUR CABIN DIDN'T SEEM TO WORK ANYMORE, NOR DID OUR PHONES. MORE TSUNAMI CASUALTIES? WE DIDN'T KNOW. BUT THE DOOR WAS PROPPED OPEN WITH OUR LIFE PRESERVERS, AS REQUESTED BY JEAN PIERRE, SO THE CAPTAIN'S MELANCHOLY VOICE WAS CLEAR, WITHOUT OUR HAVING TO GET OUT OF BED.

"INTREPID, THIS IS CAPTAIN JÖRGEN CHRISTIANSEN COMING TO YOU FROM THE BRIDGE.

"WE ARE PRESENTLY AT A HEADING OF 35 DEGREES, 37 MINUTES, 3 SECONDS NORTH BY 14 DEGREES, 58 MINUTES 21 SECONDS WEST. OUR COURSE IS 28.6 DEGREES WEST BY NORTHWEST. WE HAVE STARTED OUR TRACK ACROSS THE ATLANTIC TO THE U.S.

"YOU ALL KNOW ABOUT THE MONSTROUS WAVE WHICH TOOK US BY SURPRISE. WE WERE LUCKY THAT MORE PEOPLE WEREN'T HURT. AND IN FACT, MOST INJURIES WERE MINOR, JUST A FEW CUTS AND BRUISES.

"THE WAVE WAS THE RESULT OF THE VOLCANIC ERUPTION ON LA PALMA. WE ARE NO LONGER IN DANGER, BUT WE HAD TO CANCEL OUR STOPOVER IN THE CANARY ISLANDS.

"OUR SATELLITE AND INTERNET ARE DOWN BECAUSE OF DAMAGE TO OUR ANTENNAS. THERE ARE SOME OTHER SYSTEM ISSUES AS WELL. BUT OUR TIRELESS CREW IS AWARE OF THESE AND THEY'RE WORKING TO FIX THEM AS I ADDRESS YOU. PLEASE BE PATIENT, AS IT MAY TAKE A FEW DAYS TO GET ALL OF OUR SYSTEMS BACK ONLINE.

"NOW, LET'S FOCUS ON THE GOOD NEWS. THREE OF OUR RESTAURANTS ARE OPEN, AND WE HAVE MANY WONDERFUL ACTIVITIES PLANNED FOR YOU TODAY. ONE ACTIVITY I'D RECOMMEND YOU ATTEND IS THE OPPORTUNITY TO MEET THE FAMOUS AUTHOR T.D. BONAVENTURE. HE'S AN EXPERT IN POTENTIAL APOCALYPTIC EVENTS AND HE MAY EVEN OFFER A WORD OR TWO OF EXPLANATION ABOUT WHAT HAS HAPPENED WITH THE VOLCANOES AND THE ANIMALS, AND WHY WE THINK THE WORST OF THIS CRISIS HAS PASSED."

THERE WAS A LONG AND SOMEWHAT UNCOMFORTABLE PAUSE—FOR BOTH OF US—BEFORE THE CAPTAIN CONTINUED.

"EVEN WITH ALL THAT HAS HAPPENED ON BOARD, TRY TO ENJOY YOUR TIME WITH US. LET US WORRY ABOUT TOMORROW'S PROBLEMS SO THAT YOU CAN ENJOY TODAY.

"FINALLY, I'M VERY HAPPY TO REPORT THAT WE ARE OUT OF THE SHADOWS OF THE VOLCANIC CLOUDS, AND WE EXPECT SUNNY SKIES FOR THE FIRST TIME SINCE THIS CRUISE STARTED. WE'RE ALSO EXPECTING WARM TEMPERATURES, AROUND TWENTY DEGREES CENTIGRADE THIS AFTERNOON.

CHAIRS AND TABLES HAVE BEEN RETURNED TO OUR SUN DECK. TAKE TIME TO ENJOY THE SUN THIS AFTERNOON AND VISIT WITH YOUR FELLOW CRUISERS. I'M SURE EACH OF YOU HAVE SOME INTERESTING STORIES TO TELL ABOUT WHAT YOU WENT THROUGH LAST NIGHT.

"THAT IS ALL, FOR NOW.

"HAVE A BLESSED DAY ON THE SAFEST SHIP ON THE OCEAN, REGAL EUROPEAN'S INTREPID."

THE CAPTAIN WAS OBVIOUSLY...

31

Anniversary

"What are you writing?" TJ mumbled, her voice heavy with sleep.

"Oh, nothing important." Ted flashed her a smile and closed the leather-bound book, clutching it to his chest.

TJ leaned over and kissed him. "Morning." Then she abruptly disappeared into the bathroom.

They had remained in bed—both were exhausted—during the captain's address and for several minutes afterward. The door had been propped open the whole night, as was advised. TJ never woke once, not even during the crew's wellness check in the wee hours. A splash of light on her face from the crew member's flashlight, to verify she was in fact uninjured, didn't cause her to stir. Ted understood perfectly; it was the first time she didn't feel anxious in the last four days, and he certainly didn't want to upset that. Only when the captain's address blared through their doorway did she even stir, barely registering his words, before she rolled back over and stretched out her slumber some more. Ted, on the other hand, bolted upright in bed, terrified of what the captain had announced.

It really didn't bother him that he'd been asked to assume the role of the ship's ad hoc PR officer by delivering the captain's message that the animal attack problem had gone away, even though he wasn't yet convinced of this. It was simply that he'd have to do this in front of hundreds of people.

Far more than crazy animals attacking, or volcanoes spewing ash clouds, or even one-hundred-fifty-foot tidal waves, it was getting in front of a crowd of people which absolutely terrified him. The doctors called it enochlophobia, explaining it was a form of agoraphobia. He only knew that he'd been fighting panic attacks most of his adult life, induced by this very type of public forum. Therefore, he avoided such things like the proverbial plague.

In a former life, when he had worked as a scientist, his work activities were perfectly suited to someone who didn't like to interact with people. Ted did everything he could to not be stuck in large public places, even going so far as to do his work research at home.

When he chose his later-in-life author career, the prospect of scheduled public appearances—such as book signings or radio or TV interviews—meant he had to find a way to make them work with his needs. So his agent chose very limited venues, with only a few people or a space that allowed him to leave quickly if he felt a panic attack coming. Regardless, Ted would not take meds, although alcohol did offer occasional comfort. Instead, he'd work through his affliction.

When his agent contacted him with the idea of this cruise—turned out it was his wife through the FBI, who set everything up—Ted agreed to do the Q&A only because the venue was to be very small. He and TJ had even scouted the room on the way to the All Access Tour, and confirmed he had a quick exit if he couldn't deal with it. It was all just as his agent had said. But that was before the captain had intervened and invited the whole damned ship to come. He knew that the room would be packed with people, all crowding him, touching him, questioning him... The pounding in his chest made it hard to breathe.

To get his mind off his looming lecture and Q&A session at 08:00, he started the journal.

The whole hand-written journal thing was new to Ted: all of his writing was done on his iPad tablet or on the desktop at home. But along with the wine, the captain had given him the beautiful journal as a gift. After the captain's announcement, when he felt panic take over, and he got out of bed to pace, he finally examined the book.

It was exquisite. Fine leather protected its blank, parchment-like vellum pages. "Regal European" was richly etched in gold lettering on its dark blue cover.

He brought it back to bed and gazed at the first blank page and considered what he might scratch onto it. He started to think back over the last few days' events. That's when it hit him that it might be useful—to whom, he didn't know yet—to jot down some of the details about what they were experiencing. At this moment, he wasn't sure what the journal's purpose would be, or if it would ever be read by anyone but him. His apocalyptic mind kicked in, just for an instant, and wondered if it would be used as a historical record for some dystopian future, long after they were gone.

He shook away this thought and opened his bedside table drawer. He snatched out one of his Ultra Fine Point Sharpies, which he used for scribbling inscriptions inside his books during book signings. He brought a bunch of them everywhere he went, especially when he was potentially meeting some of his fans. This book deserved something better, but Sharpies were all he had. He popped off the pen-cap and poised the hard felt-tip over the expectant page, waiting for the words to flow out of him like a stream. He'd focus on writing slowly and smoothly so that others could read what he wrote. His cursive was nearly illegible, so he opted to write in controlled block letters and made sure that each letter was finished.

Far from being sure how best to approach this, and how much detail he should include, he just started at the beginning... "Day One." He wanted to catch up, so he wrote only a few sentences for each, intending to return with more detail, until he reached today, Day Five. His writing flowed easily and quickly, only pausing when TJ had woken.

Their cabin door clicked closed. Ted looked up to find TJ standing beside his side of the bed, wearing a big grin and clutching a small colorful object.

"Happy anniversary!" she stated jubilantly, thrusting out the colorful object. She was practically hopping. An excited squeal leaked from her pursed lips.

Dammit. He'd been so preoccupied—he had planned to surprise her with his gift first, right when she'd woken up. But she had beaten him to the punch.

He put aside the leather journal on top of the small bedside table, slid open a drawer below this, reached in and pulled out a similarly colored box. He held it out for her, offering a *you got me grin.* "Happy anniversary," he said back.

Every year, each of them had gone to great lengths to surprise the other with a small anniversary gift. It was never huge or super expensive, just a little something special to memorialize that anniversary. This being their twenty-year anniversary, he was elevating his game. He had been waiting for most of a year to give this to her.

She threw her arms around him, snatched his gift from his hand and replaced it with hers. She eyed her gift, but then looked up, flashing another big smile. "You first."

She plopped down on the edge of the bed and eyed him expectantly.

"Okay-okay." He slipped off the bright red ribbon, ripped open the festive wrapping paper, and flashed a quick glance at the Mont Blanc box and then up at her.

"When I saw you writing in that journal, I was so excited to have you to open this..."

From the box, he pulled out a jet-black Mont Blanc pen, with two gold bands. *T.D. Bonaventure* was etched on the cap. He'd always wanted one, but could never justify spending the money for something like this. But as an anniversary present from his wife... *it was perfect.*

"It's perfect. I love it. Thank you." He leaned toward her and they exchanged a kiss.

"My turn," she said, almost with a giggle. She ripped into her box, quickly exposing a similar black rectangle, only a little bigger. She cracked open the top, revealing a rich blue interior. Nested inside was something that sparkled. She flashed him a stunned look.

"It's Orion, the Hunter. Only this version is a warrior woman, kind of like my gorgeous wife."

She pulled it out of its box, letting the necklace dangle from its thin gold chain, eyeing it and then him as he spoke.

"Each diamond is a star in the constellation Orion. I know it's a bit more than normal, but I found it in London last year and knew you had to have it."

She handed it to him and turned her back to him. "Put it on me, would you?"

He did and she bounded from the bed and padded over to the full-length mirror across from the bathroom door, where she stopped and studied herself and the necklace.

She dashed back to his bedside and once again threw her arms around him, squeezing tight. "It's absolutely the best gift you've ever given me. I love it. Thank you."

She kissed him hard, like her embrace, and then looked into his eyes.

She leaned in and kissed him again, only softer, more passionately. She pulled back, smiled at him, and softly batted her eyes, fluttering them seductively. Her smile grew impossibly large as she lifted her arms in the air, beckoning him to pull her top off.

He obliged.

32

Satellite Down

TJ moaned under her breath as she slowly let her head roll around her neck, her hair snaking a trail over each shoulder blade. Her new necklace bounced playfully against her chest. Her hands were mounted above her hips, her right barely covering the large scar, a marker of a time that changed her, from when she nearly died from a dog mauling several years back. Her fingertips rested above the edges of her black Jockey briefs, legs splayed on the carpet for stability. "Geez, every part of me hurts, like after a marathon." She flashed him a smile. "What about you?"

Ted averted his eyes from her and swung his feet out of the bed. "Yeah, I can hardly move." He flashed an even larger grin at her, and she continued her stretching.

He snatched up the remote and clicked on their TV. It was a little tube-job from twenty years ago, with a screen not much bigger than his tablet. He knew the result, but he was still curious to see what would happen after the captain's announcement.

Before the tsunami, when they'd turn on the TV, the same info channel appeared, either replaying the previous night's talent or variety show—last night's show was understandably canceled, so he didn't expect to see this—or a talk show hosted by Zeka, the ship's cruise director. The talk show, often recorded late on the night before—they guessed this based on the lack of sunlight and the small number of people in the background—gave an overview of the upcoming port of call or that day's activities. He was hoping they would have done something like this to give them more details about what had happened to the ship.

There was no picture whatsoever.

The TV displayed only white static, as if it were a closed-circuit TV's view of an outside blizzard and they were in Alaska and not a more southern latitude in the Atlantic. He glanced at the outside balcony to mentally confirm this wasn't the actual weather: partly cloudy, but certainly not snowy.

He poked the channel-up button once. Then again, and again, one channel at a time. Each displayed the new channel number, but the same white snow.

"Well, the captain said the satellite was down, and this confirms it."

"So is the Internet," TJ said, surprised, and scowled at her cell phone, which she had grabbed while Ted was playing with the TV. He figured she had in fact slept through or had forgotten the captain's message about connectivity.

They both jumped, as if hooked up to electrodes, when the house phone jangled at them.

"**W**ell," Ted said sarcastically, "at least we know our phone works."

TJ was already there, receiver in hand, having moved her stretching exercises over to the more spacious middle of their cabin floor. "Hello?" There was the expected pause as she listened.

"Oh, hello JP." She smiled at Ted and nodded, agreeing with something Jean Pierre must have told her.

"Yes, we're fine." She cocked her head at an angle and crooked her brow, as if what she was hearing was painful. Then her face changed again.

"Yes, he's here. Do you—okay." She averted her gaze and nodded again.

"Yes, I'll let him know." She pulled her gaze back up at her husband, but she hadn't made eye contact with him yet.

"What? Oh yeah." She feigned a smile this time, which didn't hold. "I think he was hoping no one would be interested."

Ted eyed her back suspiciously, watching her every reaction.

"Oh, he'll be there." She laid the phone back on the cradle, but didn't say anything as she sashayed over to the chest where they were keeping their clothes and pulled out her running uniform.

"Well?" Ted thrust his hands up in the air. "Are you going to tell me what all of that was about, or are you going to hold on to your little damned secret?"

"Jean Pierre was passing along a few messages from the captain. First, the pet spa director has printed his report and one of the crew will hand you a copy this morning. He said he read it and they're breathing a sigh of relief."

TJ had already slipped on her shorts and long-sleeved sports shirt. She slid on her first running shoe, stopped before tying it, and gazed up at Ted. "Do you think this thing is really over?"

He locked into her eyes, not wanting to elevate her fear, but not wanting to lie to her either. He chose the best answer—the only true answer. "I don't know. Did he say when I'd get to read this report?"

Ted searched for his clothes, thinking that he'd have to dash out and meet this crew member who had the report. Finding his well-worn warm-ups, his preferred outfit at night and in the morning, he slipped them on over his underwear and stood up.

"Ahh, you might want to wear something else."

"Why? I don't care if someone sees me in this."

"It's not that... Remember your talk, at eight? That's where the crew member will hand you the report."

"Yes, of course I remembered, even if I didn't want to." He looked at the digital clock-radio nestled against the journal on his bedside table. It was seven-fifteen. He had forty-five minutes.

"There's one more thing..." TJ hesitated, and then looked down, knowing what she said next would consume her husband in terror, far more than any potential crazed animal attack would have consumed her. "They've moved your venue to... the main theater."

"What!" Ted hollered.

"Well, it appears," she said in an even voice, her best attempt to be calming, "that people really want to listen to your talk about the apocalypse, especially after the captain's announcement this morning. They decided to make sure you had enough room."

"But the theater?" He groaned, closed his eyes, and fell back onto the bed, his breaths becoming shorter and more uneasy.

She moved over beside him and stroked his head. "There's more. The captain wanted you to stress the point that the whole animal craziness thing was just temporary and that everyone on board is safe right now. You could just say a few words and then take questions.

You'll be into it quickly—I know you—and you'll forget the audience in no time."

She thought about the story he had told her about the death of his first wife and young child on a French vacation, deaths he was sure he had caused.

As she watched him breathe, she tried to imagine what it must have been like: watching the crowds building around him in the public square and his enochlophobia causing a full-on panic; then seeing his young wife cradling their child, walking across the street toward him; then his glancing up and seeing the madman barreling through the crowds in a truck; then Ted realizing his wife and child would be next, but because he was frozen from fear, he couldn't do anything, except watch them die.

She still couldn't imagine how devastating that was for him.

But that was so long ago, and he had been doing much better lately.

This cruise, and especially the main dining room, were big tests, which he passed with flying colors. This next one would be much bigger. Perhaps it was too huge for him to bear.

"Just tell me you'll be there," he groaned, his eyes still closed.

She didn't answer.

He lifted his head and glared at her. "Really?"

"You told me you didn't want me to come to this; I'd be bored and so on, remember? Besides I have some work-related stuff after my run.

"You mean your *work-related stuff* with Jean Pierre?" he countered.

"Yes, Bureau work, Jean Pierre is helping us with. I told you, it's the main reason we're here."

"Fine, guess I don't need to do this talk then," he huffed.

"Ted Williams, don't be selfish. You agreed to do this, regardless of venue size. I'll miss only the first part of your talk, and then I'll be there."

"Guess it's settled then." He sprang up and darted to the bathroom. "I'm jumping in the shower and going to go get a stiff drink. That way, I can really make a spectacle of myself."

She thought about saying something more, but she had already said too much. She knew he had to deal with this in his own way. At least he was dealing with it, versus just hiding in their room. She could hardly have been surprised if he did. She just didn't want to compound his problem.

As the muffled spray in the shower sounded, she slithered her other foot into its shoe and quickly tied both.

Guilt about leaving Ted to fend for himself swept over her. She had set up another meet with Jean Pierre, while Ted was giving his presentation. She decided then that her husband had to come first; she'd tell Jean Pierre that she could no longer do what she was doing. She was going to spend the rest of the cruise with her husband. She'd not waste this opportunity, feeling like maybe they'd all been given a second chance.

She stood up, truly excited. She was anxious to get going and finish this, so she could support her husband. And knowing that the threat of wild animals roving the decks of the ship had been handled, she could enjoy her run as well.

Two decks above them on the other end of the ship, completely forward, Catur, the room steward, pounded once more on the door of cabin 8500. Its occupants had not been heard from for over two days, and they did not prop their door open as requested by their staff captain last night. He had waited as long as possible, wanting to offer the couple their privacy. The Do Not Disturb card carried lots of weight for most guests on the *Intrepid's* transatlantic cruises, as some guests rarely left their cabins. This was especially true with the Royal Suite. But the time for privacy had passed. And the hotel captain now required that each room steward account for every one of their guests, DND card or not.

Cabins with doors propped open by life preservers had already been inspected and their occupants' wellness checked. Cleared cabins received a green sticker on the lock assembly. Catur had just three non-green sticker cabins. One deck 7 cabin was a disaster and a tragedy. When he first did his wellness-check rounds last night, he saw water pouring out of the bottom of 7512. He opened it to find that the slider had been left open during the tsunami, and the cabin was utterly destroyed. In a heap, among all the other debris, he'd found the beautiful honeymoon couple, naked and drowned. It was awful.

The next of the three was cabin 8504. But it was empty, so he didn't bother to check it. That left one more suite. And he had put this one off to the very last minute. He desperately didn't want to find any more dead guests.

He pounded again. "Housekeeping. This is Catur, Mr. and Mrs. Carmichael, I need to come in and check on you."

Catur pressed his ear to the door and listened. He could hear a grunt and a rumble inside the cabin. He panicked then and thought that maybe one of them was severely injured and couldn't get to the door. Mr. Carmichael was much older, and so it was very possible that he had fallen and broken something. Falls were common with older guests.

The guard normally stationed in front of the bridge entrance at the end of the hall wasn't where she was supposed to be. Probably better that security didn't see what was going to happen next. Catur imagined accidentally interrupting something he just didn't want to see: two old people having sex. Although the wife was a looker, the old man was just scary-old. He tried to shake away the ghastly image, knowing it would be something he could never unsee. He'd have to offer that mental image to Asep and Jaga, and let them share in his discomfort.

Catur smiled at that idea and rapped with a balled fist on the door, harder this time, while he fumbled with his master key-card. Almost dropping it, he regained control, slipped it in and out of the slot, and upon seeing the green light flash, he cranked the handle and pushed in hard.

It was dark inside, and only a bare channel of light flooded in from the hallway. He was immediately overwhelmed by the most horrid smell. It smelled like spoiled food. Food that had been bad before it spoiled.

He tried the light switches, flipping them on and off, but to no effect. *One more thing that isn't working.*

He took one tentative step inside and stopped, still holding the door open for light, his foot sloshing on the carpet. For a moment, he thought he saw something in the far corner of the room. Squinting, he mentally cursed the guests for leaving the curtains and sheers pulled so tightly across the slider windows.

Swift movement. A shadow, now by the couch.

Then it was closer, and Catur could see the movement was coming toward him.

"It's Catur." His voice wavered. "Mr. and Mrs.—" Something struck him in the chest with the force of a moving truck, knocking him hard into the side of the door, which he had still been holding open. At the same time, he felt something inside him break. He tried to scream, in hopes that someone would hear him in the hallway, but whatever hit him knocked his wind out. Some crazed animal screeched at his face with a warm foulness he'd never smelled before, nor did he want to. He clenched his eyes tight, afraid to look as he tried to pull in a painful breath through his mouth and nose. He'd belt out a cry for help. But he gagged at the horrid stench. Once more, he pulled in another breath—this time using just his mouth and ignoring the smell—when it felt like his entire throat had been ripped away. His gurgled half-breath bubbled out of the new opening.

Catur's dying body was released by his attacker and collapsed into the doorway, keeping the door propped open. The beast chewed the fresh piece of flesh in its mouth, heard someone else and dashed toward the call for "Housekeeping" down the hall.

33

T.D. Bonaventure

Ted—T.D. Bonaventure, as he was introduced—was being peppered with questions. Although many of the questions were coming from people who had read his books, most of the questions came from those who had no idea who he was. They had come for answers, and heard that Ted was the one on the ship who had them. For Ted, it was a catharsis. He stood in front of a huge crowd, calmly answering questions, without any fear whatsoever. He'd have to thank the captain personally for this. And Vicky, the bartender.

Ted had worked himself up to almost a full-out panic before eight. He marched over to the Anchor Bar for a drink or two to relax him. They technically didn't open for another hour. Thankfully, he was able to coax a stiff shot of whiskey out of *Vicky Smith from England*, the bartender who was setting up for the day. She said she remembered his name, although she only read romance novels. Doubtless, she took some pity on the author who admitted he was scared shitless to be giving a speech in front of hundreds of people at the theater. Ted just hoped the drink would give him enough confidence to go through with it. Turned out he didn't need the drink.

It was just a few words, offered by Vicky, a bartender's simple platitude about human fears. On any other patron, her little pearl of wisdom would have been lost. For Ted, it was exactly what he needed.

"You know why you're bloody scared of your talk?" she stated, momentarily moving her gaze from the heavy tumblers she was balancing to Ted.

He bit. "Okay, why?"

"Because you're hiding from some other shit that bothers you more."

Better than a dozen shots of heavily fortified Tequila or a doctor-prescribed sedative, her little bromide not only removed his anxiety, he almost forgot his talk altogether. He dashed down a couple hallways and a flight of stairs, before arriving at the theater, one minute late.

At the theater's performer entrance, a crew member had been waiting for him and delivered a copy of the vet's report on the crazed dogs. Because this was germane to his talk, he explored the vet's detailed findings. But he was still chewing on Vicky's words.

Ted skimmed the very thorough report for its major points, until he arrived at and slowly read the conclusion, "I recommend keeping the dogs isolated from their owners until the conclusion of the cruise, during which time I will continue to observe their behavior. It is my belief that the aggressive tendencies we saw earlier have passed, and that the dogs are no longer a threat."

Ted had rolled the report up into a tube after rereading this passage once more. Then he fist-pumped the air with it. "Yes!" he said, under his breath. His brain yelled, *I sure hope you're right*, and then he stepped through the entrance.

"I'm told he's here now," bellowed the amplified voice of Zeka, the cruise director from the theater. "Some of you know him from his international best-selling books. Others of you might be looking for answers about what's going on outside. But all of you need to welcome the

Authoritative Author of the Apocalypse, and your fellow passenger, Mr. T.D. Bonaventure."

Right on cue, he stepped through the curtains, a big smile enveloping his mustached face. He pulled his pipe from his lips and waved to the crowd.

"Thank you, my friends," he said into a microphone handed to him, his British accent—practiced for public venues—rolling off his tongue as if he were a London native.

His heart was beating like a set of bongos, and the welcome feeling of adrenaline pumped through his veins. He couldn't see most of the people because of the stark spotlight, which blinded him, and that was a good thing. He tried to imagine it was only a few dozen, even though the introductory applause sounded like hundreds. The vast room had become quiet very quickly.

"Let's see," he said, scratching his head for effect, as he looked up to the ceiling, "a giant tsunami, volcanoes erupting, animals attacking, and chaos everywhere... And you want me to talk about apocalyptic *fiction*?" He flashed a wide smile for the crowd.

The response from the audience had been a dead-quiet nothing, laced with a couple of nervous snickers, and an elderly man near the front hacking up what sounded like a lung. He'd seen jokes from comedians thud like this.

He took a puff from his pipe and decided to deliver the captain's message to set his audience and himself at ease.

"First, I have a message from our captain. We have several dogs on board with us, and like the other animal behavior we read about and many of us experienced firsthand on land, there were reports of several passengers and crew getting bitten."

Gasps billowed throughout the audience, and a woman had started weeping.

"Hang on. Before you get all twisted with worry, I'm happy to announce that the dogs have been apprehended and are locked in a protected area. Furthermore, the ship-board vet has observed their behavior and reports that all the animals' crazy behavior has passed. They are currently sleeping.

"Let me put this another way. Even though we haven't been able to communicate yet with the outside world to get further confirmations, it appears that the danger—at least on board this ship—has passed."

At first there had been just a few claps, but then the entire theater erupted in applause. The guy handling the lights turned them up on the audience and down on the stage. Ted could see the entire theater was packed to its limit and every single person was on their feet, cheering.

He clapped too. He couldn't help it. Part of him felt like maybe this thing may have passed, and he was ready to embrace this hope just as quickly as his fellow passengers were.

When the clapping subsided, Ted raised the microphone again. "Okay..." He waited for a few more slow ticks of the clock for the clapping to stop, and then said, "Okay, because this situation is unique, rather than me rattling on for a while on subjects I choose, like why you all should buy my next book, I'm going to open it up to you. What would you like to ask me?"

The early questions came from some actual fans and were centered on *Ring of Fire*, his series about the ring of 452 volcanoes in the Pacific, several of which erupted, causing a new Ice Age. They asked, "Did the rogue wave mean anything bigger?" And, "Are we going to experience more volcanic activity, and even a new Ice Age?"

By this point, even though the lights were still turned up on the house and he could see everyone clearly, Ted felt at ease. He again attempted some humor and reminded his audience that although he did a lot of research for his novels, he was not a geologist or volcanologist. Those points were not entirely true, as he had studied a lot of geology in college, and almost chose that field for his vocation. But he didn't want any more added responsibility and found it was often better to deflect.

So far, so good.

Then someone went for his jugular, and it changed everything for Ted.

A gruff-looking man wearing a red Ferrari sports shirt—Ted had seen one just like this, on the worst day of his life—stood up. "Why do most people in this room believe that a paperback writer of fictional tales could tell us anything about crazy animals?"

It wasn't the nature of the question. It wasn't even the questioner, but the shirt he was wearing and the words of Vicky Smith from England, which transported Ted out of this theater, back to that moment years ago when his life changed.

I t had been a beautiful day in Nice, France. Promenade des Anglais was bustling with Bastille Day celebrants. In the middle of it all was Ted, soaking up the culture and sun, waiting for his wife and toddler son to finish up in a restaurant bathroom across the street.

He was alerted to an odd noise before it seemed anyone else was: a large vehicle's engine being gunned, somewhere on this street clogged with people. Before he saw the truck, Ted observed his wife and their toddler exiting the restaurant, beaming a smile at Ted.

A man in a red Ferrari sports shirt bumped into Ted and scowled, as if Ted were the cause of their collision. It was then that Ted noticed the throng of people had grown. Worse, they now separated him from his young family. He couldn't easily get to them.

In a flash, the truck, its engine roaring, was barreling through the crowds of people. Without slowing, it was headed straight for his wife and son, who remained blissfully unaware and unmoving in its path.

Ted sucked in large gulps of air, while the enveloping crowds pushed at him, obscuring his view of them and seemingly taking him farther away from any possibility of saving them.

He had a scientific mind, and he understood cause and effect. His mind had already calculated, based on speed and the direction of the vehicle, what was going to happen: he was going to watch his family die.

It was a gut punch of a realization.

And rather than doing anything, he just watched. More so, he shrank back, away from warning them; saving them. He let the hordes overwhelm him.

"Hey! So what makes you an expert?" a distant voice hollered.

Ted shook his head, aware that he'd been lost in his own thoughts. His breathing had escalated, and he was uncomfortably hot. He glanced at the giant crowds in front of him—not unlike the crowds of that Bastille Day, when he watched his wife and son die. But he no longer felt possessed by the overwhelming anxiousness he always felt when he faced crowds of people. Something was different.

It was something he had not paid attention to until this flashback: his wife and boy were doomed, regardless of the crowd around him. It wasn't his fear of the crowd that caused their deaths; it was a crazy terrorist.

Vicky had said his fear of crowds was just his "hiding from some other shit that bothers you more." Ted needed to feel guilty about their deaths, and his fake disease was what he hung onto as the reason he couldn't save them. But no one could have saved them, certainly not him.

He really wasn't scared of crowds. In fact, at this moment, in front of this large audience, he felt damned good. Having TJ here would have only made it better... And taking down this little prick with the Ferrari shirt.

"What's your answer?" demanded Ferrari Shirt.

Ted focused on the man now, and his question.

When Ted had first opened up the room to questions, there were side conversations, like little brush fires that erupted around the room. At times, the room had become so loud and electric, Ted had to stop until the din quieted down. It was understandable, as everyone had their own opinions about the seemingly apocalyptic events they'd all experienced, and feeling more at ease, they wanted to share their opinions, sometimes at the same time. Now, the room fell back into its natural state of nervous silence. Literally, Ted thought he could hear a pin drop, if it weren't for the puke-colored carpet. All eyes were on Ted as he considered his answer.

He didn't want to let on that he wasn't yet convinced that this thing was over, any more than he didn't want to mute the possibility that it might be. But this guy was a heckler calling into question his abilities at getting the science right, and Ted knew the science that went into his book and the reasons for the animal population's madness were correct.

"Imagine"—he looked around the room as he spoke—"that a single-cell organism could take control of an animal's mind and reprogram it so that the only purpose of its host's existence was to kill, feed, and propagate for that organism.

"Imagine further that this organism could live dormant in the animal's brain for as long as the animal is alive, just waiting for the right stimuli to then take control of the animal and demand that it attack and follow its new programming.

"Finally, imagine that these protozoa had already infected as many as three-quarters of all animals on the planet.

"This isn't fiction, folks. This is real. That protozoa is called *T-Gondii*, and this puppet master has already been proven to be behind the aggressive behaviors of both animals and even people for many generations. Further, I believe, it's the root reason why animals appeared to be more aggressive recently."

Ted paused momentarily to study his audience. All faces, without exception, were serious and staring at him. Husbands and wives clutched each other's hands; tears streamed down the faces of some of the children; one individual literally shook with fear. Ferrari Shirt had found his seat and was attempting to disappear.

Ted had gone too far to make his point. He'd allowed his own pride and excitement at conquering his greatest fear to trump what the captain had asked him to do for the good of the ship.

His book *Madness* theorized what would happen if a small protozoa, which already infects most of the Earth's animal population, made its hosts insane. But it was still fiction. It had to be. And there was something big that he had failed to mention.

"But this was just a novel, folks! A fictional assumption of what could be. Yes, there has been some strange behavior from animals in Europe. We've even experienced it on this ship, but I'm not sure that that has anything to do with what I wrote about in a book.

"Besides, my book had anarchists manipulating the T-Gondii to make its host animals crazed, so as to usher in the downfall of humans. That's not what is going on now. It made for great reading and sold a lot of books, but it's no more real than the evil clown in a Stephen King novel... That's a bad example: some clowns are evil."

He could see some of the same people who looked terrified moments ago now wrestling with their smiles. They wanted to believe that the danger was over. And so did he.

"You're telling me that you believe that bloody rats ripping out some poor mate's eyes out of his skull is just fiction?" This came from an overly rotund bald man wearing a Manchester - MANC AND PROUD T-shirt and shoving potato chips into his mouth.

A young woman with puffy red eyes, being comforted by a man of similar age with his arm around her, squeaked, "I heard on a newscast that there was a pack of dogs in Paris attacking people in the Latin Quarter,"

A teenager grasping a hardback copy of T.D.'s book featuring the object of the Williamses' own nightmares, stood up and bellowed, "I saw some birds attack someone in Malaga."

Ted thought of when the publisher's cover artist and he went to blows over the cover. Ted wanted something scarier than what was offered. A week later, it was perfect, and almost exactly what was on the current published book: a crow with red eyes and a bloody, severed index finger held in its beak. Talk about fiction coming to life. This was the real-life image he had seen in the Alcazaba palace, the image that caused him to shiver when he'd recall it. As it was doing right now.

"Well?" bellowed Manchester, crumbs tumbling out of his mouth. "What about the bloody birds?"

He so wanted to be calming, for his audience and himself. But he was the "Authoritative Author of the Apocalypse," as he was described by his agent and the media. He was paid to think up the scariest shit and make it real, to cause people to lose sleep over thoughts of their own mortality. He wasn't someone who dished out calm, and why the captain thought he'd be able to was beyond him. But he also knew that a panic wasn't going to benefit this ship. His ship. So he tried to think of something positive to say.

"Yeah, what about the birds?" another voice warbled.

"Ahh, sorry," Ted said, snatching the rolled-up report from under the podium. "I, ahh... I mean, my wife and I saw the same thing at the Alcazaba palace in Malaga, three days ago. And I have to tell you, that was terrifying.

"But again, we now have proof that this aggression doesn't last." He held up the report he had mangled and rolled into a tube. "Until we know—not guess—otherwise, I think we have to assume that we are now out of danger."

Ted flashed an image of his dead wife and child. And a gnawing anxiousness about finding TJ and making sure she was safe burned in his stomach.

It was time to finish this talk.

"I'd suggest that all of us, me included, take advantage of today's drink special, two zombies for the price of one, and we soak up the sun, which the captain said we'll be able to see today for the first time on our cruise.

"What I am saying is, we have very little time on this big blue ball. Let's go and enjoy it.

"Thanks for being such a great audience, the largest I've ever had the privilege to speak to. I almost feel like one of the Beatles.

"God bless!"

Ted waved once and made his way back out the way he had entered.

In front of the theater was the display for him to sell his books—he'd forgotten completely about this and the long process of scratching personalizations inside the cover to each and every person. He glanced at the growing line of people already snaking from the front of the table, along the hallway, around a corner, and out of sight. One of the crew waited for him at the table, ready to ring up sales of his pre-signed books.

Conspicuously absent was his wife. TJ had said that she'd miss only part of his talk, not the entire thing. Now he was getting worried.

Before proceeding to his table to give a feeble excuse why he couldn't stay to the clamoring crowds, Ted snatched the radio the captain had given him, attached to the back of his belt. He flicked it on and turned up the volume so he could now hear the chatter, in case something important was reported.

A raspy voice interrupted, "Mr. Bonaventure?"

Ted looked up and then lowered his gaze to find an elderly woman held up by a carved wood cane looking at him over wire-rimmed glasses. Even measuring to the top of her wild hair, she wouldn't have made it to five feet nothing. He guessed she didn't want to wait in line with the others.

"I'm so sorry to be disruptive, sir. Besides being a fan of your work, I am a microbiologist—well, retired, technically. I believe you did a fine job in your book regarding toxoplasmosis."

"Thank you," he said, looking past her at the many expectant faces waiting for him to finish this business and move on to his table.

"I know what has caused the *T-Gondii* to do what it is doing, and it certainly was not anarchists. Moreover, I'm afraid the vet's thinking that this is over is terribly wrong."

A panicked voice called out on his radio, over-modulated and unclear. Ted wouldn't have heard what was said, if he had held the radio's speaker directly to his ear. He let it pass.

"What is it?"

"Thermophilic bacteria!" she stated resolutely.

For the first time, he seriously considered this woman while she readied herself to give details, her face turned up to Ted's, intense blue eyes amplified through thick lenses. It was a face carpeted by a lifetime of wrinkles. Her whole persona spoke of wisdom and decades of scholarly research. She seemed sure about what she was about to tell him.

"You, sir, I believe are completely correct on the toxoplasmosis! But the *T-Gondii* was hijacked by thermophilic bacteria. You see, these bacteria love it hot, and can even be found around volcanic vents. And as we all know, there have been an irregular number of volcanic eruptions lately. I believe that a strain of thermophilic bacteria has been released by volcanoes, and because this bacterium is wired to look for warm-blooded hosts, it sought out the warmest blood available. And that would be birds, which have an average body temperature of 104 degrees Fahrenheit. It then has been working itself down the warm-blooded mammal food chain.

"With each host, the thermophile triggers the *T-Gondii* in its host to do what it had, as you said, already reprogrammed the animal to do: attack without any personal regard for its own wellbeing."

Another voice on the radio screeched something like, "Where is it?"

"So you believe that birds must have been the first animal genus affected and they spread the thermophilic strain to other animals?"

"That's one possibility."

Ted pursed his lips, about to ask another question, but he stopped when the radio blared again, this time with a panicked woman's voice. The voice said two words that made Ted take notice: "monkey" and "killed." He held the radio to his ear.

"Hoy," a voice from the book-table line yelled out. "Excuse me, but we'd like to meet T.D. too, and get to the pool before the sun sets."

Ted turned to the voice, then back to the elderly woman, and to the radio in his hand.

"Go on, Mr. Bonaventure—"

"Please, Ted. And you are?" Ted held out his hand.

"Dr. Molly Simmons. It's my pleasure."

The radio blared, "It's been spotted on deck 8..."

Deck 8? TJ was supposed to be on that deck.

Ted lifted the radio and barked into it, "This is T.D.—ah, Ted Williams, consultant to Captain Christiansen. Are the staff captain and Mrs. Williams up there, on deck 8?"

"Mr. Williams? This is Intrepid Security... I haven't seen the staff captain or Mrs. Williams up here. And I recommend you don't come to deck 8, either. There's a wild monkey up here. In fact—" The transmission stopped.

Ted clipped the radio back to his belt. "Thank you, Dr. Simmons, for the info. I really have to go. Can we talk later?" He moved away from her, as if a force at his book table were magnetically pulling him toward it.

"Yes, Guest Services can look me up for you."

Ted nodded and dashed over to the table. He quickly gathered in the clamoring line of people. "I'm sorry, folks," he hollered so that they could all hear him.

"Something came up for the captain. I'll try to be back. In the meantime, all my books are half-off, they're all pre-signed, and this gentleman can take your payments." He pointed to the crew member, who looked a little panicked.

Ted didn't wait for a reply. He slid behind the table and darted down the long hallway of people waiting in line, away from the theater. He had to get to the forward section of the ship on deck 8 and warn his wife.

34

The Monkey

"Don't puke. You are not going to puke!" Lutz Vega of Lisbon told herself again.

It was no use. Something had gotten to her. She'd been feeling yucky all morning, and the feeling had been getting progressively worse as each minute slowly ticked by. As the guard who was stationed at the bridge's only interior entrance—*for the next four hours*, she confirmed by her watch—she could not leave her post, no matter what. Even if she were puking toenails. But wouldn't she get into trouble if she puked up her breakfast right in front of the bridge? It was a "lose-lose proposition" as her good-for-nothing boss Robert Spillman liked to say.

Lutz tried to consider her options, but there really weren't any good ones. Then she remembered the assistant director's report this morning. Included in the report was the status of rooms for each deck assignment, including vacancies. She pulled out her folded page, which listed the names of each occupant and the vacant rooms. She glanced at the starboard side, down the small bisecting hallway, and knew that cabin 8504 was right there, just out of eyesight now, but there. It was vacant. If she had an uncontrollable bout of nausea, she could just run down the hall and puke in the unused washroom, and be back before anyone noticed she was gone.

The more she thought about it, the better it sounded. She might even go there now. She could drink some water and splash some on her face, and she'd feel better. Maybe she'd even just force herself to puke up whatever was bothering her, and be done with it. Back in her bulimic days, when she was trying to fit in with her police department, she could do it on command. And although now it was more difficult, the way she felt, even without the bout of nausea, she thought it would be easy.

She looked aft, down the long highway, and then starboard again, at her destination, and didn't see anyone coming. Further, the captain's meeting in 8000 was expected to continue for at least another half hour. So this might be the best time to time go. She hesitated, and then another wave of nausea rocked her body. She ran.

Fumbling with her key-card, Lutz turned the corner and held up right at the door, card out and ready to deploy. She was a mere second or two from puking. But she stopped, the wet hairs on the back of her neck prickling. She swung a glance back forward and saw that the Royal Suite's door was propped open. Then she saw why.

She doubled over and heaved violently, tossing the remnants of breakfast, then her dinner, and probably every other thing that ever visited her stomach. A disgusting mix of yuck spilled out of her, all over the already puke-colored carpet. And then, while she was retching, she started to laugh a little at the thought that that's probably how they made this carpet: thousands of workers puking up colors that didn't belong together into one carpet. *Be serious, girlfriend*, Lutz told herself, and then stared again at what lay in the doorway of the Royal Suite.

It was Catur. The room attendant who always smiled at her in the crew mess. He was... It was too ghastly to even look at his injuries. He was literally ripped apart.

She jumped when the door to cabin 8504—her destination before she puked—shook from someone pounding and scratching on it. But this room was supposed to be empty.

"Who's in there?" she called to it.

More banging, and something else... it sounded like moaning.

"Are you all right?" She became sure that someone else was injured by whatever did that to Catur. But just in case...

She lifted the long Maglite wand from her belt and held it like a baton with her right hand while she slipped her key-card into the lock with her left. The lock flashed green, and she clicked the handle down, but hesitated. The Maglite lifted higher into the air, ready to come down on whomever or whatever, might come out.

"I'm opening the door now," she said into the thin, dark opening.

She pushed a little more and saw five hairy digits crimp around the door's edge and pull inward. The thing vaulted at her with an ear-piercing screech.

She tilted sideways and swung the Maglite, connecting with the monkey's skull, sending it hard against the hallway wall.

She spent no time contemplating the oddity of a monkey in the hallway of her ship. Having heard about the carnage in Gibraltar, and knowing she'd lose a battle going to toe-to-toe with this beast, she did the one thing that came to mind.

She dove into the cabin's darkness and simultaneously kicked the door shut. It slammed hard and continued to shudder, as the monkey, now on the other side of it, pounded on it, shrieking its anger at her through the two and a half inches of steel and plastic.

Two things occurred to her as she huffed and puffed, on her back, in the dark. First, she was sure the door would give way, as the beating it was taking was incomprehensible. Next, she realized that the inside of this room smelled so putrid that the nausea that she had momentarily forgotten about was back again in full force.

"Oh God." Something or someone else was dead in this cabin. Her skin cooled and she started to shiver, even though the air was decidedly muggy.

The pounding outside had stopped, and so did the beast's howling. She sat up and leaned forward until her ear was pressed against the door, doing her best to ignore the rancid smell. She heard the monkey breathing and something else. There was the sound of scraping against carpet, like something heavy was being dragged across the floor. The noise grew and then trailed off, becoming softer. Another revolting image popped into her head: the monkey was dragging Catur away. She was instantly sure this was true.

Although a part of her breathed a sigh of relief at knowing the killer monkey was not after her any longer, she knew she had to do something to stop it. It was wrong.

The radio!

Between her panic and desire to get away from the animal, she forgot she had a walkie. Using the door handle, she hoisted herself up to her knees and yanked the radio off her belt. Adjusting the squelch till voices could be heard, she clicked transmit and spoke over whoever was talking. "Hello! We have an aggressive monkey on deck 8. It has already killed a room attendant." She paused a moment, but still held the transmit button down. "Repeat, very dangerous and strong monkey on the loose on deck 8." She let go of the transmit button and listened.

There was an immediate response. "This is T.D.—ah, Ted Williams, consultant to Captain Christiansen. Are the staff captain and Mrs. Williams up there, on deck 8?"

That was the passenger-author, she thought. *What's he doing on the ship's private radio?*

"Mr. Williams? This is *Intrepid* Security," she chimed back, a little miffed that he was using their radio for unofficial business. "I haven't seen the staff captain or Mrs. Williams up here. And I recommend you don't come to deck 8 either. There's a wild monkey up here."

A shuffling sound in the room.

"In fact—"

A moan, followed by the sound of an object clattering to the carpet, sounded from behind her.

She spun around, held up her flashlight up and clicked it on, sending a cone of light to the floor midway through the cabin, toward the sound. Only a few feet from her, at the foot of the bed, was the body of a man—she could tell by his shoes.

She moved the light up, illuminating his body, and then gasped.

The chest and stomach were gone, emptied. It was like his trunk had exploded outward and his gore was everywhere around him. And... she caught the epaulet on his shoulder. Three bars. It was Spillman.

Another noise and Lutz moved the light up farther, casting it on the whole room.

What she saw shocked her so badly she dropped her flashlight. It bounced twice and went out.

35

TJ & Jean Pierre

"Did you hear that?" TJ asked. She shuffled over to the door on bare feet, putting an ear to it. "I swear I heard something out there."

"What? I didn't hear anything. Come back here," Jean Pierre pleaded.

She paused to wipe the sweat from her face with her palm, miffed at how hot this interior cabin was. All because the door was closed, so that no one could hear them from the hallway, or accidentally wander in, forcing them to explain what they were both doing there.

She glanced again at Jean Pierre, feeling guilty about being here and not with her husband. Her hand brushed against her Orion necklace, causing her body to shudder.

She just realized how late it was. She had missed Ted's talk, completely. "I'm going," she announced.

TJ marched over to the bed and collected her personal belongings. "I'm tired and I need to go, now."

He finally glanced up at her. "But what about, you know...?"

"I really don't care at this point. Look," she squeezed his shoulder tenderly, "I really appreciate all you've done, I just can't do this cloak and dagger bullshit anymore. And the not telling Ted everything kills me, especially since he trusts me implicitly."

"You think he would still trust you if you told him that you were in a cabin, sweating with a single man?" He smiled at his rhetorical question.

She slapped his naked dome. "You're evil. But yes, he would still trust me, even after that!"

"You Americans are so—"

"—Hey, wait. Holy shit! Did you see that?" TJ pointed at Jean Pierre's laptop screen.

He turned back around to look at it. "I know, that's what I've been trying to show you."

Ted bounded up the stairs, taking two at a time. When he cleared the deck 7 stairwell, he saw another man coming up from the other side, matching Ted's pace.

"Flavio?" Ted huffed, ascending more stairs.

"Mr. Villiams." Flavio exhaled, still countering his pace.

Each rounded deck 7 and, now side-by-side, were vaulting up the next set of stairs to the half-deck.

"What are... you doing?"

"Kill monkey. Same as you," the Romanian head waiter declared.

They turned to their separate stairwells, Ted on the left, and Flavio to his right, and made way for deck 8. They cleared the last step at the same time, but Ted turned right this time and Flavio turned left, crisscrossing each other to different sides of the deck's two hallway entrances. "I think monkey this way, Mr. Villiams," he whispered, while withdrawing a large cooking knife from a sheath with his right hand. It was polished to a mirror finish. He held up at the port-side hallway entrance.

"How do you know?" Ted whispered. He bent over, grabbed some breaths and shuffled back across the hall to Flavio.

"I do not know. I just think it this way."

"I'm not here to get the monkey. I'm here to get my wife, before the monkey gets her."

"I'll lead then." He turned right and stridently marched down the hallway, stopping only occasionally to consider each and every sound.

It was the same hallway Ted had walked down earlier with the All Access Tour group, leading to the bridge all the way forward. The tour's route began at the forward stairwell versus their mid-ship start. Now, they needed to walk halfway across the span of the *Intrepid* just to get to the bridge from here. TJ was nearby in cabin #8511. It felt like an impossibly long walk, with a crazed monkey on the loose. And now he remembered, based on the cabin numbers, the cabin he was looking for was on the starboard side of the ship.

Ted tried hard to moderate his breathing, but it was difficult because he was winded from the stairs and he feared for his wife's safety. He concentrated on taking long and deep inhalations, one for every five footsteps.

Almost every doorway they passed had a green sticker on its handle and several were still propped open, as all the passengers had been advised to do earlier. Their occupants were either away or had forgotten it was okay to shut their doors now that they'd been cleared. Worse, each open doorway presented another opportunity for a hiding, crazed monkey to leap out and kill them.

When they made it to the forward stairwell, without any sight or sound of the wild monkey, Ted bit his lip and turned right. Flavio seized him by the shoulder. "Why?" he whispered.

"My wife is in 8511."

"Dat's your cabin?"

"It's not ours... But she's there now."

"Vait." Flavio swiftly withdrew another knife from a sheath on his other hip, flipped it around with precision, and handed it to Ted, handle first. "In case you see monkey. I come around by bridge and meet you at room."

Ted nodded and pointed the shiny knife blade outward, almost more afraid now of cutting himself than getting attacked. Almost.

He studied the starboard hallway, looking in both directions. There was no movement or noise, other than an indistinguishable voice or muffled cough. But there was the blood. A lot of it.

A line of blood led from one end of the hallway to the other. It looked fresh. Leaning over, he touched a forefinger to the wetness and pulled back, his fingertip coming up red. His thumb rubbing the crimson around his forefinger confirmed it. And no coagulation meant it just happened. He shuddered just a little and clutched the knife handle even tighter. Then, he turned the corner, immediately coming upon cabin 8511, which abutted the stairwell.

He contemplated whether to knock or holler. Either would make too much noise, and he suspected if the monkey was somewhere on this floor, the noise would attract it. Deciding a short double-rap would be best, he raised his clenched fist.

Then the door opened.

It was TJ, who looked as surprised as he. Behind her was Jean Pierre.

"Ted? What are you do—"

Ted put his hand over her mouth and forcibly pushed her and the staff captain back into the room.

As Jean Pierre backed up, he caught a glimpse of the very large knife Ted was nervously brandishing. "Ah,

Mr. Williams, Theresa Jean—I mean Mrs. Williams—and I were doing nothing wrong. In fact—"

"Shhh." Ted glowered at the stammering officer as he let the door close softly behind him.

Ted glanced quickly at the room and its occupants: pages of papers taped to the walls, including schedules with times and dates; two laptops, his and TJ's; the staff captain, his bald head and face glistening with sweat, one tail of his shirt untucked. Then he noticed the bed behind him had been hastily made. For just a moment, his mind wandered, until he glared at TJ.

"Before you think anything further, I'm gay. I have no interest in her."

Ted ignored him and wrapped his arms around TJ, and hugged her tight. Upon release, he said, "I'm sorry for being such an asshole. I've been taking things out on you because of my own guilt with my first wife and son dying, and I've been shrinking away from you, and that's wrong. Please forgive me."

She hugged him back. "Of course, I forgive you."

A smile grew on Ted's face. "Also, I no longer suffer from enochlophobia."

They kissed for a long moment, while Jean Pierre waited uncomfortably.

Jean Pierre continued to scowl at both of them, before he finally shook his head and said, "Oh, you already knew what she was doing here and you knew it the whole time?"

"Yeah, she confessed to me about the whole... Affair?" Ted snickered at his pun. "I know this cruise is an FBI setup, so that TJ could work undercover—though I thought it was all about me—to catch Eloise Carmichael, because the rich son of one of her victims has a Senator uncle who pushed the FBI to send someone on this cruise, before she killed her seven-hundredth husband."

"We may be too late on that one," TJ cut in. "We were just about to open her cabin when you arrived. We were watching video recordings from her living room, when we caught a glimpse of... So did you come here just to apologize and tell me you loved me?"

Ted's face became grim. "I don't want you to freak out, but one of those damned Barbary apes got on board and was spotted on this floor. I came up to warn you both."

"Oh shit," she breathed. Her features tensed, then relaxed. "But I thought that the aggressive behavior passed after so much time."

"Me too, but the guard I spoke to on the radio said that a crazed monkey was on this deck, that it had already killed someone. There's a long blood trail just outside, spanning much of the hallway. Someone or something has been seriously injured."

Jean Pierre broke out of his gaze and grabbed his radio from his belt. It had been turned down the whole time, while they were monitoring Carmichael's cabin, in an effort to be covert. He turned it up and they heard a flurry of voices.

"Come on, let's get this over with," TJ said and bounded out the door, with the two men following.

Only a few steps later, they arrived at the Royal Suite, cabin #8500. The blood trail appeared to lead right up to and under the door, and a puddle of vomit lay off to the side of it.

Jean Pierre tentatively opened the door using his key-card, revealing the slaughter.

I t hit TJ like a shot to the head—the carnage and the knowledge that this gory mess was from an animal attack. At that moment, TJ recalled the scenes of the blood and gore from Chicago, when her actions led to a partner's death, and then to the more vivid moments from the day she was attacked.

They popped into her head in rapid succession: the vicious dog coming out of nowhere; her hand pressed against her damage; doing 180's, watching and bracing for the next strike she knew would come at any moment; the shock and dizziness from the blood loss; the extensive pooled blood and gore just inside the stables; the attack that followed.

The fear she felt from those moments ate at her every day.

It was now overwhelming.

She steadied herself on the doorjamb, reflexively snapping her head back to make sure the monkey wasn't there, before returning her gaze to the gore before her. She squeezed her eyes closed before opening them again, trying with all her will to ignore the terror that wanted to consume her. She didn't want them, most especially Ted, to see this. They needed her.

"**G**ood God, what the hell happened here?" TJ whispered, her voice scratchy. She didn't wait for an answer and stepped over the pool of blood and muck.

"Do you think that's wise?" Ted asked as he carefully navigated the large puddle of red soup: a mixture of blood and other unrecognizable organic material in it. A disgusting human bouillabaisse, Ted thought. Bile rose up in his throat.

Each of their steps into the cabin splish-splashed, indicating it too was swamped by the tsunami. Jean Pierre pulled open the sheers and curtains, to let in some light.

TJ yelped, startled as someone popped out of the bedroom. "Flavio? What are you doing here?" she asked.

"Mrs. Villiams... Mr. Villiams... Staff Captain." Flavio nodded at each, stopping in the reception area, where the gathering group held up. "Monkey not here. Also, dead man in bedroom." Flavio pointed.

They all rubbernecked, and then one by one made their way through the thousand-square-foot cabin, complete with grand piano, full-size living room, office, and giant bedroom. On the bedroom floor, among some debris, were the bloody remains of an elderly man.

Pulling a tissue from her pocket, TJ crouched beside the body and pressed it against the dead man's face. "Based on the body's morbidity, I'm guessing he's been dead more than a day."

"Just as the dark video confirmed." Jean Pierre stated while hunched over the other side of the body. He stood up and addressed the others, "We've been keeping an eye on Mrs. Carmichael during the cruise. But the video had gone dark, like much of the ship. Then we had just seen a flash of what we thought was Mrs. Carmichael. That's when we had decided to enter the cabin.

"I'm no expert, but these sure don't look like claw marks." Ted pointed to the man's stomach and chest.

TJ used her tissue to examine one of the cuts, pulling at the sliced clothing surrounding one of the stab wounds. "You're right. Eloise is probably responsible for both murders."

"I only see one body," Ted murmured, searching the shadows of the room. "How do you know all the blood at the door wasn't the husband's?"

"Besides the trail of blood in the hallway, the gore in the entrance is... fresher."

Jean Pierre moved to the living room and used his walkie to call security to find out where his guards were, including the guard who was supposed to be posted in front of the bridge. He also wanted someone posted here, to protect the crime scene, and to get an update on their crazed monkey.

"Come here. Now," Flavio said from the hallway.

They trotted out of the cabin, again carefully stepping over the gore in the entry, and found Flavio pointing down the hallway with his knife. "I think monkey drag second body this way." He didn't wait for them, stalking along the side of the corridor, just outside of the blood trail.

"How can one of those little monkeys drag an adult down a hallway?" Jean Pierre asked.

"That little monkey is many times stronger than you or me," Ted answered. His exasperation was growing. "So I guess now we're searching for both a woman serial killer and a crazed monkey?"

"It would seem so," Jean Pierre said.

"Even you wouldn't make something like this up in one of your stories." TJ turned to Ted and kissed him. "I forgot to thank you for coming up to warn us."

"Gee, shucks. Here." He handed her Flavio's knife. "You know how to handle this better than I do. And I have a feeling we'll need it where Flavio's taking us."

They caught up to Flavio, who had stopped outside of a cabin door. "Blood trail goes this way. Different blood here, into this cabin."

Flavio was right. The long blood trail almost appeared to fork a few feet from cabin 8531, with one prong, mostly blood droplets, at the threshold of the cabin and the other, more pronounced, going into a restricted crew-only doorway.

Flavio put his head to the cabin door, and then announced, "I hear nothing."

Jean Pierre had opened the restricted access door that led into the crew's mid-ship elevator and stairwell. From below, they heard distant screams.

Flavio brushed past his staff captain through the door, the others reluctantly following.

Once inside, they froze.

36

The Monkey

"His name is Catur. He's one of the room attendants," Jean Pierre said softly to the group.

"I see no knife wounds though, just bites and ripped flesh." TJ once again had another tissue out, while Jean Pierre held a flashlight on the body.

"So the monkey killed this one and Eloise—" Ted was interrupted by a terrified scream from downstairs. All heads turned.

"Enough talk," Flavio whispered and then quickly proceeded down the stairwell, using the scream and the monkey's small bloody footprints as his guides. The other three followed close behind.

They tracked the bloody marks all the way down to deck 1. When they opened the door onto I-95, everything was quiet. This was an oddity, since even during early morning hours, the area was normally abuzz with activity. It should have been bustling right now.

"Look, blood goes there," Flavio said, and then he continued his pursuit, leaving the others to ponder their next move.

"Is it just me, or is Flavio a badass?" Ted tried to crack a joke, but it fell as flat as his others earlier today.

TJ just scowled at him and then caught up to Flavio, clutching the knife Ted had given her.

"That looks like the crew's break area," Jean Pierre whispered to Ted and pointed down I-95 to where the gory impressions stopped, collected and then continued on. "It's where they can smoke and get some fresh air, outside of the view of guests."

As they continued, several crew peeked out of doorways, fearful of coming out any farther. Jean Pierre motioned for them to stay where they were. Ted would have preferred to have been in any of those places, rather than out here tracking a crazed killer-monkey. But if TJ could be tough, tracking a wild beast when she was terrified of most animals, he figured he should at least back her up on it. He had fallen behind and scurried to catch up with the group.

At the exit marked "Open Deck" and "Smoking Permitted," they examined the crimson splashes that also included boot prints, running away from the door, out of sight, toward the crew recreational areas. Flavio tentatively stepped through the door and came back out shaking his head. There was nothing. They continued along the trail, listening for any sounds that might cause them to change direction or spring into action.

They started down the smaller hallway leading to all the crew areas: recreational, admin, and even a convenience store. The hallway didn't connect with any other arteries, and the footprints only went one way. The monkey was down here.

Jean Pierre lifted his walkie to his face and spoke softly. "Security, this is the staff captain."

"Staff Captain, this is Deputy Chief of Security."

"Wasano, we've found a dead body in the deck 8 aft crew stairwell. We've followed a blood trail down to I-95, and finally to the crew rec areas. Send personnel to secure these areas. And we need a weapon or two down here to deal with a crazed monkey. Get down here on the double. I'm now off comm." Jean Pierre turned his volume down again, and trailed behind the other three, who followed two sets of fading bloody footprints: one human and one primate.

At the Slop House, the crew's mini-market, the group held up as Jean Pierre slipped in and grabbed two sets of silverware. He was about to exit when a meek voice wobbled unseen behind the counter. "Sir? You have to pay for that."

Jean Pierre grabbed his Seacard and flicked it over the counter. "Don't lose it. I'll be back." He grinned at this: even in an extreme emergency situation, they were following the rules. "No exceptions!" the captain had drilled into them.

He rushed to the group. "Here, Ted." Jean Pierre handed him one of the sets. "Didn't want you not to have some protection."

"Thanks," he said, examining the cutlery, "I'm pretty vicious with a fork on Prime Rib Day."

"Inside," Jean Pierre said as he opened the packaging, "you'll find a rather substantial steak knife."

They pulled their knives out and carefully followed behind Flavio and TJ, tracking the blood-trail to the living room, where the crew went to relax, watch TV, and play games. They held up for the next body.

It was a crew member. But other than that, it was hard to tell who it was. There wasn't the slightest amount of Regal European blue or white showing on his ragged uniform, as it was covered in blood. The poor young man's throat was ripped out and all that remained was a ragged opening.

The body also looked like it had been chewed on.

"Come on. He's dead. Monkey in here," Flavio announced and rose to proceed into the room.

"Flavio," Jean Pierre whispered, "I've called security. They're bringing real weapons. I'd suggest we wait until they get here. We'll keep the monkey in there."

"Don't want to lose more crew, sir. I go in, you stay." Flavio pushed through the swinging double doors. One by one, they followed him.

The cavernous room appeared empty of crew, and certainly held no monkey. The only sounds were that of an old movie playing on the large flat-screen TV at the other end and distant tapping.

Once inside, they all took knees and huddled closely. Flavio suggested he'd walk through the room slowly and they would back him up by spreading out. He wanted to make sure there was no crew inside. They agreed, and Flavio slowly advanced, making a trail bisecting the room, passing by a foosball table, a drum set, and a video gaming area, before he'd end up behind the couch in front of the TV.

TJ followed Flavio part of the way and held up at the foosball table, while Ted stepped carefully over to the gaming area. He tested the weight of his newly gifted steak knife and wished he had kept Flavio's more substantial one.

Jean Pierre remained at the door, so he could quietly direct security when they arrived with their weapons.

Ted noticed evidence of the crew being here besides the TV, as he negotiated his way past a couple of tables. One of these was obviously abandoned quickly, with cards splayed haphazardly across the table and on the floor. Curiously, multi-colored ravioli shells were in three tight piles in front of three pushed-out chairs, one overturned.

Ted's heart almost burst out of his chest when he saw movement underneath the table. He was ready to hoof it in the other direction, but after a moment it registered he saw no fur—only a small man, curled up in the fetal position, eyes as big as dinner plates, staring at him.

It was probably unnecessary, but Ted held a forefinger to his lips.

Ted turned back toward Flavio and almost guffawed at the movie playing on the TV. It was the original *Planet of the Apes*, and Charlton Heston was demanding, "Get your hands off of me, you damned dirty apes."

There was commotion coming toward his end of the room. Ted stood up from his squatting position to see Flavio frantically pointing at a brownish form in the corner, previously obstructed by the couch. It was the Barbary ape, and it was much bigger than what Ted remembered of these monkeys.

It was violently scratching at a cabinet, growling at it. A muffled whimper wafted through the slats of the beaten cabinet door. Someone had escaped the monkey and was hiding. But that door wouldn't hold it back much longer.

A pinball machine spontaneously sang out its rhythmic sounds, followed by a ding-ding-ding.

The beast turned in its direction. That was also their direction, and the monkey instantly saw Flavio.

Flavio reflexively tossed his knife, which sailed in a perfect arc and struck pay-dirt, hitting the beefy part of the monkey's bicep, which had moved in front of its chest, as it turned to leap in his direction.

It screeched a terrorizing racket and raced at Flavio.

TJ was next and threw her knife, but it rotated one revolution too many and hit the monkey handle-first in the face. The monkey diverted its path and headed for her, as she panicked and flopped onto her rear. She had no protection.

Ted jumped, unsure what he was going to do but knowing he wouldn't be able to throw a steak knife effectively. He did the only thing he could think of.

Clutching his knife, he leapt toward the monkey, who was completely focused on TJ. He connected shoulder and knife blade into the monkey's chest, just before it could get to her.

The monkey bounced in one direction and Ted came down hard on a guitar. A thud, a twang, and a crack, which was either one of his bones or the guitar neck breaking.

The monkey hit the wall on the other side of the room, knocking down a shelf of books. It shook its head. Ted's steak knife still protruded from its chest, Flavio's from its arm. Then it focused its red, violent eyes at Ted. It snarled its anger and leapt the short distance between them.

There was a loud explosion.

The monkey's head disappeared behind a spray of red, saturating Ted and everything around him. Its limp body crashed into a chair beside him, coming to a rest for good.

By the front entrance, Deputy Security Chief Agarwal lowered his rifle.

Ted let out a long sigh of relief.

37

Falling Apart

"I heard what happened," Captain Christiansen said, offering his staff captain a steaming cup of coffee. "Thank you, Jean Pierre, for mitigating the problem, before it got much worse."

Jean Pierre accepted his cup and sank into the sumptuous chair, one of six surrounding suite 8000's dinner table. The plush cabin, contiguous to the port side of the bridge, was unoccupied during this itinerary. Its $9,000 price tag wasn't a problem for its prospective Parisian occupants; they just never showed up. With the ready room damaged by the tsunami, the captain pressed this one into service.

The message Jean Pierre received said this meeting was "important," but no other information was given except that a similar meeting would follow with the remainder of the ship's first and second officers. The implication was huge. On the other hand, it might have simply been an opportunity to refocus the troops, and to thank each of his officers for a great job during difficult circumstances. Jean Pierre had no idea which it was. He hoped it was the latter. Still, it felt odd to know that other than him, the captain and the two lone officers on the bridge, all the ship's brass were waiting in the hallway, outside this luxury cabin's door.

"Actually, sir, it was one of our head waiters, along with the Williamses and Deputy Security Chief Wasano. They all came through and saved countless lives."

"Yes, of course. Still, I'm proud of the work you did." The captain lifted his cup of coffee to his lips and sat beside his friend. The bags under his eyes were bigger, darker. "Did you find out what happened to Spillman?"

"He was a casualty too, along with one of our masseuses and one of our guards. The three were found in cabin 8504. We're not sure what happened, as some of their wounds seemed to be self-inflicted, and there were lots of bites, too. Our best guess is that the monkey was accidentally locked in the room with Spillman and the masseuse; maybe it followed one of them inside. I'm sure you are aware they've been having an affair since the last itinerary. And I had just learned that Spillman, in an attempt to cover his tracks, was messing with the security cameras. We're also pretty sure he was the one who shorted out the electrical, and blamed it on one of his security monitors, who has since been cleared of all charges. Anyway, they were killed by the monkey and the guard must have heard it, went inside and was attacked as well, and in the process, she must have let the monkey out. Yet... some of what we saw is impossible to explain."

"Like what?"

"We found the guard's and the masseuse's bodies together, propped up against the door—this made it really hard to enter the cabin. The masseuse's body had multiple wounds, and substantial blunt force trauma to the head. It was dark, and so we believe that the guard thought the masseuse was the monkey, and because the guard's throat was ripped mortally, she must have panicked and killed the masseuse with her flashlight."

Jörgen shook his head and then said, "Okay, that mostly makes sense. So what was impossible to explain?"

"The masseuse had skin and muscle tissue in her mouth which corresponded to the bite to the guard's throat."

Jörgen looked at his friend like he'd lost his marbles; for a moment his mouth dropped open, as if he wanted to ask a question. Then his mouth closed, and his expression changed from incredulous to grim. "So our total casualties from the animal attacks and the tsunami stand at nine crew and three guests?"

Jean Pierre gazed into his coffee, and then back up to Jörgen. "Yes, sir. I'm afraid so." He'd learned of the numbers, and who the casualties were, only minutes ago, and he almost fully accepted all of this. He had to. But hearing it from his captain's lips made it seem so much more... horrible. On all the ships he'd served, after all these years, the most crew or passengers he'd lost on one ship had been two passengers. And they were fairly old folks who died of heart attacks.

Yet the *Intrepid's* circumstances were so extraordinary. And from that standpoint, any one of these issues could have caused many more deaths. It was horrible, but considering what they had gone through, they were lucky.

Jean Pierre added, "We're still looking for Mrs. Carmichael. But we think she might have gone overboard during the tsunami, after she killed her husband. Her body will probably never be found. Even considering all that's happened to us... we were damned lucky."

Jörgen was quiet. He seemed lost in his own thoughts.

Jean Pierre knew that as bad as he felt, his friend was burdened even worse for being the captain. But there was more to his friend's look than just the weight of their losses. He knew that Jörgen had something even more serious to say. That had to be the reason for this meeting, before the one with the other officers. His stomach started to churn when he asked, "We are through the worst of it, right?"

"I'm afraid not," Jörgen responded as if receiving the verbal cue he had been waiting for. He handed Jean Pierre the TV remote and looked him straight in the eyes. "No one on this ship, except me, has seen what you're about to see."

Until that moment, Jean Pierre hadn't realized they were facing the TV. But now he knew this, too, was on purpose. "But I thought we didn't have sat..." He didn't need to finish his sentence, and clicked the "On" button. This was the reason he was here, alone with the captain, with the rest of their officers waiting outside. Jörgen had been building up to this.

When the giant screen flicked on, Jean Pierre nearly dropped his coffee.

There were eight separate news channels in boxes, all displaying similar images. The volume was on for the first box, which was the Fox News Channel, but set very low, almost inaudible. Tucker Carlson was reporting about fires, mass deaths and vast damage to property. The lower-third crawl reported the numbers of dead in various countries. Every channel appeared to be discussing similar chaos and mayhem: cities damaged, fires burning out of control, people dead or dying. Intermittently among the pictures of destruction were reports of animal attacks: incidents of most every kind of mammal attacking people and other animals.

Jörgen spoke over the low chatter of the TV. "The tsunami devastated every coastline on the Atlantic, with those closer to the source suffering the greatest damage: Lisbon, Portugal; Brest, France; and Bristol, England, for example, were wiped out. The damage decreased as the waves spread farther. Large portions of Bermuda were destroyed, because it's so low-lying. The Bahamas and most of the East Coast of the US suffered significant damage, but nowhere as bad as other places. Then there are the animal attacks. They are exploding all over the world: Europe, Asia, and Africa. America has a few reports sprouting up, but not too many at present. The places least affected appear to be out of the reach of the ash cover from all of the volcanic eruptions."

Jean Pierre continued to sink deeper into his chair, letting the sounds, sights, and stories from the Chyron crawls of each program wash over him.

Jörgen said nothing more. He wanted to be sure Jean Pierre had a few minutes to process the enormity of what he was seeing. He had had all night to come to terms with this new reality.

Jean Pierre turned his watery eyes to Jörgen and said, "We need to get to Florida as soon as possible."

"I thought the same thing. But I don't believe it would be safe there, either. I used our sat phone and spoke to several port masters in Florida and one in Charleston.

"All East Coast ports are closed from tsunami damage, though all are working on repairs and should be back open soon. They haven't yet heard reports or seen incidents of animal attacks at their locations, only north of them. And perhaps the Rage disease—as the newscasters are still calling it—might not spread there, but then again it might. If when we arrive we're allowed to disembark, what if the animal attacks have started? We are safer on this ship, waiting it out. So I came up with a plan, and it was accepted by corporate.

"We were already scheduled for Nassau, Bahamas, as our last port before heading to Miami, Florida. Their port sustained only moderate damage from the tsunami. They expect to have it open again in forty-eight hours. So far, there are no reports of animal attacks on Nassau." He was going to add, *Though I wouldn't count on that by the time we get there*, he left that part out. "So our plan is to still port in the Bahamas, but we won't go ashore until we can guarantee this Rage thing has passed or the area remains unaffected. I'm still hopeful that this thing has a short fuse and will burn itself out in a matter of days. Either way, we can try to resupply and sit it out until it does."

Jörgen paused to make sure Jean Pierre didn't have any other questions. The staff captain was still in the shell-shock phase. He continued, "In the meantime, we say nothing about this to the rest of the crew and guests. We'll be in Nassau in five days. We'll use those five days to watch and carefully plan what we'll do next. I'm going to tell this to the first and second officers, right after we're done.

"The good news is, with the route I've plotted outside the ashfall, we should have sunny skies most of the way, and it's warmer outside. I intend that we all put on our best faces for the guests, and make sure they enjoy their cruise. Happy guests are manageable guests."

Jean Pierre was sitting up straight now. He turned his chair toward Jörgen. "What do we say about the TV reception and the Internet?" Jörgen could see Jean Pierre had fully accepted his plan and was already preparing himself for the days that lay ahead.

"We lie. Maybe tell them we won't be able to fix the satellite and Internet service until after we have made it to Nassau and get new equipment. We should know for sure what we're facing when we get that far. Then we can tell them the truth. But not before then."

"What about the Williamses?"

"Tell them. Keep them in the loop, as you would other first officers, at least until this crisis passes. And update the two officers on the bridge too."

Jean Pierre nodded. That was it. There was nothing more to say. Jean Pierre trusted that Jörgen had considered their options and, as he said, received authorization from corporate. They'd have five days to watch, wait, and then figure out all the details. In the meantime, their job was to make their guests feel safe. He could deal with the next five days. They'd worry about after when "after" came.

Jean Pierre stood up, straightened his uniform, cleared his throat, and saluted his captain. "Sir!"

Jörgen rose, returned the salute, and warmly shook the hand of his friend and Number One. "Thanks for being someone I can always count on."

Jean Pierre offered a small grin. "Should I let in the other officers?"

"Yes, please. Then can you go ahead and make sure all our guests have a great time today?"

"I'll do my best."

38

Sunshine and Lollipops

It was a day full of contrasts: small puffy clouds, set upon a deep blue sky; a sun revealed, now pouring out its warmth upon the cold salt water sloshing around the main-deck pool; multi-colored swimsuits covering blanched bodies swollen from this morning's breakfast; a general acceptance that all was good among the ship's guests when there were signs of potential doom all around. Otherwise, it was a day that almost seemed perfect. Almost. And if something violent was approaching, no one seemed to notice, or even care.

Once the *Intrepid* had charted a course along a diagonal arc that appeared free from volcanic clouds of soot, and the sun reigned supreme again, air temperatures rose quickly and by eleven, it was a comfortable 20 degrees Centigrade out, with the forecast of it going even higher. The crew had already cleaned up most of the debris from the public areas of the ship. The broken windows pool-side on deck 9 were cleaned up and boarded so that no one would attempt to walk through the empty frames. Only a few areas were cordoned off, not available to passengers. The passengers quickly accepted these minor inconveniences, which they were told would be fixed either in Nassau or at the end of their cruise.

All the remaining deck loungers, which had been put up before the tsunami, were laid out and were already one-third full of guests who were just happy to gather some warmth from the previously hidden sun and drown their troubles in the saltwater pool or one of the multiple Jacuzzis and the daily drink special: half-priced, double-rum zombies. It had been Jean Pierre's idea to ramp up the alcohol content

The crew expected the remaining chairs to fill up quickly once word spread that the sun was out and the world wasn't going to end. What few crew knew was that most of the guests were ill from yesterday's dinner salad, which had been tainted with a nasty mix of bacteria and other microscopic monsters.

The Williamses were among those who had decided to take temporary advantage of the warmth, finding two lounge chairs which offered sweeping views of the sun deck. Jean Pierre had wanted to meet with them up on the bridge at noon, not only to personally thank them again on behalf all the crew, but to also update them on the captain's plan for the coming days of the cruise. They had a little time to kill and it seemed like a perfect opportunity to take in some sun and reap one of the bennies given to them for their help in saving the ship from a larger disaster.

They raised their drinks in a silent toast. Some sort of red-orange rum concoction, compliments of the pool-side bartender, who informed them that all their drinks were free for the remainder of the cruise.

Ted brought the drink down to his lips and sucked down a large portion of the sweet liquid, while glancing over the entire deck and the guests who littered its surface: a multitude, lounging in chatty happiness.

After swallowing another mouthful, he said, "You know, it's funny how quickly the human spirit desires to move away from pain and tumult and set itself upon anything pleasurable. To look at the people out here, you wouldn't have even known, unless you were paying attention, that anything bad happened over the last five days. It's all sunshine and lollipops now."

"I was thinking the same thing. How quickly everyone wants to forget." She sipped her drink and then glanced tentatively up at her husband. "Is it really over?"

Ted held the bridge of his nose, fighting brain-freeze from the slushy beverage. "Not entirely. If the effect is only temporary, then maybe this will pass. I hope we'll hear of more signs from the outside that it's over with. I have a feeling one of the reasons Jean Pierre wants to talk to us is that they've made contact with other ports, and he has more of those details."

"I hope they're the details we want to hear."

"Me too." Ted finished his drink, furtively eyeing the bar only a few lumbering steps away. He decided it was better to meet with Jean Pierre with a semi-clear head. With some luck, there'd be plenty of time for drinking. He set his glass down, folded his hands into his lap, and shut his eyes, relishing the warmth on his skin.

TJ was only teasing her drink, twirling her straw around it, as if it still wasn't mixed entirely. She was worried sick about her mom and hoped that Jean Pierre would offer some way for her to call. Surely, he'd find a way.

Then she remembered the other question she had. Glancing back over to Ted she asked, "So explain to me how the volcanoes tie into the animal attacks?"

He didn't open his eyes. "Well, this is just a hypothesis. But it's the best one I've heard. They're called thermophilic bacteria. These little guys love it hot, like most bacteria do. However, this particular bacterium loves it *really* hot, even hanging around volcanoes and steam vents. They have some sort of special cellular protections that normal bacteria don't have so they can survive extreme temperatures, and they're hard to kill. When several volcanoes erupted they sent their trespassing thermophiles into the atmosphere. Those thermophiles are constantly searching for heat, and it's not too warm in the upper atmosphere. So in their search for hot, they find themselves attracted to birds, who have among the highest temperatures of all mammals. The infected birds bite other animals and transfer their infection to those other animals, who go after others, and so on."

"Wait, I thought your book was about T-something messing with an animal's brain, causing it to go all crazy-mad. What does that have to do with thermo-bacteria?"

"Right. The *T-Gondii* is a parasite already present in almost all animals and most humans. But it sits dormant in most of its hosts. The theory is that the thermophilic bacteria, once it got into the bloodstream of the infected animal, woke up the T-Gondii, which then commanded the animal to do what comes naturally, without any sense of worry about its own welfare."

"What comes naturally?" TJ asked, but she knew the answer the moment her question left her lips.

"Killing, of course."

"Thank God it doesn't affect humans too."

"Yeah, that actually puzzles me. I'm not sure why it doesn't—affect humans, I mean."

"Maybe it's because our body temperatures are different." TJ glanced at her watch and was shocked that it was already almost noon. "We need to get going to the bridge or we'll be late."

Ted didn't move. He seemed frozen in place, eyes almost glazed, staring off toward the horizon.

"Did you hear me?" TJ set her nearly full glass down and squeezed his shoulder. "Ted?"

"Sorry." Ted shuddered a little. "Your comment just got me thinking." He stared at the horizon a moment longer, and then returned his wife's gaze. "Yeah, let's go."

A cloud of darkness hung inside the bridge.

Ted and TJ didn't notice the darkness immediately when they were ushered inside: they were too taken aback by the damage. A boarded window on the port side spoke of the causeway. Together, their eyes followed what they suspected was the path from the sudden inflow of water: through the ready room—currently roped off, its windows blown inward; then into the rest of the bridge. Half of the consoles were detached from their normal places and now rested against the port-side window-wall, useless artifacts. Holes where the consoles had been were occupied by small men in black jumpsuits. Some were all the way in their holes; the rest were half in and out, all of them talking frantically back and forth in a foreign language. Bundles of wires snaked out, across the floor and into each of the holes. It looked as if they were rewiring the entire bridge.

The first real signs of trouble came from the two bridge crew members, at their posts: They looked sullen, almost dumbstruck. The Williamses hadn't expected to see anyone being overly cheery, knowing that several of their fellow crew and three of their guests had died over the last couple of days on their watch. But surely their spirits should have been lifted today after having avoided so much more death, and with the prospect that all the troubles of the last few days would pass. Not to mention the fact that even after what should have been a devastating tsunami, they still had a ship in working order—minus some obvious damage which they were still fixing—and lots of supplies. But the crew's dark mood was quickly obvious to Ted and TJ. They knew something was wrong.

Jean Pierre interrupted their mutual contemplations. "Welcome, my friends." He held out his hand and shook each of theirs warmly. "Let's go out to the starboard-side swing deck, where we can have some privacy." He walked them through the bridge and led them outside through a side hatch.

"My apologies for not offering something more comfy. I didn't realize the captain would still be in a meeting with many of his officers."

They didn't mind. In fact, they preferred the outside salt air and the stiff breeze, though the north side of the ship didn't offer any sunshine.

Neither of them wanted to hear what they suspected was coming next.

Ted deflected, partially from curiosity. "Tell me first, since both of you are here... Whatever became of Mrs. Carmichael?"

Jean Pierre looked at TJ, who looked at him. "You should explain this, since it was your investigation."

"Yeah, well we don't know what happened to her yet. We suspect she was washed overboard by the tsunami. And before that, we think she killed her husband. As you also witnessed, we found him dead in their cabin, with multiple stab wounds. As far as I'm concerned, and therefore as far as the FBI is concerned, she's on our Most Wanted list, and will remain there until she's ruled officially dead in a year."

TJ looked over to Jean Pierre to see if he wanted to add anything more, seeing the staff captain had stepped over to the north-facing railing. "This reminds me. The finger later found in their cabin—did Dr. Chettle offer any guesses on who that belonged to?"

Jean Pierre's back was to them. His binoculars were glued to his face, pointed at some wispy black cloud on the northern horizon that appeared to be moving in their direction.

"Sorry." He lowered the binoculars and turned back to them. "The finger appears to be Mrs. Carmichael's. And based on the teeth marks, it appears she chewed it off herself."

T he door rattled, stopping Paulo in his tracks. He tugged on the waistband of his borrowed black overalls, feeling his cuffs being restrained by his heels.

Paulo glared at the door, daring it to make another noise. Down the hallway, a similar shuddering sounded. He huffed, now discounting what he heard as coming from the movement of the ship, which would naturally cause things to vibrate.

He tugged once more at his pant legs and felt the pending scorn of his supervisor if he didn't hurry along. He was summoned to the bridge to assist with all the electrical problems they were having there. It wasn't his normal job—he was a janitor—but they needed all the competent able bodies on fix-up. And because he was pretty good with electronics, and after getting a recommendation from Buzz, he received a promotion today and was now a mechanic. They told him they'd find a uniform more his size when they reached their home port in Miami.

The door to cabin 8531 was once again jarred furiously from the inside. It clattered so violently, he thought it might come off its hinges.

"Are you all right there?" he called out to the person who must have been behind the door.

The response sounded like a muted grunt, and so Paulo put his ear to the door and listened carefully. Again, he called out, "Are you all right?"

Another rattle, and a longer, more pained-sounding grunt. The person behind the door was obviously in distress and couldn't answer. The previous wellness check on the guests must have missed this one. Or maybe their condition had worsened.

Panicked, Paulo looked up and down the hallway, searching for any crew member who could take over responsibility. He assumed this floor would be a buzz of activity, but it seemed empty now. There was no other crew to be seen or heard, though he did hear some more rattling far down the hall. Its hollow echoes only added to Paulo's building anxiety.

He was certainly overdue on the bridge by now. But he couldn't ignore the cries of a potentially injured guest. He withdrew his new Seacard from his pocket, not convinced it would work on this door. But with the elevation in title came increased access.

"Hello! I'm going to come in and help you, okay?"

The drumbeat rattle on the back of the door continued, more furiously, followed by another long groan.

Paulo slid his card in-out, the lock flashing its green acknowledgment.

He pushed the handle down and nudged at the door, just enough to crack it open. "I'm coming in to help," he hollered louder, so that the injured occupant and anyone else around could hear.

There was pressure from the inside, so he pushed harder, but the pressure was building by an equal portion, as if the injured guest was working against him.

Maybe the guest was pressed up against the door and couldn't move.

Paulo, as determined as he could have been, dug his heels into the carpet and pushed low into the solid door.

When he had it wedged half open, he stuck his head into the black opening.

Lights must be burned out here, too.

Paulo focused on the floor, figuring the injured guest would have been there.

He was startled to see bare feet and legs, and as his eyes continued up, the pelvis of a naked female. He blinked his eyes and moved his head upward, attempting to avert his gaze. Instead, he caught a glimpse of the woman's mostly exposed breasts. He pawed on the door, intending to push himself away from it and the woman.

"Ah, oh my," he stammered. "I'm so sorry, miss. I didn't know. I thought you were hurt. I—"

A vise-grip clutched his hand, clamping it to the door.

It was a female hand, bloody. It was missing a finger.

Paulo yanked his own hand loose and skittered backward, his legs and cuffs tangling. He was going to fall. He glanced up, his eyes meeting hers. They were bright red and so angry.

She screeched an unearthly noise.

He attempted to scream back, but was cut short.

No one heard Paulo die, as all around the ship, the doors began to rattle.

Epilogue

"Is that a ship, out there to the southeast?" The man pressed the binoculars to his eyes and focused all his attention on the ship south of them. His vision was blurred, but the image was clear. "It's a blooming cruise ship!"

His partner bounded over to him, causing their little aluminum boat to pitch violently.

"You idiot. Do you want to toss us over?"

The smaller man immediately sank to the floor, his rear splashing in a couple of inches of water. "Sorry, Thomas," Phillip said, looking down at his pants. They had finally dried out and now they were sopping wet again. He glanced at the distant ship, ignoring his friend's gaze. "Yeah, I can see it. But it seems... broken."

Thomas glared at him for a moment longer, before returning to his binoculars and the cruise ship in the other direction off their bow. The ship was already plainly visible without the help of the binoculars, but he couldn't see clearly since his glasses went overboard. "It's the smokestack. You're right, it's bent over. They must have survived the tsunami, but it still got busted up. You want to see?" Thomas held the binocs behind him, expecting Phillip to snatch them from his hands. He turned back to find his friend sitting in the water gathering in the bottom of their little boat, staring downward. "Phillip, what's wrong?"

Phillip looked up. "I miss our friends, and I don't feel well."

"Me too." Thomas thought about what they'd been through, the only two out of a crew of twenty who survived the tsunami. How he and his friend Phillip made it, he had no clue. But somehow, after it passed, he found his friend and then this boat, floating beside them. The boat had no oars, but at least they were out of the water. That was, until it sprang a small leak, which required them to bail constantly. If they could stay ahead of it, they'd stay afloat long enough to be spotted. And they had a good chance of being spotted since they were floating in one of the busiest shipping lanes in the world. At least, it had been the busiest before the tsunami.

Thomas turned back to the cruise ship.

It looked like it was headed in the normal westerly route all transatlantic ships took from Europe, when they were first headed to the Azores. Unfortunately, their little skiff was probably too small and too far away to be seen by anyone on that ship. Just in case, he put the binoculars down and held up the broken oar they had found in the debris of another destroyed ship. With a T-shirt tied to its flat end, he waved it furiously from side to side.

"Will they see it?" Phillip asked, and then dry heaved over his lap. "I don't feel too good." He moaned and then slowly hoisted himself back up on the second seat in the battered rowboat to get a better look.

"Doubt it. But we gotta try. No telling how many ships survived the tsunami."

"I sure am thirs..." Phillip's voice trailed off.

"I'm thirsty too, Buddy. But what I'd *really* love is one of those rum-filled drinks that they serve to all their guests. You know, one of those fruity things with the umbrellas in them?" Thomas closed his eyes and licked his lips, almost tasting its cool yumminess. "A zombie! That's what it's called. Remember when—"

Thomas turned back to his friend, wondering why he hadn't heard a peep from him while he was yapping on about the rum drink. Phillip had loved those things when they stopped at a beach bar on holiday in the Canaries a couple of years ago. He found Phillip staring into the heavens at a giant black cloud that moved rapidly over them. This cloud screeched and crackled.

"It's a flock of blackbirds. Probably coming from the Canaries," Thomas said, as he watched the swarm of them pass overhead, all flying toward... the cruise ship he'd been watching.

"Philip?" Thomas begged, pointing back behind his friend, who was stooped over in his seat.

There were dozens of stragglers, flying irregular patterns, rather than the normal sinewy lines of a flock. In fact, the flock had looked rather irregular as well. The stragglers were flying lower too, so he could hear their cackles more prominently. Several of these seemed to be flying toward them.

The attack was quick, and before either of them knew it, they were overwhelmed by the demonic-looking blackbirds. The birds screeched at them and dove into Thomas, burying their beaks into his flesh, followed by clawing and ripping.

Thomas got turned around while swinging at the offending birds, when he heard gasping and cries from Phillip, and then a scream. But it wasn't a scream of terror. It sounded like frustration, or anger.

Thomas batted away two of the birds, and this gave him enough of an opening to turn to see his friend Phillip—his buddy since childhood—leap off his seat and land on top of him. Phillip dug his fingers into Thomas' skin, and his friend opened his mouth wide, like he was going to take a bite out of him. "What are you do—"

Shock stopped his words as he saw Phillip pull away from him with a chunk of Thomas' own skin in his mouth. This part horrified him, as did his friend's insane behavior. But what made him piss his own pants was his friend's red eyes.

Preview

The following is a chapter from PARASITIC: MADNESS Chronicles II

Fifteen Years Ago

The dog came from out of nowhere, completely silent, rather than the usual vicious pooch announcing its terror long before it reached you. It crashed into her right side like a freight train. She only heard the briefest sound of the monster gulping one last bit of air, before it struck.

When she hit the ground, she heard the animal grunt from their impact and then growl as it attempted to get a better grip on her side, so that it could set itself to ripping her flesh.

If she had any time to think about her situation, she would have probably panicked. This was where her training kicked in. Her gun was already unholstered, and so she quickly fired off a shot. But it was from the same side as the mutt. She missed. Quickly, she switched hands and shot once more from her left.

A long moment of quiet passed. Not more than maybe twenty heartbeats.

They both lay in a heap, but only she was panting.

Upon quick inspection, she concluded this was not your back-yard, shit-bird variety of pit bull; this was a pure-bread Vizsla: slick, muscular, and very powerful. The Bureau already knew that the dog's owner had bought a half-dozen over the years from a breeder in Jackson, about ten miles South.

Of course it never occurred to her superiors in the FBI, who put together this raid, that the dogs might be a threat; only their owner.

Well, they screwed the pooch on that one, she thought.

"Sitrep, people," blared her earpiece.

"Taggert here... Wren here... Anderson here..."

With some effort, TJ pushed herself onto her knees. She lifted her mangled shirt edge to inspect the wound. It looked pretty bad.

"Sitrep, Williams."

Her black FBI jacket came off—*damned thing was too hot anyway.* She pulled off her shirt with a grunt and groan, thankful she was wearing her sports bra and not one of the frilly Victoria-Secret-things Ted bought her. Folding it length-wise until it was a long thick strip of fabric, she wrapped it around her side, making sure both ends of the wound were covered enough. Holding the ends of the jacket arms, she spun it around, turning it into a cord, with most of it bunching up the middle. It too was placed over the wounded area. Finally, she tied the jacket's arms tight around her other side, cinching it down to hold the field dressing, and hopefully stem the flow of blood.

It would have to do, until this was done.

"Williams, report," her earpiece hollered at her, again.

"Williams here. Damned dog fricking bit the shit out of me. Had to shoot it. I'm good to go. 10-76."

"Roger."

She should have called in 10-52, Ambulance Needed. But then she'd have to walk ten times as far back to their mobile base, and she really wanted to get this sonofabitch, especially after now learning he was training vicious dogs.

She drew her weapon again; it had been holstered, while she'd rendered herself aid.

Each step forward elicited a painful grunt, and she could feel a warm trickle of blood drip down her backside.

Worse yet, she felt a building anxiety giving way to a constant need to check her twenty for another crazed animal.

The ranch house was only a hundred yards away, and no doubt, their perp would be looking out his window, in her direction. So she had to approach it covertly, which was damned hard to do without much natural cover. With any luck, he'd think her gunshots were from a hunter, illegally shooting on the Yellowstone National Reserve property, contiguous to his. He had often called in complaints to Game and Fish about this.

The worst case scenario, would be the guy coming out, guns blazing, and then they'd have another Waco on their hands. And that they did not want. The guy may have been a murderer, but they didn't want his dozen-member family hurt too. They were the reason TJ had to keep going.

It was because the kids hadn't been seen for several weeks, and all of them missed the first two weeks of the fall semester, a couple of deputies from the Jackson Sheriff Department were dispatched to check on the family. Upon arriving on the scene, there was a single panicked radio broadcast from one deputy. The dispatcher claimed the caller said only, "He's crazy." Nothing more. An hour later, the FBI stepped in as they were not coincidently investigating two missing hikers from Prague, who were last seen wandering in the same direction as TJ was now.

She stopped to regain her breath, and to readjust her field-dressing, which was already coming loose. She was sweating like it was ninety out, when it wasn't much more than sixty. She pressed her palm to her bicep. Her skin felt cool. Do not go into shock, she told herself. As if one could coax one's self into not doing so.

She cinched her jacket-pressure-bandage even tighter, moaning at the pain, while she trudged forward the last few steps.

The moaning continued, but this time, it wasn't her.

"This is Williams," she whispered. "I'm at the South-West corner of the corral fence-line, about fifteen yards from the home. I'm hearing some sort of... moaning. Going to investigate."

"Hold up Williams. Wait for your team."

The rest of her advanced team reported in, but much further away. She would be there long before the others, which meant no backup. Yet, if the moaning was from an injured family member or the hikers, waiting longer might end up killing one of them. To buttress her argument for moving forward, she was feeling queasy. It occurred to her, she'd have to finish this pretty quick, before she passed out. The last thing she wanted to do is blow the whole operation passing out before they got 'em. She'd rather accept a verbal tongue lashing, if it meant they could catch this SOB.

Maybe I could claim delirium from the dog-bite. It wasn't too far off, she thought.

She'd press forward, moving along the back fence line.

Within a minute, she heard the moaning-sound again, only it was more of a groaning. It was coming from the dark opening of the barn, diagonally across from the corral.

TJ slipped in between the rough slats of the split-rail fence and yelped when she saw where she stepped. She thought for a moment, it was another dog. But it wasn't.

Below her foot and against the fence, lay a dead horse. Practically gutted. A dark stain circled the carcass, the blood had mostly seeped into the corral's soft dirt. There were multiple small-round-puncture wounds and deep gashes in its throat and sides, like it had been mauled by a wild animal.

Her head pivoted, searching around her twenty for the wild animal that did this. Her breathing accelerated, to the point of hyperventilating. The perp had more dogs. What if they were just as vicious as the one that attacked her. She felt a chill shoot across her spine.

TJ bent over to catch her breath. It was either the blood loss or her hyperventilating or both: her dizziness turned to double vision. At any moment, she felt certain she'd either panic or pass out. Touching the lower edge of the bunched up shirt against her side, her fingers came away very wet and dark red. She was losing too much blood. She needed to call it. Losing any more blood, she'd surely loose consciousness, maybe even die.

A low growl, like a dull echo, pulled at her. Her head drew up, attempting to find the sound, and she instantly saw it.

Or rather him.

Their perp, Jim Tanner. Father of ten. Multi-millionaire, ranch owner. Perhaps, even mass-murderer. Was the one growling. And running.

He was running toward her. In his hand, he brandished a metal rod, like a piece of rebar.

"Subject is running toward me, yelling," she warbled over their comms.

More like screeching, at her. He sounded and looked like some crazed wild animal. An insane thought hit her:

maybe their perp, and not one of his dogs, mauled the horse.

"Mr. Tanner. FBI. Freeze!" she demanded, but it came out a weak croak. Her Glock 29 raised. He was sighted in, with only the slightest of twitching. Good thing, there were at least two of him coming at her.

He kept coming, only faster.

"Mr. Tanner, I'll shoot you," she hollered, her own voice sounded distant, like it was someone else's.

TJ dropped to her knee, not just to keep her gun hand steady: she was seeing three of everything now.

"Stop!"

He didn't.

She fired. Three times. One for each of him.

Then she tumbled to the ground, her strength leaving her.

"Subject down. Officer needs assistance," she whispered over her comms, and then passed out.

Before The Next Book

Find out how the madness of the Rage Disease spreads around the world and on the Intrepid when the *MADNESS Chronicles* continues in *PARASITIC: MADNESS Chronicles II* (http://mlbanner.com/madness2). But before you do...

I'm an independent writer who relies on ratings and reviews to help get the word out about my books. This is why reviews are so important to me and why I truly need your help. Leaving even a short review would be greatly appreciated.

Please post a review on Amazon

https://www.mlbanner.com/madness-review

Madness Fact vs. Fiction

S cience fiction is a wonderful genre because it takes science and adds layers of fictional what-ifs. Storylines are crafted around scientific precepts, and set upon a foundation of reality. At least that's how most science fiction should be. Unfortunately, it's often more fantasy than reality, where the foundational world is almost entirely made up, or the science is bent to the point of breaking. I prefer fiction that sounds and feels real.

I'm not saying that there isn't creative license built into every sci-fi story. This is often necessary when trying to track a story's narrative around the science. But such license—think warp-drive technology in *Star Trek*—is still completely different from ignoring scientific facts. I offer zombie-apocalypse (zompoc) fiction as one such example.

The preponderance of zombie fiction involves the reanimation of the dead, often giving these ghouls super-human powers they'd never had when they were alive and setting them on the unending course to eat the brains of the surviving humans, unless of course you're able to "kill" the already dead zombie by puncturing its brain (doesn't matter where), at which time the reanimated zombie dies, losing all animation forever.

This whole concept is utterly ridiculous and for me, makes it hard to accept the rest of the story. And that's because the whole zombie-thing is scientifically impossible. Every part of it. I won't go into the whys because others have done a much better job at debunking the whole zombie concept, in scientific and medical terms, and in all the major flaws of the zombie world narrative. Yet, I'll admit to you that I've garnered a love for some zombie fiction. Some.

Let it be known, I have been a closet *Walking Dead* fan. At least the first few seasons. Yes, I know this flies in the face of what I've just said, making me a zombie hypocrite (would that be a zombocrite?) of sorts. But I haven't spent endless hours watching *TWD* because of its zombies. My enjoyment was in spite of its zombies, and bad science. It's the characters and their constant struggles to survive that captured my attention. The zombies are often a storyline after-thought. I also love the story concept that everyone (in *TWD's* case, when taken by death) will eventually become a potential monster; when each person's internal "evil" is released upon the world.

It's that concept of internal "evil" that you're starting to see in the pages of the *Madness Chronicles*.

But I'm jumping ahead of myself, as I've only hinted at this at the end of this book, *MADNESS*. You'll have to read *PARASITIC (MADNESS Chronicles II)*, and of course, the finale, *SYMPTOMATIC (MADNESS Chronicles III)*, to really understand this. The real question I want to explore here and my purpose for giving you this additional back-of-the-book segment is... how much of what I wrote in *MADNESS* is science and how much is fiction?

I'll explain it this way, just about everything in the book describing the *T-Gondii* protozoa is absolutely correct. Walk into a room with nine other people, and most likely half of you are already infected with *T-Gondii*. Where this room is located in the world will determine the numbers more precisely: in Paris, probably eight out of ten; New York, maybe five out of ten; in other places, it may be even ten out of ten. This infection is truly wide-spread, and scientists are only just now starting to understand what the *T-Gondii* does to peoples' brains. Some say that the current wave of aggressive behavior we see around us (think road rage, school shootings, etc.) is directly related to *T-Gondii's* reprogramming your brain to be more angry and aggressive. Have you been feeling angrier lately? You might be suffering from toxoplasmosis, where the *T-Gondii* puppet master is actively pulling your strings. Scary stuff, huh?

It's worse for mammals.

The creative license I took in giving you the *MADNESS Chronicles* is the introduction of a thermophilic bacterial infection, which I have flipping the switch on the *T-Gondii's* reprogramming. Thermophilic bacteria do exist around volcanic vents. But could they actually cause this reaction to *T-Gondii*-infected hosts?

Anything is possible.

Finally, you may ask what was with this graphic during each chapter break?

These are actual images of T-Gondii parasites. I was probably having a little too much fun with this. But hopefully it didn't take away from your reading pleasure.

Thank you for reading!

FREE BOOKS

Sign up for ML Banner's *Apocalyptic Updates* (VIP Readers list) and get a free copy of one of my best-selling books, just for joining.

In addition, you'll have access to our VIP Reader's Library, with at least four additional freebies.

Simply go here:

http://mlbanner.com/free

(give me an email address to get your free book)

Who is ML Banner?

Michael "ML" Banner is an award winning,
USA Today Bestselling author of Apocalyptic Thrillers

Michael writes what he loves to read: apocalyptic thrillers, which thrust regular people into extraordinary circumstances, where their actions may determine not only their own fate, but that of the world. His work is traditionally published and self-published.

Often his thrillers are set in far-flung places, as Michael uses his experiences from visiting other countries—some multiple times—over the years. The picture was from a transatlantic cruise that became the foreground of his award-winning *MADNESS Series*.

When not writing his next book, you might find Michael (and his wife) traveling abroad or reading a Kindle, with his toes in the water (name of his publishing company), of a beach on the Sea of Cortez (Mexico).

Want more from M.L. Banner?

MLBanner.com

Receive FREE books & *Apocalyptic Updates* - A monthly publication highlighting discounted books, cool science/discoveries, new releases, reviews, and more

Connect with M.L. Banner

Keep in contact – I would love to hear from you!
Email: michael@mlbanner.com
Facebook: facebook.com/authormlbanner
Twitter: @ml_banner

Books by M.L. Banner

For a complete list of Michael's current and upcoming books:
MLBanner.com/new-projects/

ASHFALL APOCALYPSE

Ashfall Apocalypse (01)
A world-wide apocalypse has just begun.

Leticia's Soliloquy (An Ashfall Apocalypse Short)
(Exclusively available from a link at book #1 end)

Collapse (02)
As temps plummet, a new foe seeks revenge.

Compton's Epoch (An Ashfall Apocalypse Short)
Compton reveals what makes him tick.
(Exclusively available from a link at book #2 end)

Perdition (03)
Sometimes the best plan is to run. But where?

MADNESS CHRONICLES

MADNESS (01)
A parasitic infection causes mammals to attack.

PARASITIC (02)
The parasitic infection doesn't just affect animals.

SYMPTOMATIC (03)
When your loved one becomes symptomatic, what do you do?

The Final Outbreak (Books 1 - 3)
The end is coming. It's closer than you think. And it's real.

HIGHWAY SERIES

True Enemy (Short)
An unlikely hero finds his true enemy.
(USA Today Bestselling short only on mlbanner.com)

Highway (01)
A terrorist attack forces siblings onto a highway, and an impossible journey home.

Endurance (02)
Enduring what's next might cost them everything.

Resistance (03)
Coming Soon

STONE AGE SERIES

Stone Age (01)
The next big solar event separates family and friends, and begins a new Stone Age.

Desolation (02)
To survive the coming desolation will require new friendships.

Max's Epoch (Stone Age Short)
Max wasn't born a prepper, he was forged into one. (This short is exclusively available on MLBanner.com)

Hell's Requiem (03)
One man struggles to survive and find his way to a scientific sanctuary.

Time Slip (Stand Alone)
The time slip was his accident; can he use it to save the one he loves?

Cicada (04)
Cicada's scientific community... the world's only hope, or its end?

Made in the USA
Monee, IL
10 June 2023

35553432R00167